T0207886

My
Shorts

My Shorts

A Collection of Short Stories about Life, Death, and Laughter

Bert G. Osterberg

MY SHORTS
A Collection of Short Stories about Life, Death, and Laughter

iUniverse books may be ordered through booksellers or by contacting:

*iUniverse
1663 Liberty Drive
Bloomington, IN 47403
www.iuniverse.com
1-800-Authors (1-800-288-4677)*

*ISBN: 978-1-5320-0088-1 (sc)
ISBN: 978-1-5320-0089-8 (e)*

Library of Congress Control Number: 2016910393

Print information available on the last page.

iUniverse rev. date: 08/05/2016

Dedication

To Armaine

CONTENTS

DEATH

LAUGHTER

CODA

FOREWORD

When I first contemplated putting together this collection of my short stories I thought of limiting it to one subject. Because I had a few horror stories and tales of death, I thought that I would publish a collection of those stories only. I could call it "Death Stalks My Mind" and create a market among the Goths of America.

Then I thought better of the idea. My life has been one ruled by thoughts of death (my own mostly) and sustained by my view of life (Christ's) and a great deal of laughter. When I took a job at the Henry Ford's Greenfield Village in Dearborn, Michigan to present a character who was a barkeeper in 1850 at a stagecoach stop, I created a character filled with jokes, puns and wild stories to entertain my customers as I informed and educated them. When I preach the Gospel of the Lord Jesus Christ to congregations in my role as preacher and teacher I use a great deal of humor to inspire and challenge. Laughter has always been important to me and I saw no reason why it should not be included in a collection of stories that would include dark tales like **The Crimean Horror; To Make Themselves a Home; The Connoisseur; The Castle** and **Russell School** that are five of my stories with the theme of death.

Beanwacker and Dudley had to be included if I was going to provide laughter, as it was one of my favorites among my lighter works. **The Livonia Rats** came upon me one day after a real-life conversation with a neighbor that begins the tale. The two Christmas stories, **Christmas of the Mind** and **Five Christmases**, I include because I think they both convey an important message. **The Colony**, although a little dark, well very dark, I like because of its irony.

Terror in the Jungle and **Emma F. Beetlebiter** I wrote for my daughter when she was in grade school. She liked them.

The Hitchhiker had been kicking around my mind for a while and recent NASA probes to Mars makes it fresh.

The Option was written while I contemplated my past.

Now a word about **My Aunt Ruth**. The Ruth Clift in the story is a real lady who lived in Michigan all of her life. After her death many people told me that I wright down the things she had done and the things she had said and "do something with them." Well, I did.

High School was inspired by a plot twist in Tchaikovsky's opera, *The Queen of Spades*, and recalls my own tortured high school career. I wrote **To Amerikay** because of my love of history as told in the stories of ordinary people who do extraordinary things. **Three Views** is my political statement. I wrote **Nettie's Triumph** for my granddaughter for her to illustrate when she was in grade school. **A Day at the Eagle Tavern** grows from my work at Greenfield Village and recreates the character I presented there. **A Death with Dignity** grew from the event of the death of my wife's uncle, Detroit Fire Department Lt. Ray Owens. **Black and White and Read All Over** is an adaptation of a play I wrote of that name. It is, by far, the longest short story in this collection.

The only story in this collection that I did not write is **A Dog's Tail.** It was written by my dog, Co-Co. I included it at Co-Co's insistence and because she sleeps with me and could bite me in my sleep.

I conclude the collection with a very short story called **A Walk after my Wife Died**. It is a fitting ending for my look at Life, Death and Laughter and is dedicated, as is the entire book, to my wife, Armaine Yvonne Lacen Osterberg, the most remarkable person I ever had the privilege to love.

So there they are: **My Shorts.**

LIFE

NETTIE'S TRIUMPH

"Mama! Look!" Nettie Cully said as the little girl looked out of her family's home through a heavily frosted window. The eight-year-old wiped the very cold pane of glass with one of her small hands, an action she instantly regretted. "It has snowed," Nettie called to her mother as she blew on her hurting hand.

"It surely has, dear," Isabelle Cully observed as she looked out through another window. "It has snowed heavily."

"School!" Nettie said. "How can I get to school?"

Her mother smiled. "I'm sure there will be no school today. No one will ever be able to get to the school house through snow this deep."

"But I must go to school today, Mama. I must."

Isabelle knew why. Nettie had spent so much time the evening before studying and preparing her presentation for the classroom. The eight-year-old's teacher, Miss Harris, had selected Nettie from all the children who sat in the third grade section of the one-room schoolhouse to make an oral presentation on slavery. Nettie had talked to her Papa, Silas Cully, and her father and mother about it. She had listened to her grandmother's tales. Sadie, the child's paternal grandmother, was a woman of African descent who had been born to a woman who had been enslaved in her youth. Sadie had told Nettie what Sadie's mother and grandmother had told her. She shared their stories of courage and struggle. She told the little girl about Sadie's grandmother's flight from slavery; of that horrible night when the woman, then a young child, hid in her mother's arms as the patrollers searched the underbrush along very road where they were hiding; of the people who had helped them along the way north and of the people who tried to capture them.

The eight-year-old listed with wide eyes as her grandmother told her how she had been born to a slave and that slave's white master and how she had fought to be something more than what people expected her to be. Nettie was so proud to be descended from such proud and strong people that she wanted so much to tell their stories.

But as the little girl looked out through that cold pane of glass she doubted she could do it. "I *must* go to school today," she said ever so softly.

Isabelle Cully crossed the room to her daughter and knelt on the child's bed beside her. She put an arm around Nettie who was crying by then. "If no one can get to school, I'm sure your teacher will postpone your presentation until some other day," she assured the girl.

"She said today," Nettie whimpered.

"There is no way," Sadie insisted.

Nettie looked out at the deep snow. It had blown up the side of their house and drifted in banks between the house and the road. Snow obscured the road and no traffic, not even wagons with the runners of sleighs, was to be seen upon it. The road was impassable.

"I could walk," Nettie offered.

"There is no way," her mother repeated.

Nettie fell silent. She pressed her nose to the cold glass window and cried. She just knew that if she did not make her presentation on slavery that day that there would never be another chance to do so. Her grandmother's story and her great-grandmother's story would never be told. It would be like those women had never lived. The little girl felt like a vessel that held the truth and now that vessel was to be emptied at home. It was useless.

Isabelle hugged her daughter again and tried to reassure her. Nettie just cried. Suddenly the little girl pulled her nose back from the window and, ignoring the frozen condition of its tip, she smiled. "Papa!" she declared.

"What about Papa?" her mother asked.

"He'll know what to do. He always knows what to do."

Papa was Silas Cully, Nettie's grandfather. Silas was working in town as the barkeeper and resident manager of the Eagle Tavern in Clinton, Michigan. He and his quadraloon wife, Sadie, lived upstairs from the barroom and looked after the guests and travelers at the stagecoach stop.

Because Clinton was fifty miles from Detroit on what was called the Chicago Road, it was normally the first overnight stop on that eight to ten day stagecoach journey from Detroit to Chicago. Silas and Sadie Cully ran the Eagle tavern; Silas keeping bar and seeing to the finances of the establishment and Sadie overseeing the cooling and overnight accommodations.

"Papa will know!" Nettie said again and she jumped off the bed to put on her clothes.

"Even Papa cannot make the snow go away," Isabelle Cully cautioned.

"He'll know what to do," the child uttered excitedly as she pulled on her clothing. "He always does."

Isabelle let young Nettie go out into the deep snow after she made sure that the little brunette's long brown hair was carefully tucked up under her hat and her coat was securely latched up. The tavern where Papa and Sadie were was only a little way from the Cullys' house and Isabelle was sure that when her daughter got there she would be given a cup of hot soup and good advice by Nettie's grandfather. The little girl would be comforted and become resigned to the fact that there was no way that she could go to school that day.

Nettie trudged through the deep snow the short distance to the tavern. The sun was brightly shining but it was still bitterly cold outside. There was a bit of a wind that blew up powered snow and whirled around in the air at the corners of buildings and along mostly buried fence posts. Nettie pulled the scarf she wore up over her lower face and held it there as she made her way to her grandfather's tavern.

"Papa!" Nettie called as she pounded on the barroom door. There were two front doors to the tavern: one that led into the sitting room and one that opened directly into the barroom. Travelers and the general public used the former while exclusively drinking men used the latter. "Papa!" Nettie said again and the door was pulled open inward.

"Why, Nettie! What on earth are you doing here?" Papa asked. He pulled his little granddaughter into the barroom. The room was warm because Silas had a nice fire set in its fireplace. The barroom smelled of the burning wood and also of beer and liquors. Silas closed the door behind his granddaughter. "Why are you here on such a morning?"

"You must get me to school, Papa," the eight-year-old announced.

"School? There ain't gonna be no be classes today, I'm sure." Silas pulled the scarf down from Nettie's small face. "Would you want some soup? Nana's warmed some from last night for the travelers to have this morning. It is a good soup – root vegetables with some beef." He paused. "No one's goin' nowhere today."

"I must go to school, Papa. Today is the day I give my presentation for the class."

Silas smiled. "The presentation on slavery?"

"Yes, Papa, and I must be there."

The barkeeper smiled again. He was so proud of his determined granddaughter. Just then Sadie came into the room.

"Nettie!" the woman exclaimed.

Silas raised a hand. He explained why the child was there.

"But, surely there will be no school today," Sadie proposed.

Nettie's grandfather looked down at the girl. "There ain't gonna be no school today unless I get this child there."

"Will you, Papa? Will you?" Nettie threw her short arms around her grandfather's legs and hugged them. "Thank you," she said.

"But how?" Sadie asked. "And why?"

"Why? Because she must. You heard her. And how? Let me think about that part." Silas pulled Nettie's hat off the child and removed her scarf from her neck. "In the meantime, dear, get this frozen child some soup."

"Certainly," Sadie replied and she took her granddaughter into the tavern's kitchen to ladle some hot soup into a large cup for her.

Normally there would have been several travelers at the Eagle Tavern spending the night before their morning coaches left east to Detroit or west to Chicago, but the blizzard that had hit Lenawee County the day before had kept the travelers from their journeys and the tavern only had two overnight guests: two salesmen who had already eaten their breakfast and were both sitting in the barroom, each sipping a mulled cider.

Nettie held the cup in both of her cold hands and sipped the delicious broth until there were only vegetables and meat left in the ceramic cup. Her grandmother gave her a spoon and she finished the warming food.

"Have you a cup of soup for the man who'll be gettin' his granddaughter to school today?" Silas asked as he entered the kitchen.

"How, Papa? How?" Nettie asked with a great grin on her pretty face.

Silas smiled. "Champ and Wolf will help you," he proposed. Those were the names of his two large dogs.

"But how?" Sadie asked.

"I'll make a sled and they'll pull it, and Nettie."

"Over the snow?"

"Yes, as if flyin'," the man smiled.

"Do you think that this is a good idea, dear?" Sadie asked.

"It'll work." Silas replied. "I'll use that flat board in the shed that came offa the old wagon and some rope. The dogs'll do the rest. It ain't that far."

Sadie stepped closer to the man as Nettie ran toward the back of the tavern to go out to the shed. "For what purpose?" Silas' wife asked

"Because our granddaughter's determined," Silas told her. "She'll get there and find out that there ain't no school and come home. It'll be an adventure and no more dangerous than lettin' her play in the snow as she would have done anyway on a snowy day when there ain't no school."

"I suppose you are right, dear," Sadie said.

"Papa is always right," Nettie said as she reentered the room. She had dragged the flat board from the shed into the rear door of the tavern and was looking for rope. Silas helped her find some and he lashed the rope to the board then fastened a harness for two dogs.

Champ was asleep under a table near the dining room's fireplace and Silas roused him to his work. Wolf was lying nearby but not asleep. The two dogs were soon hitched to the board, which Papa carried out to the back of the tavern.

"Give my regards to Miss Harris," Silas called after his granddaughter.

"I will, Papa," Nettie called back.

"Silas, you're quite the schemer," one of the salesmen in Silas's barroom laughed.

"Oh, shut up and order another drink," the barkeeper smiled. "Nettie might be gonin' to school but you ain't gonin' nowhere." The man poured another cup of hot apple cider that he laced strong with dark rum. He handed it across the wooden bar to his guest. "Drink up," he urged.

Nettie lay on her stomach on the board and held tight to the reins that guided the two dogs. The unlikely sled avoided trees and other obstacles and was guided closer to the town's one-room schoolhouse.

Despite the blowing snow and the cold, young Nettie Cully arrived at her school not much later than was the normal start of school time. She held the ropes that were attached to her grandfather's dogs and pounded on the closed wooden door. "Teacher! Teacher!" she called out.

Mrs. Harris pushed the door open. "Why, Nettie Cully!" she said, looking down at the snow-covered child. "What on earth are you doing here?"

"My presentation," the girl said.

"But..." Emily Harris stopped short. "Of course," she smiled. "Come in. Everything is ready." The woman led her charge into the empty schoolroom.

Emily Harris, Clinton, Michigan's only schoolteacher, lived in a small room behind the schoolhouse, a large one-room affair with three neatly arranged rows of wooden desks. She, of course, had expected no students to arrive that morning and was in the school room only to straighten things and tend to the Franklin stove that provided heat to the room.

"You are the only one who was cleaver enough to get here this morning, Nettie," the widowed schoolteacher announced. "But, pay no mind to that. Take off your outerwear and you shall make your presentation." The wise woman had her student hang her snowy coat, scarf and hat on wooded pegs on the wall and take her usual seat in the third grade section of the room. All the other desks were unoccupied but that did not matter. The roll call began.

"Martin Alby?" Mrs. Harris called and when there was no answer she marked Martin absent

Mary Browning? Joshua Faulklam? Joseph French?"

As each name was called, Mrs. Harris marked a student absent.

She called the names by grade, beginning with the upper form. When she got to the third graders, she called Nettie's name.

"Nettie Cully?"

"Here, ma'am," Nettie said, holding up a hand.

The roll call continued until each of Mrs. Harris' students were marked absent except for one third grader. When that task was complete, Mrs. Harris led her one-person class in the recitation of the Lord's Prayer, as was their daily routine, then had Nettie sit.

"It is time for oral presentations," the teacher announced. "Who is ready?"

Nettie's hand shot up into the air.

Mrs. Harris purposely looked around the all but empty room. "Nettie Cully," she said, calling upon the only child there.

Nettie got up from her seat and walked to the front of the classroom.

"Begin," Mrs. Harris prompted.

"My oral presentation is about slavery," the little girl began. "My grandmother's mother was a slave and she escaped to become a free person. This is her story."

Nettie went on to tell in remarkable detail the story she had been told of her great-grandmother's escape from Maryland and her harrowing journey to Pennsylvania. She told how the men looking for her and her mother, a young child at the time, carried torches and how they also had ropes to tie up those whom they caught. The little girl said how proud she was on her grandmother's mother and all those Africans who dared all for freedom. When she was done her teacher's eyes were filled with tears.

"Nettie," the white woman said, discreetly dabbing her eyes with a handkerchief, "that was so good that I would like you to do it again when the snow melts enough to allow the others to be here too."

"Yes, Mrs. Harris," Nettie said and she retook her seat.

"Students," the teacher said, "because of the inclement weather I am going to allow all those students who have made their oral presentations to be dismissed early. You may go home."

Nettie got up and her teacher hugged her.

"I am very proud of you, child," she said softly.

"Thank you, ma'am," the little girl said.

The dogs carried Nettie and her homemade sled over the snow back to the tavern where Nettie told her grandparents of her triumph. "Thank you, Papa," she said, hugging the man. "I knew you could do it."

"It was you who done it, Nettie," Silas said. "You and your great-grandmother."

HIGH SCHOOL

I was a junior in High School and Bobby was my best friend. Bobby Richmond had it all. He was the captain of the football team, our winning football team, and good-looking. His dark eyes and black hair gave the 17-year-old a very Elvis look just when Elvis was at the height of his popularity. Bobby was getting laid all the time and I was still a virgin.

Bobby and I were friends like so many oddly matched youngsters are friends. He was athletic, handsome and popular. I was his counterpart: a skinny, clumsy intellectual who talked to the girls at a party while Bobby was off drinking and talking sports with his fellow athletes. The girls liked talking to me and then they'd have sex with Bobby. I was his opening act.

"Hey, Pete. What's up?" my best friend smiled as he and I met in the hallway of our high school.

"Not much," I said. I opened my locker and exchanged my first period books for my second period ones. "Got a date for the dance Friday?"

I looked over at Bobby whose grin and rather incredulous look told me that had been a stupid question. "Yeah. You?"

"Not yet," I said. I locked the combination lock to my hall locker.

"You can come with us," my friend offered. "It's just her and me. There's plenty of room in my car and if you get a date…" The boy left that sentence hanging as he knew there was a strong likelihood that I would be going stag to the school dance. I had tagged along with my friend and a date many times before.

"Thanks," I smiled. I went off to class and so did Bobby.

My second hour class was math and the teacher taught us something about cosines, an entity I think I understood at the time but in the thirty years since then I have never met. I'm sure that cosines are great things but I never worked with one and my neighborhood was, and is, pretty much cosine-free. After taking copious notes on the benefits of cosines I returned to my locker to exchange books once more. To my right, Lisa Bowman, a girl I knew from my neighborhood, was standing at her locker with another girl. Lisa was a heavyset, black-haired girl with glasses with thick black frames. She and I knew each other from the neighborhood and from the grade school we had attended.

The girl with Lisa was the most beautiful female I had ever seen. She was thin but shapely with long blond hair and pale blue eyes totally unobstructed by glasses. I had seen her around the school but I had never had the courage to talk to her.

"Hi, Pete," Lisa Bowman said. She was opening her locker too. She looked at that gorgeous girl with her. "You two know each other, right?" she said. "You're in the same study hall."

"Sure," the blonde smiled. "I know Pete."

I looked at her and she looked at me. There it was: that magical look, the one that fixes eyes together, locks souls and brings instant love. She looked deeply into my eyes and

I looked deeply into hers. We were in love. Just like that, she and I were in love. There was no way I could tell her that I didn't know her name.

At study hall, an hour later, I looked across the student-filled room at the blonde and she was looking at me! I was stunned. Maybe the feeling I had experience during that magical moment in the hallway near my locker was real. I fidgeted with a pen on my desk and kept looking over at her. She smiled and nodded in my direction. I was tempted to look to my rear to see whom this incredible beauty was really acknowledging but I restrained myself. I could tell she was looking at me. There was no doubt.

I looked over at the wall clock, mounted high on one of the study hall's walls. It was encased in screening, I suppose to keep us highschoolers from throwing things at it, but it could be plainly read. Below the clock that told me I had twenty more minutes of study hall was a sign that read, "TIME IS PASSING. ARE YOU?"

Cute. I looked back at the blonde who was still looking at me. Her incredibly sexy lips formed words but I could not read them. I shrugged, looked over at the study hall monitor to be sure she wasn't noticing me, then at the blonde again. I held up a finger and smiled. I wrote out a note. "Are you going to the dance Friday?" I asked. I folded this note three times and handed it to a girl whose desk was across from my desk. I pointed toward the blonde.

The girl smiled. "Her?" she asked in a whisper as if I didn't stand a chance.

I nodded and she passed the note to her right. The note was secretly handed across two more rows of desks and up one seat until the blonde had it in her hands. I watched her read it then write her reply. The note returned to me and I unfolded it.

She had a date for the dance, she had written, but she hoped I would go so we could talk. "I'll save you a dance," she said.

That settled it. Once more I was going to sit in the back seat of Bobby's car and go with my friend and his date as a third wheel but this time for a purpose. I nodded at the blonde and then tried to concentrate on my homework.

This was incredible. There was no doubt that the two of us were in love. I kept looking over at her and she kept looking over at me. After study hall she tarried by the door – her desk being closer to the exit than was mine – and she waited for me.

"Hi," I smiled.

"Hi," she smiled back. The beautiful girl slipped a hand into mine and it felt like fire to me. "I'll see you at the dance," she smiled with a squeeze to my hand then she was off to her next class. I wiped my very wet hand on my slacks and made my way to my locker, my mind filled with her.

"So, ya goin' to the dance Friday?" my best friend asked after school. He and I were finishing our homework together at his house. Bobby's mother worked and we had the place to ourselves. We usually went there after school so we could smoke cigarettes as we did homework. Bobby's mother worked and smoked. Mine did neither.

"Sure," I answered.

"Got a date?" Bobby asked, blowing a cloud of blue grey smoke into the air over us.

"Nope. I'm goin' alone but there's a girl whose gonna be there waitin' for me.

"Who's she?" Bobby wrote an answer on one of his worksheets then took another drag on his Chesterfield.

"Just a girl," I said in a way that Booby knew she was more than just a girl.

"From school?"

"Yeah, she's in my study hall."

My friend smiled. "Good for you. She goin' stag too?"

"No, but she wants to talk."

"So talk to her, pal. That's your high card. The girls love to talk to you. I'll be busy with Karen so you'll be on your own."

"Karen?"

"Yeah, I met her last week after the game. She's hot. What about yours?"

"Hot," I grinned.

"Great." Bobby took the last puff of his cigarette then snuffed it out into an ashtray we shared. "What ya got for number seven?" he asked, looking down at his homework's answer sheet.

Bobby pulled up to my house in his car. Bobby drove a '57 Ford Fairlane 500 - a black convertible 1957 Ford Fairlane 500 with red upholstery – the most beautiful car I had ever seen. It was long and sleek with jutting tail fins and cowled headlamps. I know, some people say that the '57 Chevy Bel Air was the better of the two but, to my mind, there was never a car better than the '57 Fairlane 500 convertible.

Bobby parked his two-year old car, top down, in my driveway and honked his car's horn.

"See ya," I yelled up the stairs at my mother. "Bobby's here."

"Okay. Have fun," my mom called back.

I grabbed a jacket and went outside. It was September in Michigan and the nights were getting cool so I needed to take a jacket. I knew my friend would have his car's top down no matter the evening temperature.

As soon as I stepped onto my front porch I saw her. There, in the passenger side front seat of my best friend's car was his date, my beloved - the blonde from study hall. I paused then sucked it up and went down to the car.

"Pete, this is Karen Cobert," Bobby said.

"We're in study hall together," I said.

"Hi, Pete," Karen said. "I didn't know you're friends with Bobby."

"Best friends," Bobby smiled. He was out of his side of the car and opened the door where Karen sat. "Come on, pal," he urged. "We'll be late."

Karen sat forward and pulled her seat with her to allow me to climb into the rear seat. I took my place behind her. Bobby returned to the driver's side. We drove off, the cool wind blowing Karen's long blond hair back at me.

Bobby had the top down and the radio up. In the back seat I could hear Rob Orbison singing *Only the Lonely*, one of my all-time favorite songs. I looked up at Karen's hair and sang along with the words.

We parked in the school's parking lot and Bobby put his car's top up as Karen and I watched. She kept looking over at me and I at her. Neither of us wanted Bobby to see.

Bobby walked into the dance holding hands with his date and I followed. Soon they were dancing and I was watching.

We had records played for our dance that night. I stood against a wall of the gym with my right foot put back against that wall and listened to the Ames Brothers sing *China Doll* and Bobby Darin's *Beyond the Sea*. A couple of rock and roll songs followed those and a girl with stringy hair asked me to dance with her to one of them. I did and she went back to her side of the room after it was over.

When I listened to Paul Anka's *Puppy Love* I watched Bobby and Karen dancing on the gym floor. He was close to her and she didn't seem to mind it.

"Pop anyone?" Bobby asked after he walked Karen over to where I was standing. The two were still holding hands.

"Sure," Karen answered. "Pete?" she asked me for her date.

"Yeah," I said.

"I'll get 'em," my friend offered and he left his date there with me as he went to the stand where the PTA was selling soft drinks. The gym filled with the sound of *The Theme from A Summer Place*. I looked at Karen and she looked at me.

"Dance?" I asked.

"Sure," she said and we stepped away from the wall to the dance floor. I took her right hand in my left and, put my other hand around her thin waist and we began to dance. She moved in to me and I felt her ample breasts push against my thin chest. The beautiful blonde squeezed my hand.

"I really didn't know that Bobby was your friend, Pete," she said to me.

"That's okay," I said. "I didn't know he was bringing you." I kept myself from telling her that I hadn't known her name until Bobby introduced us that night. "It's just that…"

"We're in love," Karen said, completing my sentence.

I leaned back and looked at her gorgeous face. "Yes," I said.

"We are, you know," Karen told me. "I felt it right away, when I first saw you."

"Yes! Me, too," I said. I squeezed her hand and hugged her closer to me. "As soon as I saw you," I said.

We danced and Bobby returned with the three bottles of Vernor's Ginger Ale. When the music ended I walked my love back to my best friend. "Thanks," I said as I took my pop from him.

"No problem, man," he smiled. "Thanks for keeping my date warm," he added.

"No problem," I said. I sipped my ginger ale through the straw that the PTA mother had placed into the bottle. Bobby pulled his straw out to toss it aside and drink directly from the bottle. That was my way and that was his.

I danced once more with Karen before the dance was over. She and I danced to *Moonlight Gambler* sung by Frankie Laine, holding each other tenderly as we danced. Bobby talked with fellow jocks.

"I really am in love with you, Pete," Karen said.

"What are we going to do?" I asked. "About Bobby?"

"What about Bobby?"

"He's my best friend and he obviously likes you."

"He's a nice guy," Karen said. "I love you and he's a nice guy."

"So, stop seeing him and start seeing me. Bobby's got any girl he wants."

"I know that, Pete," Karen said. "That's the whole point. He's captain of the football team and he likes me."

I stopped dancing and just stood there with Karen in front of me.

"And?"

"And I can't just stop seeing him because I'm in love with someone else. I mean, he's the captain of the football team."

I struggled through the rest of the dance and took Karen back to Bobby. The three of us stayed a little longer then Bobby drove me home. As my friend had so many times before, he dropped me at my house although Karen's house was closer so he could be alone with his date. I'm sure the red leatherette upholstery got a good workout that night.

I never stopped loving Karen Colbert, I suppose. I still think about her on occasion. Bobby ended up getting her pregnant and her father forced them to marry. Bobby and Karen were divorced within a year after Bobby caught her with the boss at the clothing store where she worked. Karen went on to marry a couple of other men.

Bobby and I were never close after his forced marriage. After the divorce he went into business with his father and I was at school. He really couldn't go to college what with the child support he had to pay. At the University of Michigan I began seeing Lisa Bowman, the heavyset girl who had her locker next to mine in high school. She had lost quite a bit of weight and became the University of Michigan's Homecoming Queen in 1964. We married a year after college graduation and have two children, neither of which is named Bobby nor Karen.

TO AMERIKAY

I.

There it was – Amerikay. After three long horrible months at sea in the stinking "coffin ship" Maggie Madigan and the others were looking at what they hoped – prayed - to be their new home. Refugees from the Irish Potato Famine were they. They crowded the rails of the sailing ship that had been their home and dungeon for the almost thirteen weeks since they left Cork and stared out at the hope, the promise, that was America.

"'Tis really Amerikay?" Maggie asked, her lips blustered with the salt air and heat of July.

"'Tis," a fellow traveler said. "I heard a sailor say it. 'Tis New York City herself."

The ship was taken to its mooring and tied off at a pier in New York's harbor. The passengers gathered up their belongings, often no more than a sack of clothes and a few mementos of home and family, and they crowded the gangplank to the wharf. A gang of nativists was there to meet them.

"Protect the women!" an Irishman yelled as men with sticks, clubs and knives set upon the group.

"America belongs to Americans," one of the attackers shouted.

There was pushing, yelling and blows being delivered all around Maggie Madigan. She shoved her way up the dock, protected by two Irishmen with clubs. Her dress had blood on it when she reached safety.

It was 1850 and the horrible calamity of the Potato Famine had been going on for five years. The potato was a New World crop that had been introduced to Ireland where it grew well and in abundance. By the middle of the Nineteen-Century the average Irish farmer rented lands from a landowner and farmed potatoes. Margaret Madigan, whom everyone in her family affectionately called Maggie, like most in Ireland had lived on potatoes. Their diet of this healthy tuber, augmented from time to time with a bit of meat or fish, sustained them well. They ate potatoes roasted, boiled and in soups and stews. They dried the skins to be used during the winter. They lived on potatoes.

Then, in 1845 the blight began. Maggie and her mother pulled their potatoes from the rocky ground to find them covered with black spots. A rot had been was introduced from the New World that attacked the potato in the ground as it grew. At first there were enough potatoes to see the Madigans through the winter then it got worse. By 1846 potatoes were rotting in the ground. By "Black '47" famine stalked the island. The Madigans and their neighbors became desperate. There was less and less to eat and little help from the ruling English government.

Taxes were imposed to raise funds to feed the starving but because the landowners were getting no rents from those who had no crops to sell, mass evictions followed the imposition of the new tax. People who were starving now were without homes as well. Those who could leave left and wave after wave of disparate Irish sailed from Ireland in converted slave ships they called "coffin ships" to England, Scotland, Wales and North America. By 1850 the port of St. John's in Canada was closed to any more Irish immigration. Those who had already arrived overwhelmed it. Boston, New York, Baltimore and New Orleans had their Irish populations increase from almost nothing to twenty-five percent or more of the general population.

Maggie boarded her "coffin ship" in Cork. She hugged each member of her family, one by one until only her mother was left. The two embraced, each knowing that they'd never meet again in this life.

The Irish came to America with three things that were unwelcome. They were poor; they were sick and they were Catholic. These new arrivals had little money. Cholera outbreaks were blamed on them. The Protestant majority of the United States feared the upset of the balance of power that kept the Protestants in charge of government.

Maggie Madigan was poor, that was for sure. She was Catholic from birth but, unlike many of her fellow passengers on the coffin ship that had brought her to her new home, she was not sick. Her blue eyes were clear and her skin, although marked by streaks of dirt and soot, was clean of any lesions or pox. Once she presented herself to the government official at the docks and her papers were checked she was on her way to her sister's house in Michigan.

Those who arrived in America from Europe were always confused by the size of this country. Michigan, Maggie Madigan knew, was well beyond New York City, farther into the interior of the continent but she never imagined that it could be so far. Back home most people never travel fifty miles from where they were born. In America fifty miles was but a day's journey. Michigan lay three weeks or more from where Maggie had first set foot on the shore of the New World and the trip would prove to be a harrowing one.

Maggie Madigan had little when she stepped into New York City. Her sister had sent her the money that had bought her passage to America, all of thirty American dollars, and fares money for her trip to Michigan. She had the clothes she wore, a shirt and a pair of stockings wrapped up in a bag with the catechism her father had given her on the day of her confirmation, a lock of her mother's hair that was folded into that book and a comb. A handful of other things, buttons, ribbons and a small mirror completed Maggie's treasures.

The steamboat that Maggie was to take into the northern parts of New York State was tied along the dock on the Hudson River. The young Irishwoman found her way there after asking several people on the streets, most of whom ignored her. The streets were teeming with people, a sight Maggie had never seen before that day. The population of America's largest city was over six hundred thousand souls and Manhattan Island was developed all the way up to 40th Street. The homes of the rich, the Astors and the Vanderbilts and others, lined Fifth Avenue. The slums of the Five Points and the Bowery housed masses of destitute poor. Garbage was thrown into the streets in both rich and poor neighborhood to be rummaged through by the poor and by the herds of swine that roamed freely through New York's streets and avenues.

P. T. Barnum's American Museum, a six story tall wooden structure housed oddities and humbugs. People lined up to see a "Six Foot Man Eating Chicken" complete with a drawing of a huge bird with fangs, only to sit before a curtain that, when drawn, revealed a six foot man eating a chicken dinner. The customers laughed then invited their friends to the Museum to be fooled too.

Barnum was from Connecticut but in 1850 lived in New York where he had his museum. He featured the famous Siamese Twins and Tom Thumb, the world's smallest man - at least according to Barnum. He had an Egyptian mummy (although no one really knew what was wrapped up in those linens) and the "Fiji Mermaid", a creature preserved in a bottle of alcohol that looked suspiciously like someone had sewn a monkey's head onto a fish's body.

Maggie passed the American Museum on her way toward the Hudson River and paused on the street outside.

"Can you believe it!" a laughing woman said as she passed.

"That's Barnum, all right," her male companion said. The man stepped to the museum's ticket booth to buy two more tickets. "He got us good," the customer said as he put fifty cents on the counter. "We fell for the sign that said 'This way to the Egress.'"

The ticket seller, knowing about that sign, smiled. "We get a lot of folks that way," he said.

"'The Egress'. We thought it was a bird. That's what was pictured upon the sign. It was only when we were out in the alley that I realized that egress means exit!" The man paid for two more tickets and he and his lady friend reentered Barnum's museum.

"Is it a cheat, then?" Maggie asked the ticket seller.

"No, miss," the man said. "It's all in fun."

The young Irishwoman looked up at the many signs that were displayed on the façade of the tall building. She looked at them then moved on.

Street vendors were selling sausages on the next block and the pungent aroma of those roasting meats made Maggie realize that she was hungry. Breakfast had been on the ship and was no more than porridge with water. The young woman surveyed the cooking foods but forwent them. She had no money to spend on food in the city. They would feed her on the boat to Albany.

After the sausage vendors there were men and women selling live chickens and butchered meats. Then the bakers tempted shoppers with the smell of freshly baked breads and buns. Maggie so wanted a taste but she knew she could not.

As she approached the Hudson, Maggie smelled fish. Fish shops and fishmongers lined the streets as she neared the water. Fish hung from hooks in windows and lay on tables atop beds of ice in the streets. The blood of those fish made the wooden sidewalks slippery and Maggie had to be careful as she walked past them.

The ship to which Maggie Madigan walked, her small bag of belongings tightly grasped in her hands, was a steamship. It had two tall stacks from which billowed white and black smoke. It had two paddles, one of each side of the thirty-eight foot long craft that, when powered by the shaft that was powered by the boiler, would propel the small ship through the water. Maggie went to the dock and paid for her ticket.

"The Canal?" the agent asked and she nodded.

"Yes, the Erie Canal and on to Michigan."

"Cabin or deck?"

The young woman looked puzzled.

"Ya want sleeping quarters in a cabin or will ya be asleepin' on the deck. We feeds ya no matter which way." The man paused. "A cabin's two dollars and the deck's fifty cents," he explained.

"The deck," Maggie answered and he stamped a hole in her ticket and waved the young woman aboard after she gave him two quarters of a dollar.

The boat steamed up the Hudson River past Fishkill and West Point. It passed barges and steamboats coming down for New York. For twenty-five years, since its opening of the Erie Canal, this had been the main route to and from the West. Before New York governor, DeWitt Clinton, inaugurated New York's grand transportation project, the way west was overland along what became the National Road through the Cumberland Gap to the Ohio River. That was why the states of Ohio, Indiana and Illinois developed in the south along the Ohio River before the northern Great Lakes area. Cincinnati, Jeffersonville and Cairo were thriving centers of commerce when Cleveland, Detroit and Chicago were small frontier settlements. Then the Erie Canal was opened and hordes of people floated west and great barges of goods floated east.

At Albany, Maggie changed for a packet boat for the Erie Canal. Within sight of New York's capitol building where Governor Hamilton Fish held forth, the Irishwoman stepped carefully onto the deck of the long and narrow canal barge.

A packet boat was only for passengers and their hand carried luggage.

They carried people while other larger and heavier canal boats, barges, carried goods. The shallow-draft packet boats could go up to fifty miles a day on the canal while the larger and much slower barges were limited to no more than fifteen.

Maggie took a seat on the deck and watched as the mule was hitched to a long rope that would pull the boat along the waterway. The mule, like one other, was kept in a stall on the boat's deck. It was pulled braying, and pulling back from it enclosure by the canalman and his hoagie.

The hoagie, a boy of no more than eleven, had a dirt face and torn clothes. When he let the rope he held slip and the mule stumbled the hoagie was beaten by the canalman.

"My God!" Maggie said as she watched blows rain down on the lad.

"'Tis nothin', Miss," a fellow passenger, a tall and thin American man, said. "He's just a hoagie. 'Tis his lot in life."

"He's just a boy, don't you know," Maggie protested.

The hoagie retook the rope and pulled. He seemed none the worse for his beating. The barefoot lad led the mule to a well-worn dirt path that paralleled the canal. The canalman oversaw the boy secure a long rope to that animal's harness. The man returned to the boat and left the hoagie to guide the mule. The packet boat was pulled along the Erie Canal by the big mule that the hoagie led. The boy trod the mule path along the canal bank and guided the beast. When all was set, the canalman gave orders to his crew and lines were loosed from the dock. The hoagie began his long trek ashore. The long rope extended from the animal the boy led to the boat's prow and propelled the craft slowly through the water.

"We'll be eatin' soon, Miss," the tall thin man told Maggie. "The food'll be good."

Maggie had forgotten how hungry she was until the man spoke. She put a hand to her belly and held it there but not for long.

"Dinner," someone called out and Maggie, the tall thin man, and the other passengers rushed below deck to a long dining table. The man was right. The food was excellent, the best that Maggie had eaten since she left Ireland and, really for quite a while even before she left home. There were roasted potatoes, corn - maize to the Irishwoman -, boiled beef and turnips. Hard cider was available to the men and water and sherry to the women. Maggie passed up the sherry for it was at an extra charge, and ate heartily of the foods. This was the first time in her life she had seen so much meat on a table. She ate the beef and enjoyed it all.

"Is this a special day?" Maggie asked the tall thin man.

"No. Why?" he asked back.

"So much food!"

The man laughed. "Welcome to America, Miss." He stabbed a piece of beef with his two-tined folk. Maggie took another helping too.

"I surely will be fat as a porker by the time I reach Michigan if I continue to eat like this," Maggie smiled.

From the beginning of the Erie Canal its cuisine gained a reputation for goodness. The toll was typically a penny a mile so the entire trip from Albany to Buffalo would cost $3.84. That included food and the food was good. With little else to do but cook and the availability of fresh food all along the way, the canal cooks gained a reputation for grand style. In the early days people would get on a packet boat just before a meal would be served, eat, and then exit paying only a cent or two of the small amount of distance traveled. A minimum charge was adopted by the canalmen to stop that practice.

Maggie Madigan ate well then returned to her place on the deck.

"Yer allowed to sleep below, Miss," the tall and thin man told her as evening neared.

"Without extra charge?"

"Without extra charge."

Supper, leftovers from dinner, was served at about six in the evening then, as night fell the passengers retired. Maggie sat out on the deck for a while before going below.

She watched the sun set over a hill in the west. She held her knees to her breasts and looked at that red setting sun. She wondered what it saw out there where she was going.

II.

The night passed peaceably for Maggie and her fellow passengers. The young Irishwoman slept on a bench below deck with a light blanket that she found there. There was no pillow but she didn't care. She put her head down on the wooden bench and was asleep before her prayers were over.

The morning of the next day was clear and sunny. The morning sun poured across the packet boat's deck from behind and the cabin caused a long shadow to form across the fore part of the deck that shortened as the day progressed. Maggie ate breakfast, a meal again filled with meat. There was fried bacon, and sausages served with potatoes sautéed in the bacon grease, toasted bread with plenty of butter. Coffee and tea were poured from pots passed around the table. Most of the men drank hard cider or beer, as well.

Maggie ate below and rested after eating, on the deck. She watched the shore pass to see dense forests, small villages and growing towns. When a bridge was neared the canalman would yell out "Low Bridge. Everybody down!" and all on deck would have to duck to keep from hitting their heads on a stone bridge as the packet boat was pulled beneath it.

From time to time the packet boat would encounter another packet boat or heavier barge coming back from its journey to Lake Erie and the man at the long wooden tiller at the stern would pull hard to port to swing the boat closer to the shore. The returning boat would have to pull to the opposite shore of the canal as the westward bound craft had the right-of-way.

Soon after one of those encounters that first morning, passengers on Maggie's boat were dipping water from the canal.

"Fer washin', dear," a woman told Maggie and she joined in on the water collection. She and the other women went below and washed with the cold water. They stripped their dresses to their waists and washed as best they could in the cramped quarters. When they came up the men replaced them.

Maggie had not felt that clean in months. On the ship she had washed with seawater but that made her feel salty. The brine evaporated and left a crusty feeling on the young woman's skin. On the ship fresh water was rationed for drinking only. The canal water, although a bit muddy, was fresh water and used with a little lye soap it made Maggie feel clean.

After her clean-up, the young woman sat on the deck and watched the hoagie guide the mule along the canal's shore ahead of the boat.

The hoagie, a boy named Calvin, walked barefoot along the narrow mule path with the reins of the beast of burden in his left hand. He led the large mule avoiding briars and thorns. Calvin Lipscomb was born in 1839 in the state of New York in a small town. He ran away from home when he was ten and fell in with other runaways. By the time he was eleven he was employed as a hoagie on the Erie Canal. That night the boy sat on the deck with Maggie Madigan and told the Irish woman his story.

"My Ma died when I was born," he reported. "My Pa always blamed me fer it. He beat me bad a lot. When I could, I took what I found and run off."

Maggie patted the child's hand. He looked up at her and smiled. "I wish you was my Ma," the boy said.

Maggie smiled. "You'll make your own way," she assured him. "Amerikay is a grand place to make your way."

"Well, it ain't been so grand fer me so far." The eleven-year-old settled back against the packet boat's cabin. It was night and the mules were tied in the deck-top cabin. At dawn he and the animals would be put to work but until then Calvin could sit on the deck next to Maggie and hold the young woman's hand. He wanted to smoke a cigar but did not. He figured that the young woman would not approve. She wanted to go below to sleep on her bench but chose instead to stay with Calvin.

"What ya doin'?" Calvin asked Maggie the next morning. He was preparing to help get one of the mules its enclosure and start another day's journey on the canal. She was on her knees, facing the rising sun. She did not answer him.

"Ya prayin'?" Calvin asked.

Maggie silently nodded.

"Why?"

The young woman said nothing. Her lips were moving but she said nothing aloud.

Calvin got up from the deck and moved toward the door that led to the mules' quarters. "Hope it duz ya some good," he said back to Maggie.

She nodded and kept praying.

Maggie Madigan always said her morning prayers. She prayed to the Virgin and to Ste. Catherine, her patron saint. She prayed for her journey and those whom she had left behind. She prayed for her sister who was awaiting her in Michigan. That morning she also prayed for the young Calvin as well as for the captain of the packet boat and for the mules. When she was done she crossed herself and pulled herself up from her knees on the wooden deck.

"Cath-lick?" a voice asked from behind Maggie.

The young woman turned to see a tall man standing there. This man, bewhiskered and wearing round rimless glasses, was standing upright. He wore a dark suit of clothes with a gray waistcoat. A golden watch chain hung from one side of that waistcoat to the other.

"Yes, sir," Maggie answered his question.

"There's too many of you here already," he replied. The man stepped around Maggie, avoiding getting too close to her as if her Catholicism could rub off of her.

"We don't hurt nobody," Maggie offered.

The man did not answer. He just went below deck for a breakfast he ate as he sat on the far side of the long table from where Maggie came down to sit.

There were other Roman Catholics on the packet boat and as the trip continued they congregated together on the deck. They soon were saying he Rosary together, much to the annoyance of their fellow passengers.

"The Papists should stay where they came from," the man in the dark suit offered.

"I don't mind them bein' here but why don't they keep quiet 'bout that sort of thing?" another added.

That night once more Calvin sat with Maggie on the deck. "Why do you pray like that?" the boy asked.

"We're supposed to," the young woman said. "The Virgin appeared to two children in France, Melanie and Maximin, and she asked if they prayed. They said 'not very well' and the Virgin told them to pray a Hail Mary and an Our Father every morning and every night." The young woman looked down at the eleven-year-old boy. "Maximin was no older than you," she told him.

Calvin looked up at Maggie. "If she tells me to pray, I will."

"She told us all through those two children in France," Maggie insisted.

Calvin shrugged. "Maybe," he said. The boy settled back against the packet boat's cabin. He looked up at the star-filled sky. There are so many stars, he thought.

Days passed and the packet boat finally reached Buffalo. It was nine days after it had left Albany.

Buffalo was a large town to Maggie's eyes – not as large as New York City, certainly, but large to this Irish country girl. Near where the packet boat ended its journey a railroad train was sitting on tracks. The great steam engine puffed and spit steam that formed large clouds beside it. Passengers were boarding for stops along the way: Syracuse, Rochester, Troy and Albany. They will travel the 384 miles that had taken the packet boat nine days in thirteen or fourteen hours. The railroad train would chug through the forests and fields day and night at up to thirty-five miles an hour. The cost of railroad fare was $6.00 instead of the $3.00 fare on the Canal. To someone like Maggie Madigan the three-dollar difference was a deciding factor. Three dollars was what an Irishwoman could expect to earn working for six days or more and a week's wages was too much to spend for the speed of the railroad train.

Maggie said good-bye to her fellow Catholics on the packet boat and to Calvin who was hard at work pulling the mules from their enclosed stall to feed and water the beasts before the packet boat was refitted for a return trip to Albany.

"Good bye to ya, Ma'am," the eleven-year-old said. Then he leaned close to the young woman. "I prayed last night," he whispered.

Maggie smiled and kissed Calvin's forehead.

The boy withdrew with a start. Then he smiled and returned to his work.

III.

Maggie was guided from the packet boat dock to a tavern by one of her Catholic fellow travelers. The steamer for Michigan would not be leaving until the next day and the young woman and other Westerly-bound passengers needed a place in which to spend the night. She found her accommodations at Harper's Tavern, a hostelry near the Lake Erie waterfront.

Harper's Tavern was a typical inn with two floors and white painted columns that held up the front porch's roof. The lower level consisted of but two rooms: a sitting room that was rimmed with many chairs and benches upon which travelers would sit as they awaited the next boat or stagecoach or tarried while awaiting a meal, and the barroom. The barroom was the haunt of the men and off limits to Maggie Madigan and other female guests. From its doorway poured both cigar smoke and ribald conversation. Maggie and the other women there sat in the sitting room after they made arrangement for their night's stay.

Supper was served in a small kitchen off the back of the tavern, before the fireplace in which the food had been prepared. It was served on metal plates that were nailed to a long table around which men and women sat to eat their meals. Supper was made up of meats, all left over from the earlier dinner at the tavern, freshly made bread with jelly and butter and onions and potatoes that had been newly roasted in the fireplace. Maggie, as did all there, ate heartily and when she was finished she left the table for the sitting room.

"I be from Ireland," the young woman told another woman when asked her origin.

"My Pa was from Ireland," that other woman said, her round face smiling as she spoke. "Roscommon?" That statement was more of a question because she did not know if she had remembered what her father had told her correctly.

"Yes, 'tis north of where I was born," Maggie said. She held up a hand to show a rough map of her homeland. "Here be Roscommon," she said, pointing a finger to the approximate center of the back of her other hand. "And here I was born," she added, moving her fingertip a bit down. "I'm goin' for Michigan to be with me sister."

"Michigan, eh? There's plenty of Irish there. You'll do well."

"I hope so," Maggie replied. "Me sister lives near Detroit."

"Corktown," the other woman said.

"Maggie looked puzzled.

"There's a place just outside of Detroit for the Irish. They call it Corktown 'cause of all the Irish there."

"Cork is where I sailed from."

"That's why they call it that. So many coming from Cork."

Most cities and towns in America by 1850 had a "Corktown", an Irish section. They were called Corktowns because the city of Cork was the point of exit from starving Ireland for so many. Their papers would read "Cork to New York" or "Cork to Boston", and they'd live in "Corktowns" in the new world.

The woman with Maggie took her hand. "You sleep with me tonight. I don't snore none."

Women, like men, were expected to share a bed at a tavern like Harper's Tavern. The luxury of having a bed to one's self was reserved to the rich whom could afford to stay at hotels such as the Astoria in New York City. Common people, businessmen, doctors, lawyers, judges and other traveling folk slept two or three to a bed at taverns and inns along the way.

The fifty cents that Maggie had paid for her overnight at Harper's Tavern entitled her to a place in a bed and two meals. She had eaten supper. She would eat breakfast the next morning. She slept with that half-Irish woman in a straw mattress bed on the tavern's second floor. There were two large room upstairs, one for women and one for men. The men's room was the larger of the two because more men traveled than women did. Men on business; traveling salesmen; doctors and lawyers on circuits; itinerant preachers and teachers; knife sharpeners and hawkers would fill the sleeping rooms of taverns in America each night. The only women who traveled by coach, train, canal, or steamer were the occasional schoolteacher going to a new assignment, a widow going to a new husband, a journalist or artist looking for adventure and women like Maggie who were called "movers", ones looking for a new home.

The bed was lumpy and hard but Maggie slept well. Her bed companion had not lied. She did not snore.

In the morning water was brought to the rooms and the women washed up in a shared basin that was filled with warm water from a pitcher.

There was a washstand for this purpose. After washing, the ladies, only four of them in all, came down for breakfast.

The breakfast at Harper's Tavern was all as good as breakfast had been on the canal boat. There was ham, sausages, bacon, pork chops, eggs – both fried and boiled - and toasted bread. The tavern owner's daughter made the toast in the fireplace. She slid slices of bread into a wire toaster with long handles then held the bread before the fire and turned from side to side to evenly toast them. When she removed the bread pieces from the toaster the wires that had held them in place left a pretty pattern of untoasted bread. Maggie lathered great quantities of freshly churned butter onto her toast and spread some jam on it too. Poor Ireland seemed so long ago.

The omnibus coach for the steamship left the front of the tavern at eight in the morning. The long and narrow coach had seats facing each other behind the driver and was tightly closed to the weather. There were glass windows that could be opened and on that pleasant morning most of them were open. The sides of the wooden coach were brightly painted with the name of the coach company and with a lively pattern of flowers. A team of four horses pulled the omnibus the several blocks to the dock. Maggie bounced in the back of it along with the others as it was taken over Buffalo's rut-filled dirt roads. Pigs ran to get out of the way of the coach in the streets and men stepped aside to let it pass. When the omnibus reached the docks it stopped and unloaded its passengers.

Maggie Madigan stepped down the three steps at the back of the omnibus and carried her meager belongings to the steamer. She bought a ticket, spending three more of the few dollars she had left. Then, ticket in hand, she boarded the steamer that was bound for Michigan.

The steamer was quite different from the canal boat. It provided meals as did the packet boat but the meals were neither as all-inclusive nor as well-prepared. The food was adequate and Maggie certainly did not complain.

The sleeping accommodations, however, were better that of the canal boat. There was a real bed upon which to sleep with a feather filled mattress. Maggie slept with the same woman with whom she had shared her bed at Harper's Tavern.

The woman's name was Sarah. She was a pock-faced woman of forty-years who was on her way to California to find herself a husband.

"There's a thousand men to every one woman out there," Sarah told Maggie, "sos my chances are pretty good." The woman laughed, showing her missing front tooth.

"Never married?" Maggie asked.

"Oh, no. I was married," Sarah said. "He died of cholera three years ago and I just got sick of folks lookin' the other way when I walk down the street. I don't like to be pitied."

"How long to get to California?" Maggie asked.

"Depends," Sarah said. "I'll be headin' for Missouri there to join a wagon train. I got three hundred dollars fer the trip." Sarah whispered that last part. "So we'll head west from Independence. I'll have to hook up with someone else, another woman or two. They say that'll be no problem. There's plenty of us headed for California."

"Then what? After you join a wagon train?"

"Don't know. They say it'll be a hard trip – mostly walking- but I'm up to it." Sarah leaned close to where Maggie sat. "It's been three years since I've been with a man sos my strength's all stored up," she grinned. The older woman laughed and moved her head around in a circle, stretching her sore neck. "This bed's hard," she said.

"Ain't too hard to me," Maggie reported. "The bench on the canal boat I took to Buffalo was much worse."

"Canal boat, huh? Food as good as they say?"

"It was wonderful," the young Irish woman said. "And bountiful."

"I took the train, myself," Sarah said. "It was five dollars but worth it. "Like I said, I'm flushed."

That was the second time that Sarah had mention the money she had and Maggie wondered about it. Even she, a foreigner, knew that talking openly about money one had while traveling was not a good idea.

"So, anyway, they tells me that it'll be 'bout six months a'walkin' to get all the way to California," Sarah said.

"Six months!" Maggie exclaimed.

"Truly. But what from what I hears, it's worth it. There's gold and, better – men who've found it. I'll be a'marryin' one of those fellahs and live out my life out there in the lap of luxury."

"Well, I wish you well, Mistress Sarah," Maggie Madigan smiled.

The two women settled into their shared bed and soon both were asleep for the night.

When the two awoke the next morning the steamer was tied up off of Erie, Pennsylvania. During the early hours it had berthed at a dock there and as breakfast was being prepared for its passengers the side-paddle steamship was off-loading cargo and taking on other goods to be sent west. Some passengers disembarked and others embarked there.

Breakfast was served in a small dining salon in shifts. The first ones there ate first then the latecomers would replace them and eat off the same plates used by the first shift. That was not unusual. Plates and silver then would only have to be washed once after each meal.

Breakfast was bacon, thick and fried; sausages; eggs and untoasted breads. There were small pots of butter and jelly on the table and they were all empty by the time the meal was over.

Maggie ate with Sarah in the second round of breakfast dining. She used a piece of bread to wipe up some of the butter the first person to use her plate had left upon it and she ate heartily of the other foods. The young woman was still amazed as to how much food was available in America. This ordinary breakfast was made up of more food than Maggie had ever seen at one time. In Ireland meat was a rare treat and so much meat at one time was unheard of outside of the big manor houses. What a rich country she had come to, the Irish woman thought.

Sarah talked during breakfast and, once more, mentioned the money she had with her but this time not only to Maggie but also to others at the table too. As she spoke Maggie put a hand over onto one of her hands.

Sarah only laughed. "I ain't worried, Maggie," she said. "These is all nice folks."

The men and women at the small dining salon table made up a mixed crew. There was a preacher heading west to a new posting; a farmer and his wife moving to Michigan for cheap land; two men going to California to pan for gold; a widow like Sarah who was headed for Illinois to marry a banker in Chicago; a tall man who always wore a top hat, even while dining who had not revealed his plans, and several salesmen who worked the Great Lakes region to sell their wares. None of them, not even the man in the hat, seemed menacing but one never knows.

After breakfast Maggie sat on deck watching the ship's loading come to an end. Soon the crew was casting off lines and the steamer was under way to Cleveland. Sarah joined her.

"Do you think I talk too much?" Sarah asked as she sat beside Maggie.

"'Tis no good thing to talk openly 'bout money you may have," the Irish female cautioned.

"I can take care of myself." Sarah patted her side as if she had something hidden there.

Maggie looked at Sarah. "I'm new to this country, Sarah," she said, "but I know this: no matter where you are in this world a woman has to be careful. Men will take advantage of her."

Sarah put a hand over to Maggie and ran it over the young woman's auburn hair. "Did a man take advantage of you, dear?" she asked.

"Not in that way," Maggie answered, "but back home there were plenty who would have. I was careful and so should you be."

Sarah laughed and spat over the rail of the steamer. "I've been takin' care of myself ever since my husband died and, to tell the truth, for quite a while before that too. I ain't no fool, girl," she said. "What I have, I'll keep."

Maggie smiled and looked out at the disappearing shoreline. The steamer was leaving Pennsylvania behind and heading out into Lake Erie to turn from the sun to head on a westerly tack. Great clouds of smoke billowed from the boat's two stacks and cinders fell onto the afterdeck and into the water astern of the stream boat. The captain, a slightly built man with a menacing face, stood on the bridge, a platform that connected the two paddlewheels that propelled his boat through the water. He looked steadily forward with an occasional glance about the deck.

Sarah leaned back against the cabin of the boat and closed her eyes. Maggie kept looking out over the rail to see gulls and other birds fly by. The shore was only a thin strip on the horizon now and Maggie's eyes strayed from it to look out into the lake.

Lake Erie was a vast fresh water expanse to young Maggie Madigan's sight. She had never imagined that a lake could be this big. As she sat there she thought of Jesus on Lake Galilee she had heard about at Mass and imagined her Lord in a fishing boat somewhere between her and the thin shoreline.

By nightfall the steamer and its passengers had reached Cleveland, Ohio and all would spend the night on the boat as it was tied to the dock there. More loading and unloading took place as the passengers looked out at the Ohio town.

Cleveland was founded by Moses Cleaveland but its name got shortened when a newspaper could not fit the full spelling of the place into its masthead in the size of type it had. The newspaper solved its problem by dropping the extra A and Cleaveland, Ohio became Cleveland, Ohio. It like all Great Lakes ports languished until the opening of New York's Erie Canal. Then, with the construction of the Erie and Ohio Canal that connected Lake Erie with the Ohio River, Cleveland began to flourish. By 1850, when Maggie was looking at it from the steamer, Cleveland had a population of several thousand people.

All of the passengers stayed the night aboard their steamer except those disembarking there. It was just too unsafe to go ashore and wander around because the boat, like most boats in Cleveland, was tied to a dock at The Flats, a dockage on the Cuyahoga River that was inhabited by gangs of thugs, longshoremen, whorehouses and saloons. It was hardly a place for a passenger to visit.

That night Maggie and Sarah shared a bed again. The two women talked but briefly then they were both asleep.

The next day was a stormy one and the captain of the steamer chose not to venture out onto the lake. Sailing ships went to reef points and dared the storm, heeling over sharply. Steamers were at the disadvantage of having no deep keel and in a storm they were not as safe.

Maggie, Sarah and the rest of the passengers spent the day below deck, two of them getting seasick and vomiting a lot into buckets given to them by the crew. That made breakfast, dinner and supper not as enjoyable as they could have been without the pungent smell of vomit below. With the day wasted as far as travel was concerned, Maggie and Sarah settled into their bed early.

That night the storm subsided and the lake became calm. The captain decided to leave Cleveland at daybreak and all was quiet about the streamer.

The women were both asleep when a figure quietly crept into their tiny cabin. It was a dark night. It was a moonless night and after the storm had subsided the sky was dark. Tightly drawn curtains on the cabin's lone single porthole kept out what light might have shown into the women's cabin. Before she could react a hand was clamped down over Sarah's mouth. The startled female reached a hand down to her thigh but the knife she had strapped there was gone from its leather scabbard. Its point was at Sarah's throat, held there by one of the salesmen with whom she and her bedmate had eaten their meals.

"If I couldn't take a knife off a sleepin' woman I'd find other work," the invader whispered in a hoarse whisper. He pressed the knife to Sarah's neck, its point pressed dangerously to the woman's skin. "Where is it?" he demanded, still in a whisper. The man looked over at Maggie who was obviously still asleep.

The Irish woman had her face pressed to the rail at the other side of the bunk she shared with Sarah. She was quiet but was not sleeping. The terrified young woman listened and pretended to be asleep.

"Where is the money," the man demanded with another poke of the knife he held. He had his bewhiskered face down close to Sarah and raised it a little when the woman looked up at him. He wanted that three hundred dollars Sarah had admitted to possessing.

Maggie Madigan eased a hand from under her pillow. She had its fingers wrapped around the handle of her own knife. Without looking the young woman with a sudden motion swung her hand over her friend and it cut into the man.

"I'm cut!" the salesman shrieked. He grabbed his neck from which now was spurting blood. He stood and his hand left Sarah's face. As her mouth was uncovered the woman screamed and sat up. The man fled the cabin holding a hand to his injured neck. He bolted toward the port side of the steamer intent upon escape. Before he could throw himself from the boat he was swept up into the arms of the tall man who was still wearing his tall hat.

"The bitch cut me," the panicked salesman said. His right hand was covered with his own blood.

"He tried to rob her," Maggie, who had followed the man's flight, called out from the hatchway that had brought her from below.

"As I thought," the tall man said. He held the salesman tightly until relieved by a sailor who was on duty on the deck.

Sarah was behind Maggie, shaking as she stood on the stairway. She had a blanket wrapped about her. Maggie Madigan was only in her heavy nightgown. Both were barefoot.

The man in the hall smiled. "Well, you've certainly met your match," he said to the restrained thief.

The salesman was taken ashore by the sailors and handed over to the police. Sarah was calmed with a cup of tea and the consolation of her fellow passengers. She sat on the deck, holding hands with her savior.

It was two more days before the streamer reached Detroit and when it did Maggie had convinced Sarah that her future could be more secure in Michigan with her and her family than in California.

"Three hundred dollars will buy quite a farm or quite a business here," Maggie's sister told her sister's new friend.

"I owe your sister my life," Sarah told Maggie's sister.

"You're welcome to stay here, with us, until you're ready to go on your own."

"Thank you," Sarah smiled. "I shall."

Sarah settled in Michigan, buying a boarding house in Detroit with her three hundred dollars. She later married a widower. Maggie lived with her sister for several years. She married a man she met at Ste. Anne's Church where her sister's family worshipped. She had seven children and often told them of her adventurous journey from Ireland to Michigan in "Amerikay".

A DAY AT THE
EAGLE TAVERN

In the Barroom

"Well, look at what just came in!" Silas Cully grinned David Paul entered the barroom. "My favorite foil!"

The two patrons of the Eagle Tavern barroom looked up from their drinks at the man entering.

"Amber ale, coming up," the barkeeper declared without waiting for Mister Paul to order. As he poured an ale into a ceramic mug, David Paul, a local tradesman, took his usual place at the end of the bar. "Here you go, David," Silas said, shoving the beer-filled mug toward his customer. "I'll be akeepin' track so don't you worry."

David Paul took the mug by its handle and sipped at his beer.

It was May 17th of the year 1850. The Chicago Road that linked Detroit to Chicago had mostly dried from the previous week's rain and stagecoaches were making the six to eight day run between Detroit and Chicago. Business at the Eagle Tavern in Clinton, Michigan, fifty miles, or one day's journey out of Detroit, was recovering. The two other men in Silas' barroom were both stagecoach travelers who had spent the night and were awaiting the next coach west.

"David here is a local fellow who haunts my barroom regularly," Silas announced. "He's a regular sorta fella," he added, meaning the pun.

"Gentlemen," David smiled, nodding to the two other men there.

"Just don't gamble with him," Silas warned.

"Hey! Thanks, Silas. You're cuttin' into my income."

"Just protecting my clientele." Silas wiped the bar with a white cloth he wore draped over his left shoulder. "These fellas are on their way to Chicago and if they start up a game with you, they'll not have enough to pay their fare. That'd keep 'em here, but without no money, how does that help me?"

"Thanks, Silas," one of the travelers said with his drink lifted in the barkeeper's direction.

"If a barkeeper can't take care of you, who will?" Silas smiled. "So, David, what's goin' on today? Avoiding work?'

"Naw, just relaxing a bit before I begin."

Silas looked over at the clock on the mantel above the barroom's fireplace. "Ten o'clock," he reported. "And you ain't started work yet?"

David shrugged.

"I want his job," one of the others laughed.

David just smiled and sipped at his beer.

"The next coach will be stopping here at ten-thirty, or so. Your things all ready to go? The driver don't wait long."

"All ready, Silas," the man said.

"Me, too," the other man joined.

"Good 'cause the road from here through the Irish Hills is pretty much dried out now and the coaches want to make up for lost time."

"No more plank?"

"Nope. The Chicago Road's only planked from Detroit to Saline – forty miles. The rest's dirt, or mud last week."

"I've rode it many a time," the other man said. "Plank for eight hours, then dirt for the rest." He looked at the other man. "First time to Chicago?"

"Yep. I'm from Ohio but got hired in Detroit by T.C. Miller, the tobacconist. I'm on my way to Chicago to interest the men there in our fine Detroit cigars."

"Best in the West," Silas smiled. He held up his own unlit cigar.

"That one of ours?"

"Surely is. Ain't no better smoke than Miller's smokes. How does he do it?" The barkeeper looked at the cigar salesman expectantly.

The salesman smiled. "You expect me to tell you about the stable, right?"

"Of course," Silas said.

"Well, I ain't affirmin' it and I ain't denyin' it, neither." He looked at the other traveling man. "The story goes that when Miller first set up his cigar rollin' business in Detroit it shared a space with a stable and some of the, let's say – 'horsy material' – got mixed up with the tobacco to give Miller's cigars a particular horsy smell and taste that became so popular that the other cigar rollers had to stop by stables to get stuff to add to their mix to keep up with the competition."

"That true?"

"Like I said, I ain't affirmin' it and I ain't denyin' it. It's what we call a trade secret."

"Well, true or not, Miller's segars are still the best," Silas offered.

"You know, I've been buying Miller cigars every time I pass through Detroit and I've noticed the difference." The man plucked a cigar from his waistcoat and sniffed at it. "Horsy, huh?"

The cigar salesman laughed. "You didn't hear it from me," he said.

The next half-hour passed with more chatter in the barroom until the stagecoach formed in front of the Eagle Tavern. The two travelers finished their drinks, gathered the belongings and headed out of the barroom from the tavern's front door. "Remember where we are on the way back," Silas called to them as the departed.

"Nice fellas," the barkeeper said.

"And leavin' with more money than they woulda if you hadn't said what you did," David Paul mused.

"You got plenty of pigeons right here in town, David. You don't need to be afleecin' the travelin' men, too."

David just smiled, drained his beer mug and slapped a five cent piece onto the bar in front of him. "There you go, Silas. If it weren't for what you said, there would be more there."

"And I'd have to put up with you even longer," the barkeeper laughed.

As David was exiting, four men who had gotten off the stagecoach entered the barroom. "Keep agoin', David," Silas warned as the prospective gambler eyed the men. He did.

"Welcome to the Eagle Tavern, fellas," the barkeeper welcomed. "What can I be agettin' you?"

Drinks were ordered – two stonewalls, a stout and an Irish whiskey.

"Stonewall?" the Irish whiskey-orderer asked as Silas began making the drinks.

"Yep. Very popular around here. Where you from?"

"Pennsylvania."

"Rye whiskey country," the barkeeper observed. "So why you orderin' Irish?"

"'cause of my Pa. He was Irish and put that taste in my mouth."

"Understood. My Pa was Irish, too. Good folks them. If it weren't for the Irish and the Germans I'd have no body in my barroom!"

All laughed.

"But, stonewalls are the most popular whiskey cock-tails here in Michigan. It's made with corn whiskey and simple syrup with a splash of bitters. Very refreshing."

"I'll stick to Irish – for now," the Keystone-Stater said.

Silas finished making the four drinks, passing each to one of his customers across the pock-marked wooden bar. "Everyone staying the night?" he inquired.

All were.

"Well, you'll find good accommodations here. We got plenty o' room in the beds upstairs what with the road clearing and the men who were here now on their way and all. We'll sleep no more than two to a bed and, like I always say – you never gotta sleep with strangers at the Eagle Tavern 'cause we'll properly introduce you before you go to bed."

"Meals?" the Pennsylvanian asked.

"Your fifty cents includes three meals and a place in the bed – breakfast, dinner and supper. We shake out the sheets in between each and every use and we wash 'em once a month, whether they need it or not. And this bein' the middle of the month, them sheets all got a lotta clean still in 'em."

"So, you own the place?" one of the other men asked.

"Oh, no. The Eagle Tavern's owned by Mister Calvin Wood, late of New York State, and his wife, Harriet. Calvin's a local farmer who bought the place a couple of years ago. He hired me and my wife, Sadie, to run it for him."

"Your wife do the cooking?"

"Sure does, along with Calvin and Harriet's daughter. They're both good cooks, especially my Sadie."

"So what your story, Silas?" one of the others who had taken a seat at one of the six small wooden tables in the barroom asked.

"Sos how do you know my name?" Silas asked back. "I don't remember you from bein' here before. Have you?"

"Nope, but I've certain heard of Silas, the bestest barkeeper on the Chicago Road."

The barkeeper laughed. He straightened the black high felt hat he wore and looked over at the man. "Thanks for sayin' that, but you're still apayin' for that drink."

"Don't hurt to try," the man grinned. "So, what is your story?"

"My story? I've got a story?"

"Everyone's got a story," the man insisted. "How'd you come to be here?"

"Well, my Ma and my Pa loved each other and…"

The man laughed. "No, I mean, how'd you get here to Clinton, Michigan and barkeeper at the Eagle Tavern?"

"Well, it ain't all that remarkable. I was born in Kentucky. My Pa had fought on both sides in the Revolution…"

"Both sides?" the Pennsylvanian asked.

"Yeah. He was recruited in Ireland to fight for the English against the Boys of Freedom here. He was in a pub – that's what they call barrooms over there – and he took the King's shilling."

"What's that?"

"What's what?"

"The King's shilling."

"That's what they call joinin' up the army. The recruiter offers you a shilling and, if you take it, you're enlisted. In Ireland, my Pa said, they put a shilling in the bottom of a beer mug, offer a fellow a free beer and as soon as the shilling touches his lips – he's in the army!"

"Aw, come on,"

"Well, that's what my Pa said and he never lied. He was Irish, you know."

Everyone there laughed.

"So, anyway, my Pa, Daniel Patrick Scully, come over to fight for England against his will and at one of them battles he saw all them guns lined up apointin' at him so that night he decided to become an American. He changed his named from Scully to Cully, just in case the English won the war and the King was alookin' for him. We've been Americans and Cullys ever since."

"That true?"

"That's what my Pa said and…"

"He don't lie."

"Got that right. Anyway, after the war he married my Ma, Isabel Grace Currier, an English girl, so I'm the product of a mixed marriage – half Irish and half English. Out of the shame of it my folks had to move from Virginia to Kentucky where that sorta thing is allowed."

"So you grew up in Kentucky?"

"Yep, for the most part. We farmed there until the Harrison Land Act in 1809 allowed folks to buy land in Indiana. But when we got there we found out that it was a cheat - you had to pay cash money for the land - so were farmed for others until 1811 when the government was sellin' off what had been Indian lands on credit. That's when we became official Hoosiers."

"Where'd that come from?"

"What?"

"Hoosiers. Why do they call people from Indiana Hoosiers?"

"I started it, actually," Silas said.

"You?"

"Yep. I was aworkin' for General Harrison who owned a barroom in Vincennes, which was the capital at the time, and one night, after a big donnybrook fight – they had Irish in those days, too – I was asweepin' the floor and reached down to pick somethin' up. 'Whose ear?' I called out and, I guess, it stuck."

"Now, Silas. Your Pa may not have ever lied but…"

The barkeeper smiled. "You don't have to believe me, you know. It's a free country. Everyone's got the right to be wrong."

"So you're workin' for General Harrison – then what?"

"I joined up with him and Indiana militia to fight the Shawnee. We heard they was amassin' at the Tippecanoe River for an attack on us so we attacked them before they could organize it. We whipped 'em good but it only made them mad so a year later, in 1812, they joined up with the English and we had to fight them all over again. They had two great leaders, Tecumseh, the war chief, and his brother, the Prophet. Over the next couple o' years we fought them fellas up and down the Wabash River and even into Michigan and Canada."

"The English and their Indian allies captured Detroit during the war and slaughtered a group of Kentuckians that had been sent to oppose 'em. They caught them poor fellas acrossin' the Raisin River and cut 'em to pieces. It was horrible. Later, after the Shawnee went with their English partners from Detroit through Upper Canada, our forces caught them unawares and we sent in the Kentucky troops first. They shouted 'remember the Raisin' and got their revenge. Tecumseh fell there and that pretty much ended the Shawnee involvement. Things settled down in Indiana and, after the war ended in 1815, I left for other things. I had my fill o' war so I didn't wanna be a soldier none and, unlike my brother who stayed on the farm in Indiana, I didn't want to be no farmer, either. So I moved to Chicago where I learned barkeepin'. Speakin' of which, who's ready for another drink?"

"Stonewall, Silas," the Pennsylvanian announced.

"Ah, another convert!" Silas Cully poured a good amount of corn whiskey into a short glass that he had filled with ice. To that absolutely clear liquid he then added simple syrup had had earlier made by boiling sugar with water so the resulting liquid remained unclouded. With a hard splash of bitters he finished the drink, adding a macaroni sucker to it before he handed the stonewall to his customer.

The man took the drink and sipped it through its hollow pasta tube. "Delicious," he declared.

"Welcome to Michigan," one of the other stonewall drinkers called out with a raised glass.

"Looks pretty empty," Silas noticed.

"Sure, Silas. Another and for my friend, as well."

The barkeeper prepared to more cock-tails then poured a second stout ale for his remaining customer.

"Come on. Come on," that man urged. "Back to your tale."

Silas smiled. "Well, where was I?"

"In Chicago, after the war, learning barkeeping," the Pennsylvanian reminded.

"Oh, yes." Silas adjusted his cravat, tucking an end under his frock coat between that black trimmed grey wool garment and the colorful cotton waistcoat he wore under it. The cravat, a red and yellow polka dot strip of cloth, was tired into a large bow at the barkeeper's throat. "Well, like I said. I moved to Illinois to get off the farm. By then my Ma and Pa were both dead and my brother was operating our farm. I had two children in tow so…"

"Two children? How'd that happen?" The beer drinker was confused.

"Oh, I left that part out."

"Pretty important part, I'd say."

"Well, I married before the war and had two children, twins – Hezekiah and Dorcas. My wife, Rosemary, was killed by the Indians during a raid on our town and I was stuck with the youngin's with no wife to care for 'em. When I was off to war, my Ma, then my sister-in-law, saw to the children but, afterwards, it was all my job. I went to Chicago to find work and a ma for the children."

"And, of course, you did."

"I sure did – both. A great job – barkeepin', and a great wife – my Sadie. Both at the same time, too. My wife was the daughter of Mac McAllister, the owner of a tavern in Wolf Point – that's what Chicago was called in those days. He taught me his trade and I fell in love with his daughter. Sadie's ma was an Indian woman sos she's half Scottish and half Shawnee. But with me bein' half English and half Irish, it was acceptable."

"You have children by her?"

"Just the one – Megan. She's living right here in Clinton along with her daughter, Nettie. You might see Nettie in here soon. She likes to come here to help her grandpa."

Silas Cully finally pulled his cigar from his waistcoat. The man held the finally rolled Detroit cigar in front of his face, looking at its beautiful summitry. He smiled and clipped its head. Silas put the cigar to his lips to take a dry draw. "Perfect," he reported.

"Now," Silas said as he lit his Lucifer match to put its flame to the foot of his smoke. He toasted the end of the cigar before fully lighting it. The barkeeper drew in a mouthful of rich smoke then expelled it into the air over his bar. "Horsey," he smiled.

"What do you say to people who say that cigar smoking is not good for you?" one of the customers asked.

"Are you serious? Cigar smoking was proved to me to be good for you."

"How so?"

"Well, last month I went over to Ann Arbor, Michigan where they just opened a school for doctors. You know now, in Michigan, to be a doctor you've gotta go to school for a full year – quite a burden on the young men, but they gotta do it. Anyway, I met with a man there, his name was Doctor Cocker, an Englishman. On a series of shelves he had all kinds of bottles and jars and inside each one was a dead frog or squirrel or other critter. He said they use them for dissection. I figure that means they died and they section 'em up to see what's inside 'em. Anyway, I said, 'Doc, these must be all fresh kill, huh?' and he said, 'No, some of 'em have been dead for a long time.' So I said, 'Then what keeps 'em from rottin'?' He told me that they preserve them in alcohol and that keeps 'em from rottin'."

"Then the other day, I went to a butcher shop here in town and the butcher had a whole bunch of hams, turkey breasts and sausages all ahangin' right out in the open and they weren't rottin', neither. So I asked him, 'What do you do, dip 'em in alcohol?' 'No,' he says, 'I take 'em out back to the smokehouse and smoke 'em and that keeps 'em from rottin'.' So, between the segars and alcohol, I figure, I'm gonna last forever!"

"Good thinking, Silas," one of the men laughed.

"Now I got a sister-in-law who insists that my whiskey drinking is a sin. What should I say to her?" the Pennsylvanian asked.

"Well, tell her that I had scientifically proved to be otherwise," Silas offered. "I asked my own doctor about it. He was a teetotaler and wanted to show me that drinking whiskey was bad for me. What he did was to set up a demonstration. What he did was he took two glasses, one filled with corn whiskey and the other filled with water. He dropped a live worm into each of 'em and, sure enough, the one that went into the whiskey curled up and died whilst the other one was swimmin' around lookin' kinda happy. He says, 'Silas, what does this prove to you?' I said, 'Doc, it proves to me that if you drink whiskey, you'll never get worms!' And I've been worm-free most of my life."

"You're a wise man, Silas," the customer smiled.

"Thank you, but it's pretty obvious, ain't it?" Silas took another drag on his cigar, expelling the rich and slightly horsey smoke into the barroom air. "There's a jar up there on the mantle with some segars in it. You fellas are welcome to partake of 'em, if you wish. Most of 'em have been smoked only once so there plenty of smoke still in 'em."

"Thanks, Silas, but I've brought my own," the Pennsylvania man smiled. He produced a cheroot from his waistcoat, clipped its head and lit it. "Not Detroit, but still good," he maintained.

"Supper's gonna be ready by four," the barkeeper proclaimed. "My Sadie and Harriet's daughter, Irene, have been cookin' all day to feed you.

They've got roasted pork, roasted potatoes, root vegetables, a fine cabbage soup, shredded beef and chicken pie for you. They've made an apple pie for dessert along with tea or coffee, whatever is your preference."

"Sounds like we've chosen the right place to spend the night, Silas."

"Darn right you have. Ain't no better food anywhere along the Chicago Road then right here."

"I hear that Walker's Tavern at Cambridge Junction serves good food," one of the men proposed.

Silas sneered. "Walker's? Let me tell you about Walker's Tavern. Last year Walker was accused of puttin' horsemeat in his rabbit stew. Well, he denied it for months but was finally taken to court about it. Well, the judge asked his directly, 'Do you put horsemeat in your rabbit stew?' and, being from Michigan, Walker had to answer truthfully – I understand It's different in Washington – and he told the judge, 'Well, your honor I do put a little bit of horsemeat in my rabbit stew.'"

"Well, the judge was from Michigan so he was used to that equivocation talk so he asked directly, 'What do you mean by a little bit'"

"Walker answered, 'half and half'"

"The judge asked 'what do you mean by half and half?'"

"'One horse and one rabbit,' Walker said."

"Alright, Silas," the cigar salesman laughed. "You warned us."

Silas lightly stroked his beard and took another puff on his cigar. The man was over six feet tall and had a burliness to him. As he wiped down his bar, he kept his Detroit cigar in his mouth. He redraped his bar cloth over his left shoulder and looked around his barroom.

The room was about twelve feet by twenty feet, not including the bar area. Behind Silas was a tall rack of shelves that held beer mugs and the various liquors of the trade. There was one bottle each of Holland gin, Irish whiskey, Scotch whisky, corn whiskey, rye whiskey, and applejack. There also were bottles of wine: ruby and tawny ports, rainwater Madeira, a claret and a hock. Nearby were bottles of bitters and simple syrup. The kegs for hard cider, pale ale, amber ale, stout and porter were placed off to a side as were bottles of non-alcoholic beverages like lemonade, cherry, orange and strawberry syrups. All these libations filled the air with a pleasant aroma that even the smoke from the lit cigars could not overwhelm.

Adding to it all was the smell of the fireplace in which burned one log. It was May but still a bit damp and cool in Michigan. The small fire made the barroom a pleasant place to be.

"So, Silas, when did you come to Michigan?" the Pennsylvanian asked, sipping his stonewall.

"Thirteen years ago in 1837," the barkeeper replied. "Sadie and I left Chicago when Michigan became a state. We thought a new state would give us new opportunity. At first we went to Detroit where I kept bar at the Rail-road House Hotel. Then I worked in Pontiac for a while before we came here to Clinton. I met a lot of good people along the way."

As Silas was speaking, a tall man wearing a tall black hat entered the barroom. He and his hat were so tall that he was compelled to duck to get through the doorway. "Well, look who's here," Silas said, interrupting his story. "Gentlemen, this here is Mister Dan'l Brown. Dan'l's a salesman for the McCormick Reaping Machine Company of Chicago, Illinois. How are you today, Dan'l? I haven't seen you in a while."

"I'm just fine, Silas," the tall man said. He crossed to the bar. "Thirsty, 'though."

"Well, I can solve that problem. What will it be?"

"A Liberty."

"Of course." Silas began to prepare a Liberty cock-tail – a blend of hard apple cider, applejack brandy and simple syrup. The barkeeper stirred the drink with ice and decorated it with a small macaroni sucker. "Here you go, Dan'l: a Liberty cock-tail. God bless America!"

"God bless her," the reaping machine salesman agreed, lifting his drink.

"Spendin' the night, Dan'l?" Silas asked.

"Sure am. I'll be starting out for Detroit in the morning. Got a fella there who's interested in stocking our machines. I have hopes to open up a whole new territory outta Detroit."

"Good luck to you. All these fellas are travelling men, too."

Daniel Brown looked about the barroom and each man there tipped his hat to him. "Can't ask for better company," he smiled.

"Silas here's been telling us his life story," the stout-drinker reported.

"I hope you ain't in no hurry to get somewhere," Daniel Brown laughed. "Once someone's got old Silas talking 'bout himself – look out."

"So, how far did you get, Silas? The time you invented fire or how you won the War of 1812 all by yourself."

"Now, Dan'l, you know I don't tell no fanciful tales. I just say the truth and if it feels like a lie – so be it."

"All right, then, tell these gentlemen how you started the gold rush in California."

"You did what?" the Pennsylvanian asked.

"Oh, that weren't nothin' I planned."

"I thought you said you worked in Michigan ever since you left Chicago."

"Well, I did except for the time between 1845 and last year. Those four years were spent in California."

"Well, let's hear it."

Silas smiled. He knew his customers were in for a treat.

"In 1845, my Sadie and me were workin' right here in Clinton before Calvin and Harriet Wood bought this place. I had already turned fifty-two years old – that official life expectancy, you know – and I decided that, since I had nothin' much to lose, we should go off on a final adventure. Sos she and I travelled West to Missouri where we joined a wagon train for California which was then still Mexican territory, we kicked in three hundred dollars to buy a wagon and team and pay our part of the wagon train fee."

"That's a lot of money, Silas," the stout-drinker said.

"Surely is. We saved for a long time to get it. So, we're off to California, followin' the Platte River to the North Plate then down through the Great Salt Valley, across this horrible desert to the Rocky Mountains. That's when Chief Truckee, an Indian, joined up with us to guide us through the mountain passes. Six months after leaving St. Joe, Missouri, we were there, in Yerba Buena."

"Yerba Buena?"

"That's what they called San Francisco in those days. It means 'good grass' in Mexican talk. They called it that 'cause it was a good place to graze animals. We settle in, takin' up with one of the greatest men I'll ever met – William Alexander Leidesdorff."

"Never heard of 'em,' the Pennsylvania said.

Silas winced. "William Alexander Leidesdorff was the first man of African descent to become a millionaire in America. He was born in the Caribbean Islands to a Dutch planter and his African wife. The man was so fair-complexioned that his pa sent him off to New Orleans to be reared in white society by his uncle. He grew up there and when an adult he became a lion of high society. He was sought out by the high-born French families there and manya fine French young lady hope to be his bride. He met and fell in love with one a strikin'ly beautiful girl named Hortense. Well, he and Hortense were about to be married when Leidesdorff's father died and when his will was published, Will's secret was revealed."

"Hortense's father broke off the engagement and at their last meeting, Will gave Hortense a gold ring as a symbol of their undying love. Each promised never to marry another and they parted."

"All this true, Silas?"

"Let him finish," Daniel Brown insisted. "It's true."

"Well, Will Leidesdorff sold all that he had and bought a sailing ship to become a trader. Just a few days before the ship was to depart, Will made a final stroll along the streets that he and his beloved had walked together. It was then that he saw a funeral procession passing. It had fine coaches and on each black horse was a white plume that signified the death of a young person. Then Will saw many of Hortense's family inside those coaches. He asked someone nearby and was told that the deceased was a young white girl who had become involved with a mulatto and had taken her own life. Will was devastated. The next day a priest came to ill Leidesdorff to hand the man the gold ring that he had given

Hortense. 'She said that, if anything happened to her, I was to give you this ring,' the priest told him."

Silas paused. He looked across the bar to see the men in his barroom in rapt attention. "He wore that ring on a chain around his neck. He never took it off and he never married."

"That's such a sad take, Silas," the Pennsylvanian said. He sipped at his drink and asked the barkeeper to go on.

"Will Leidesdorff took us in, puttin' me to work in a barroom he owned in Yerba Buena and hired Sadie to do laundry for him. We got to know him well. Many an evening he and I'd sit on the bluff of the South Beach that overlooked the harbor, smoke cigars and talk of life and love. That's when I learned his story."

Will became rich, trading in California, and after the revolt that freed California from Mexico and the arrival of the American Army and Navy, he was elected to the city council and became its treasurer. There was no man more respected that William Alexander Leidesdorff in what they then were acallin' San Francisco."

"What happen to him?"

"He died of the brain fever just months before gold was discovered on the American River. He died in my arms with my Sadie lovingly wipin' his fevered brow. At the end he looked up and called her Hortense. She didn't correct him."

Silas paused again. He ran a hand over his face to secretly wipe a tear from his eye.

"So, what about you causing the gold rush?"

"Well, after Leidesdorff's death I went to work of a squirrelly fella name Captain John Sutter."

"Oh, here it comes," the stout drinker laughed.

"'tis true," Silas maintained. "Captain Sutter was a Swiss fella who had a fort and he us marchin' around every day like we was his army. Well, I had been a real soldier back in 1812 and I had no need to do all that again so, when Sutter asked for volunteers to go to the American River to build him a mill, I joined John Marshal and others to do so."

"That's where the gold was discovered, right?"

"I'm getting' to it," Silas said. "I was a cold day in early 1848 and it rained almost every day. Well, this one morning dawned clear and Johnny Marshal and me was workin' near the river when I spied a critter comin' out of the woods to get a drink of water. It looked kinda like a possum to me and, me being from Michigan, and all, I figured – there's lunch. So I said to Johnny Marshal, 'Hand me one of them stones over there and I'll chuck it over and hit that citter in the head and we'll have a fine stew today.' He said 'Sure, Silas. Which stone?' And I said, 'Gimme that shiny one over there' and the rest is history."

Everyone laughed. "So that started it all, huh?" the Pennsylvania asked.

"Yep. A Mormon fella by the name of Sam Brannon got ahold o' that stone and ran through the streets of San Francisco ayellin' 'Gold! Gold from the American River.' That changed everything. Men left their businesses and rushed out to get rich. The onlyest schoolteacher in town joined them and the school was closed. Soon people were apourin' in from all over, hundreds of ships filled the harbor, all abandoned by their crews for the gold fields. That's when Sadie and I decided to come back to Michigan. William Leidesdorff was dead and the men replacing him weren't the kind I wanted my wife to be around. So we sailed on a ship – six months around the bottom of South America to New York. From there we went by train to the Erie Canal then by steamboat to Detroit. Our daughter, Megan and her daughter, Nettie, were sure glad to see us."

"You know, Silas, you tell that story so well, I'm actually tempted to believe it," Daniel Brown grinned.

Silas gave a sly grin over at his customer. "I find that 'true' is more often than not different to different folks. What's true for one, ain't necessarily true for another."

"And everything you say is true?"

"To me it is," the barkeeper smiled.

The chatter and drinking continued in the barroom of the Eagle Tavern. Silas interrupted with another fanciful tale much to Daniel Brown's delight. The barkeeper's stories were one of the reasons the salesman always stayed at the Eagle Tavern rather than one of the other taverns in Clinton.

"So, anyone here because of the big funeral?"

Daniel smiled. He knew what was coming.

"No," the Pennsylvanian answered for him and the others, "but I'm sure you'll tell telling us about it."

"Sure. One of the local men died three days ago. His name was Brother Odd Fellows. Ain't that somethin'? His folks named him Odd. And, of course, Brother Fellows grew up ahatin' that name. In fact, his final request was that they don't put that name on his tombstone. Sos they buried him yesterday with a stone that ain't got nothin' written on it at all. People walk by, see that stone and say, 'That's odd'. Sometimes you can't win for losin'."

Daniel Brown laughed, as did all the others. "That's why I love you, Silas," he proclaimed.

Silas just shook his head. "Another Liberty, Dan'l?"

"Sure, Silas. I think I earned it listening to your stories."

"Us, too, Silas," the stout drinker said, raising his nearly empty beer mug.

The barkeeper went to work, pouring drinks. When each mug or glass was refilled he collected the money for the drinks as well as fifty cents from each of the travelers to pay for their overnight stay.

"Dinner's gonna be ready shortly, gentlemen," he said. Silas finished his cigar, tossing the butt of it into the fireplace. He walked around his barroom, wiping tables and straightening up a bit. On each of the tables was a small redwear saucer that Silas put there to collect the ashes from his customers' cigars or pipes. At other taverns, smokers were allowed to use the floor for that purpose but not at the Eagle Tavern. Silas considered it a better way. Also on the tables, as well as on the bar, Silas had placed a bill of fare that listed the drinks available and offered information about stagecoach routes and schedules.

As Silas was at work on the floor, David Paul reentered.

"Oh, no!" Daniel said when he saw that man come in. "I thought I be avoiding you today."

"Well, Mister Brown," Paul smiled. "Still stingin' from the lesson I taught you last time."

"Don't gamble with this man," the reaping machine salesman warned.

"Why does everyone have an interest in cuttin' into my income?" David laughed as he went to the bar. "Beer, Silas," he said when he got there.

The barkeeper returned to his place behind the bar and dipped a mug into a keg of amber ale which he passed to the newly arrived man. "Thank you, Silas," David smiled. He lifted the mug to his lips and sipped through his beer's rich foam. "Delicious," he smiled.

"So, you're a gambling man, huh?" one of the others there asked.

"I've been known to risk a bit from time to time – just for fun, of course."

"Of course. "What's your pleasure?" the other man asked, picking up a deck of cards from a table near him.

"It pleasures me to win," David answered, "At whatever game you like."

"You know poker?"

Poker was a rather new relaxation that had spread inland from the Mississippi river boats. Few in Michigan knew it but, the, David Paul was not like the average Michigan farmer who worshipped the game of euchre. "I've played it once or twice," Paul answered.

"I'm sure glad I got your overnight fare already," Silas warned as the man and David Paul took a table together.

The cards were dealt and the game began. Seven card stud was the most popular version of poker and that is what the two men played. The others watched. By the time that Sadie Cully stuck her head into the barroom from the adjoining sitting room, David was down three dollars.

"You can't eat now. I gotta catch up," Paul protested.

"Finish after dinner," Silas insisted. "Let that deck cool down a bit. Dinner is served and if your poker mate there don't get to it, the others'll eat it all. And no discounts on your fares, if he don't eat."

"I'll be back," the man smiled, pressing his money into his waistcoat pocket. "I ain't missin' dinner."

"I'll be here," David Paul promised.

"Just warming him up, David?" Silas asked after the other men had left.

"Playin' him like a fiddle," Paul grinned.

In the Dining Room

The men from the barroom joined two more men who had been waiting in the sitting room and two women whom Sadie had called out of the ladies' sitting room. The bonneted mixed blood female's face clearly showed her heritage with a broad Scottish forehead and high Indian cheek bones. She was very attractive, even in her fifties, and carried herself with authority as she guided the tavern's guests to their seats in the small dining room. But there was something else that at least a few of those in the dining room saw. From under the woman's tight fitting bonnet protruded brown curly hair and her skin tone suggested more of African heritage than simply Indian and Scottish.

"Ladies, here, please," Sadie directed and had the two women travelers, both movers – people moving from one place to another – sat side-by-side on one side of one of the two wooden tables in the room. "Gentlemen, wherever," Sadie announced and the men took their places at the two tables. They, along with the women, immediately began eating, grabbing at the bowls of freshly baked breads that were already on the table. Small dishes of butter were passed as Sadie joined now by Irene Wood, the tavern's owner's daughter, carried two large terrines of soup into the dining room. The soup – cabbage and onions – were dipped into and served to the guests in bowls that were passed.

"A great soup, Sadie," the Pennsylvanian told Silas' wife.

"Thank you, sir," she replied.

More bread and butter were brought in from the nearby kitchen then Sadie and Irene began carrying in platters of food.

Sadie toted two large platters, one piled high with roasted pork and the other with an assortment of roasted root vegetables - potatoes, parsnips and onions. As the woman placed those platters onto one of the tables, Mister Wood's daughter placed two others – Chicken pie with a crust draped over what was really a chicken stew and shredded beef in a thick gravy – on the other table. As the diners filled their plates, the platters were rotated to the other table so all could have some of it all.

Coffee and tea were offered. Some of the men had brought in their drinks from the bar and drank them with their meal instead.

Salt was found on the tables in small salt bowls and dipped from them by the diners' increasingly greasy fingers. "Use your knife," Sadie suggested. She demonstrated, picking up a nearby unused table knife. The woman used the tip of the knife to dip salt from a salt bowl and sprinkle it into one of her palms. "And if the knife's been used, use the heel of your fork," she suggested.

"Such a gentile place," one of the women smiled.

"So, Sadie," the Pennsylvania said as he hacked at piece of pork on his plate with his table knife, "Your husband's been regaling us with some pretty interesting tales."

Sadie rolled her eyes toward the ceiling. "Silas's been known to do that," she said.

"And everything he says is true, right?" one of the other man asked between bites.

"To him," Sadie said with a bit of a smirk.

She and Irene continued to serve the men and women in the dining room as Silas stayed in the barroom with David Paul. Those two men talked and lit up cigars. Sadie and Irene covered used platters with napkins to leave them there until supper and poured coffee and tea. Unlike some taverns the Eagle Tavern used a china plate for each diner. Other places simply nailed tin plates to the table and mopped down the whole lot of them after a meal was finished. Not doing so meant that the two serving females had to gather up those used plates after the meal was over, as well.

But, before the plates were removed, apple pies were brought in and great chunks of the pies were distributed. More coffee and tea was poured as the men and women finished their meal.

Just as the plates were being cleared from the table a young girl entered. The child was dressed in a day dress with a white day cap. She, too, had dark curly hair and dark eyes like Sadie.

"You must be Nettie," the Pennsylvanian said when he saw the girl.

"I am," she replied.

"And Silas and Sadie are your grandparents?"

"Yes, sir."

"Well, Nettie, your grandfather has told us good things about you."

The girl smiled and helped her grandmother and Irene finish carting the used dishes from the two tables then went into the barroom to greet her grandfather.

"Beautiful child," the Pennsylvania told Sadie.

"Thank you," she smiled.

Back in the Barroom

With the meal completed, the overnight guests left the dining room. Most of the men went to the barroom. The two women and one of the men, a Baptist who could not join the men where liquor was served, repaired to the sitting room.

"Well, hello again, Nettie," the Pennsylvanian smiled as he saw the child helping her grandfather sweep the barroom floor.

"Hello, sir," Nettie answered.

The men took seats. The poker game resumed. Drinks were ordered and conversation restarted.

"So, Silas, Sadie's father, Mac?"

"Mac McAllister."

'Yes. You say he was a Scotsman?"

"Yes." The barkeep looked over at the man. 'Why do you ask?"

"Well, it's just that Sadie has a bit of an African look to her."

"And?"

"And, is she?"

Silas hesitated. The man looked at the long ash at the foot of his Detroit cigar, holding his smoke up in front of his face.

"No matter to me. I'd just like to know."

"Well, Mac was a mulatto. His ma was mostly African. That gonna be a problem for you?"

"Not at all. Why didn't you say so in the beginning?"

"Well, I hesitate to be open about it 'cause I don't know the politics of my customers."

"We're all free-soilers here, certainly." All the men but one nodded. The stout drinker just looked down at his newly filled beer mug. "Your wife's a handsome woman, Silas. Her blood don't matter to me. I've known a few free African men and I've found them to be as good as white men."

"That's why you tell that story about that Leidesdorff fella, ain't it?" another one of the men suggested.

"Well, he and I are kindred, in a way, ain't we?"

"So, do the people here in Clinton know?" the man asked.

"Mostly. It don't matter to most, once they get to know Sadie and me."

"I can see why," the Pennsylvanian said. "From what I've seen so far, you're both good people."

"Thank you," Silas smiled.

"So, come on, Silas, tell us another of your stories."

The barkeeper smiled.

"Tell 'em 'bout the time you almost got killed by that bear, Papa," Nettie urged.

"Yeah, that sounds like a good one."

"Well, it was a bit ago and I was awalkin' in the woods just outside o' town when I came upon a she-bear with her cubs."

"And you survived it?" one of the men asked, knowing that a she-bear with cubs was the most dangerous animal in the world. She will attack anything in sight.

"Yep, but I almost didn't. As soon as I saw her, I started running but I knew I couldn't outrun that bear so I scrambled up the nearest tree I could get to. The bear tried to get up to me but she was too fat and the branches broke off under her weight."

"And?"

"Tell 'em, Papa," Nettie prompted.

"I will. So the bear just growled a while, then left. I thought I was safe but then I sees her comin' back with a skinnier bear."

"Oh brother!" the Pennsylvania laughed.

"And that skinny bear tried to get up with me but he was too big to do it, too. Sos they both went away and I thought I was safe. That tree saved my life. If it weren't for that tree, the bears woulda got me."

"And that was it?"

"No, sir. Just when I thought I was over it, I saw the bears acomin' back and they had a beaver with 'em!"

Everyone, including Nettie, laughed.

"But I was able to jump down and get away 'cause that beaver slowed 'em down."

"Doesn't my grandpa tell the greatest stories?" Nettie proudly asked.

"Sure does, child. Sure does."

Silas dropped his cigar's ask into a dish on the bar and put the head of that smoke into his mouth. He took a long pull on it and blew the smoke toward the barroom's ceiling.

Conversation and drinking continued. Nettie excused herself and left. David Paul started winning and by the time supper was ready he had won his three dollars back and pocketed two more.

Supper and to Bed

Supper was served in the dining room. It was not much more than the leftovers from dinner with the addition of a cherry cobbler that Sadie had made. The diners ate then returned to the sitting room or the barroom to be soon taken upstairs to their beds. Sadie led the two women up first. The two movers followed the mixed race woman who carried an oil lamp to light the way up the narrow stairway that led from the first floor to the long bedroom upstairs. She had the women follow her to a heavy curtain that separated the small ladies' quarters from the much larger men's quarters.

On their side of the room, the female overnight guests found a wash stand with a bowl and pitcher that would be filled the following morning for face washing. There were two beds and, because there were only two women staying at the tavern that night, each got her own bed – a rarity while traveling in Michigan in 1850.

Sadie stayed with the ladies until each was in her bed then left, taking the oil lamp with her. That put that end of the Eagle sleeping room into total darkness.

The men in the barroom tarried a bit before going up to their beds. Each had one more drink before retiring for the night. The other man, the Baptist teetotaler, stayed in the sitting room, trying to read a book by the dim candlelit there. When Silas led the other males up the stairs, he joined them.

"You two gentlemen here in this bed," Silas directed. "And you two in this." Each man was assigned a sleeping spot and told to be up and ready by six the next morning so as not to miss breakfast.

"We'll be presentin' fried bacon, fried potatoes and onions, fried eggs, toasted breads and plenty o' coffee and tea. The barroom will be available beforehand for an eye-opener, if you wish." Silas turned toward the door then looked back. "Chamber pots are under the beds. Please be careful in their use. Candles are on the wash stand if anyone needs to get up during the night."

The barkeep left the men as soon as the travelers were all to bed, walking down the narrow stairway with the lamp he carried.

Morning

The next day as the sunlight poked into the sleeping room on the second floor of the Eagle Tavern, the travelers were all up and dressing. Before dawn Sadie had brought up hot water for face washing and towels which she left beside the wash stands. The men filtered down, mostly to the barroom for that suggested eye-opener, while the two women stayed on their side of the long sleeping room until it was their time to come down, too.

Sadie Cully and Irene Wood carried platters of food into the small room and breakfast was served. All the travelers came in to enjoy that hardy meal, most of the men carrying drinks from the barroom. Silas joined them all.

"The first coach west will be forming in front of the tavern at eight," he announced. "The first coach east will be arriving at about that time, as well. You must have your belongings on the porch and ready to load or they'll be aleavin' without you and you'll have to spend some more time with us."

"That wouldn't be such a bad thing, Silas," the Pennsylvania smiled as he put a forkful of eggs to his mouth. "I've never heard such wonderful tales along my travels than the ones you spin."

"Amen," one of the other men agreed.

"Well, folks, just remember where we are when you are called to travel back this way again. We'll be right here, awaitin' you."

"With new stories?"

"A few, I'm sure," the barkeeper grinned.

BLACK AND WHITE
AND READ ALL OVER

Our story opens in the office of the Detroit Observer, a black-owned newspaper in Detroit, Michigan early in 1967. Seated at desks are Christine Johnson, a busty woman with blond hair wearing a sweater that shows off her "assets"; Martha Adrian, older and not so busty; Leon Simmons, an older man, conservatively dressed and Harold Williams, a younger man, also conservatively dressed. All are African-Americans.

Christine is talking to Martha. "You know, Stewart's just about perfect for me," she says. "He's everything I want in a man…except for the one thing."

"And that is?"

"He's an alcoholic.

"He is?" Martha asks, now actually looking at her co-worker.

"That's what Stewart says and he don't lie," the chesty black female insists.

Martha is concerned. She likes Christine and is well aware of the attractive young woman's limitations. The busty blonde black young woman was assigned to the Detroit Observer by a Federal anti-poverty program named "Total Action Against Poverty" or TAAP. "Does he go to meetings?" she asks.

"No. He goes to bars. I told you he's an alcoholic."

"You mean he's a practicing alcoholic."

"Well, he's not all that religious, but he drinks."

"But you don't drink at all, do you?

Christine looks a bit confused at Martha. "I sure do," she says. "Pepsi, mostly." She pauses. "Well, sometimes water, but not much. I stick pretty much with Pepsi."

"I mean you don't drink alcohol." Martha smiles, partly in condescension and partly in sympathy.

"I don't think so. Is there alcohol in Pepsi?

Leon has been eavesdropping with Harold. "You know, a woman's IQ is in inverse proportion with her bra size," he offers. "The bigger the boobs – the smaller the brain."

Harold laughs. "A bit of a crude theory, isn't that?"

"No, just true." He looks over at Christine. "Christine is a case in point. It's like this - those boobies hang down and pull all the blood from her brain. That's why she's the way she is. She can't help it. It's anatomy."

"But there have been intelligent women who've had big breasts hasn't there?"

"Never. Name one."

Harold thinks. "Jayne Mansfield was said to be pretty smart and she had huge hooters."

"That's the best you can do? Jayne Mansfield? She pretends she an actress, marries a Hungarian weight-lifter and gets killed by driving under the flatbed of a truck. Real bright broad her."

"What about Pam Greer?" Harold purposely counters.

Leon gets angry. "Now don't be talkin' bad 'bout Pam Greer. You know how I feel about her."

"Intelligent?"

Leon scowls. "Who the hell cares? She's the Goddess, you know. Pam Greer's the most beautiful woman in the world."

Harold laughs. "Yeah, yeah. Okay, I won't use her as an example, but that's just out of respect for your unnatural fixation on her. How 'bout Sophia Loren? She's smart."

Leon smiles, once more. "Seen that man she married? Carlo what's-his-name. She coulda had Cary Grant, for God's sakes, and she picks that short, bald Italian clown over him? A real brain all right."

"Small breasted women do stupid things, too."

"Not as much as the heavy hooters."

"Heavy hooters?" Harold looks around. "Anyone from Labor Relations around? Man, you're treading on dangerous ground now. Ever heard of Women's Lib? That means no sexual talk to the ladies and I think *heavy hooters* comes pretty damn close."

"We're just talking science, man. Besides, our Christine has the double disadvantage of being blonde."

Harold looks over at Christine. "I don't think it's natural," he says.

By then Christine has taken a phone call at her desk and is now holding a hand over the mouthpiece "Leon?" she calls to the older man.

"Yes?" Leon replies.

"I have a story follow up on the Westside. Want it?"

"What street?"

Christine looks down at her note pad. "Gil-Christ," she reads.

"That's Gilchrist," Leon corrects, pronouncing the west side Detroit street as Gil-crest. "It's pronounced Gilchrist."

Christine looks at her note pad again. "But it's spelled G- I- L- C- H- R- I- S- T." she insists.

Leon winces. "I know, but it's pronounced Gilchrist."

"That's stupid. What do they do that?" Christine asks.

"I don't know, Christ-ine," Leon grins.

Without comment, Christine returns to her call. Leon pokes Harold then makes a motion with both his hands in front of his chest to refer to the young woman's big breasts. Both men laugh.

The workers do paper work at their desks and answer phone calls. Martha restarts her conversation with Christine. "I hope things work out with you and Stewart, Christine. But I think you should be a little careful with him being an alcoholic and all. I dated a drunk for a while before I met my husband. It wasn't pretty."

Christine smiles. "Stewart's more handsome than pretty."

"I meant that the relationship wasn't pretty. At first a drunk might be exciting to be around, but that changes soon. Just be careful, okay?"

"Oh, we use protection," Christine said with a slightly embarrassed smile.

"That's not exactly what I mean, but that's a good thing too. Gettin' knocked up is one thing. Gettin' knocked up by a drunk is yet another."

"Stewart's not really a drunk. He's sober a lot. Well, not a lot, but he has his times."

"Just be careful, and I'm not only talkin' sex. That man I dated before I met my husband?"

Christine nods.

"He was a charming man – I mean charming. He charmed the pants off me – literally." Martha looks to see if the men are listening. She doesn't think they are. "He was the best in bed. And out of bed he was really good too. Except when he was drinking. When he was drinking, he thought he was all that, but he was really somebody you didn't want to be around. He got loud – that was the beginning. Then he got mean. At first I thought I could control him. I thought if I showed him how much I cared, he'd cool the drinking, but it only got worse. Pretty soon he was drinking all the time. One time we were supposed to be going to a movie. He picked me up and I could tell that he had already been drinking. We drove to the movie theater – the Beverly on Grand River – and we parked the car in the lot. He pulled out a bottle and offered me a drink. I took one, just so he'd be satisfied. Then he took a drink too. You know, we never went into the movie. We just sat out in the lot in his car and he drank until the bottle was empty. There we were, two colored people sitting out in our car in that parking lot, drinking, while white people walked by us to go into the movie. We were lucky no one called the police.

He drove me home and I was terrified because I could see how drunk he was. From the Beverly to where I stay on Broadstreet – it seemed like a hundred miles. We made it but, after that, I broke up with him."

"Stewart's never done that. He doesn't like to go to the movies."

"Just watch out, Christine. You never know what a drunk's gonna do. You deserve better than that. You deserve a man like my husband."

"Does he drink?"

"Only Pepsi," Martha smiled.

"Like me!" Christine declares with a broad smile.

Martha and Christine return to their work.

Harold looks over at Leon. "Speaking of drinking, Leon. You wanna stop by Gary's after work and the two of us can get a drink?"

"No thanks, man. I got stuff to do," the older man replies.

"Stuff? What stuff?"

"Just stuff. Maybe some other time."

"You're the hardest man to pin down," a frustrated Harold says.

81

"Well you know what they say – A hard man is good to find. Ain't that right, Martha?"

"Mind your own business, you dirty old man," Martha says, half smiling.

"Dirty, but hardly old," Leon insists. He looks over at a radio that is near Christine's desk. "Hey, isn't the Tigers game on?" he asks. "Lolich's pitching, right?"

Harold looks at his watch. "That's right. It should have started by now. Christine, get it on the radio, okay?"

"Okay," Christine says and she turns on the radio. There's music – Motown tune.

"No, the game," Leon insists.

"It's the right station," Christine maintains.

"Let me see." Leon rises from his chair and goes to Christine's desk to check the radio. "It seems to be," he says, looking at the radio dial.

"Maybe the game was rained out," Martha suggests.

"It's raining? You can't see nothing in this tomb," Leon says, exasperated.

"It was raining a little when I went out to lunch," Martha reports. "It probably got worse and they cancelled the game."

Leon smirks, "We work on a newspaper and we don't even know if it's raining out. Someday they'll put a roof on Tiger Stadium and they'll never be a rain-out in Detroit."

"Or they'll build a new ballpark," Harold suggests.

"Never!" Leon said. "We'll never let that happen. The Tigers have always played at Michigan and Trumbull and the always will. Navin Field. Briggs Stadium. Tiger Stadium. I don't care what you call it – it'll always be the home of the Detroit Tigers. No doubt about that. Besides, if Tiger Stadium goes, what's gonna happen to Lindell's? Do you think those Butsicaris boys'll let that happen? Never in a million years." He turns off radio and returns to his desk.

"Who's your favorite Tiger, Leon?" Martha asks.

Harold speaks a second before Leon. "Willie Horton."

"Willie Horton," Leon says, a second behind Harold.

Harold laughs. "How'd I guess?"

"Hey," Leon says, "Gates Brown is good, but Horton's the best."

"What about the white boys. What about Kaline, McAuliffe, Lolich and Denny McLain?" Martha asks.

"Oh, no. Don't get Leon started, Martha," Harold cautions.

Too late.

Leon shouts, "McLain? Denny McLain ain't worth shit. Sure, he's off to a good start this year, but he'll fade. He'll be lucky to win fifteen games in '67. Come on. He's a flash in the pan. That arm of his is hanging by a thread to his shoulder. By the '68 season, no one will even remember his name."

Christine jumps in. "I think he's cute," she says. Leon glares over at her.

"For a white boy," she adds.

"What about that colored pitcher they got in St. Louis?" Martha asks.

Leon smiles. "Bob Gibson? Now there's a pitcher. If he ever squared off against McLain, McLain would have to retire."

"The only way that could happen is if both their teams were in the World Series," Harold reminds Leon.

Christine is puzzled. "Why's that?" she asks.

Leon turns fatherly. "'cause the Tigers are in the American League and the Cardinals are in the National League. The two teams could only play each other if they both made it to the World Series and what's the chance of that happening?"

"It could happen if the Tigers keep playing like they are," Harold insists.

"Not with McLain fading like he will."

"He hasn't faded yet."

"He will," Leon says, confidently. "Them white boys just can't stand fame."

"Like Babe Ruth, Joe DiMaggio, Ty Cobb, Lou Gehrig…," Harold grins.

"A few exceptions. Just mark my words; Denny McLain will be playing the organ for twenty-five cent tips in some Jew-owned bar next year."

"Or win the Cy Young award."

"No chance in hell." Leon folds his arms in front of his chest. There can be no chance he is wrong.

The employees' boss, Charles H. Webb, publisher of the Detroit Observer, enters the office. Charles is the second generation publisher of Detroit's only black-owned newspaper. He walks into the office and moves directly to Leon's desk.

Leon looks up from his work. "Yes, Charles?"

"There's a new man starting today and I want you to show him around."

Christine, Harold and Martha are listening.

"Sure. No Problem. What's he, a reporter?"

"A feature writer."

"Great, more competition for me."

Charles laughs. "Get real, Leon. No one's competition to you. You're a legend here at the paper."

Leon laughs, too. "That's what it says on my column anyway. A legend in my own mind, some say. But, you're right, boss: no one's competition for "Tan Lines" by Leon Simmons, featured feature writer for this here newspaper."

"Anyway, show the new man around, will ya? We'll give him Duff's desk. Help him settle in. Okay?"

"Sure. Where's this guy from?"

"He's a young fellah. Just been graduated from Wayne State. The highest in his class in journalism."

Leon smiles. "Top of the class, huh? Well, we colored are finally breakin' to the top, are we?"

Charles pauses. "Well, he isn't exactly colored."

Leon looks concerned. "'Not exactly colored'? What, exactly, is he?"

"He's white."

"Say what?"

"He's white. You know - Caucasian?"

"I know Caucasian. You hired a white man to work here?"

Charles stops smiling and looks serious now. "Yes. We're Detroit's only colored paper and there are those of us who feel we need to do this. My God, this is 1967. Integration is all around us. Negroes are moving into white neighborhoods. We're getting into the best schools. We got colored men in Congress and colored judges. Thurgood Marshall sits on the Supreme Court. White and colored are marching together in the South. Walter Reuther and Martin Luther King marched down Woodward side-by-side. Things are changing. If this paper is to grow in Detroit, it's got to broaden its appeal."

"Broaden our appeal? Are you nuts? What are we gonna do with a white feature writer at a colored newspaper? We gonna have a polo section on the sports page?"

"Bob's gonna write a general interest column and cover stories we've missed in the past."

"Like Elvis Presley concerts? A feature on the Beatles?"

"He's okay. I interviewed him myself. Damn it, he knows who Ahmed Jamal is."

"I don't care if he's the distant cousin Ramsey Lewis doesn't talk about. He doesn't belong here."

"Look, Leon, it's done. Bob Weingard starts today. I'm the publisher and owner of this newspaper and I've been so ever since my father died. My sons'll be the publisher-owners after I'm dead. Bob Weingard starts today and that's it."

"Okay, okay. Where's this honky now?"

"He's on his way up. And that's the last of that honky shit, right?"

"Right, boss man." Leon puts his head down. "Bob Weingard, Goddamnit? Damn! That's the whitest name I've ever heard." He looks back up at Charles, "Bring him on."

Charles leaves the office to return with his new employee: Robert James Weingard. Bob, as he likes to be called, is a tall and slender white male, fresh out of journalism school. He sports a thinly developed van dyke bread – mustache and goatee – and wears his brown hair long but not too long. It gives the young man a nonconformist look without being mistaken for a hippie.

"Gentlemen…Ladies." Charles says as he stands in the office with Bob beside him, "This is Bob Weingard. He's our new feature writer. Bob, this is Christine Johnson, our secretary; Martha Adrian, our copywriter; Harold Williams - features and sports and the great Leon Simmons, features."

All stare at Bob without speaking.

Christine turns to Martha. "Is he white?" she asks.

"He's white," the older black woman answers.

"Damn!" Christine says under her breath.

Charles makes a speech, pretty much repeating the same things he had said to Leon. He says he hopes all will make Bob feel at home. "We've always been a family here at the Observer and I know we are going to stay a family," the man says.

Leon makes a face that the others pretend not to notice.

Charles leaves after assigning Leon, of all people, to show his new employee around. It is a test for both Leon and Bob.

Leon shows Bob where to put his things in his new desk. Bob has a briefcase and unloads various office items including a coffee cup with his photo on it.

"So, put your shit anywhere in here you want," the black man says. "This was Duff's desk. He kept it messy but you'll, no doubt, have it all neat and crap."

Bob begins putting things away in the desk. "Who is Duff?" he asks.

"Was Duff," Leon corrects.

"Huh?"

"It's not who is Duff. It's who was Duff," Leon says.

"Oh, he's dead?"

Leon looks at the young white man. "Yes. He was killed by the Klu Klux Klan just before Charles hired you. They strung him up right here in the office. The body swung from the ceiling fan and the cops wouldn't let us take it down for three days. They said it was evidence. Every time someone turned on the fan, there was old Duff swingin' around the room. It was very disconcerting."

Bob looks incredulously at Leon.

"He's shitting you, Bob," Harold tells the young man. "Duff retired last month. That's all. He moved home to Mississippi."

"To be lynched by the Klu Klux Klan," Leon added.

"To grow soybeans and watch sunsets."

"And hide from the Klu Klux Klan," Leon says.

"Quite shitting the boy, Leon. You're scaring him."

Leon looks at Bob. "You scared of me?"

"No," Bob replies.

"You should be. I'm one bad ass black man, you know."

"I know you're a great writer," Bob offers.

"You do? How do you know that?"

"I've been reading this paper since I was a kid."

"Like photos of black women, do you?"

Bob laughed. "No, that's Jet."

"You know of Jet Magazine. You sure you're white?"

"I just liked to know what was going on in my community."

"Your community? This isn't the Rosedale Park Observer, you know."

"I don't live in Rosedale Park," Bob said as he put his coffee cup on the desk.

"I'm sorry – Grosse Pointe Park, then."

"I live on the Westside. I went to high school at Mackenzie."

"I was Northwestern, myself."

Harold looks at the two from his desk. "I know people from Mackenzie. Do you know Elroy Pratter?"

"No," Bob answers.

"Leroy Johnson?"

"Uh uh."

"Big surprise," Leon smiles. "So where you stay?"

Bob looks back with a questioning look.

Harold translates. "Where do you live?"

"Oh. Schaefer and Joy area."

"Any colored there?"

"A few."

Leon laughs. "That means two. When someone says a few colored live somewhere that means there's two. If there's more than two, they say there's a lot."

"I haven't counted, but I think there's more than two. Where do you liv.. er stay?"

"Around Dexter and Davison."

Bob's eyes widen a little. "Really? You know that church right there on Davison and Dexter?"

"Yeah?"

"That's where I was baptized."

"You were baptized in a colored church?"

"It was a Swedish church then. My grandmother went there. When it was time for me to get baptized that was where they did it."

"You were baptized in a colored church. Son-of-a-bitch!" Leon looks closer at Bob. "You went to Wayne State, right?"

"Yeah. I was just graduated."

"Top of the class, I hear."

Bob nods.

Leon crows a little closer to the young white man. He looks him over. "So why did you interview for this paper?" he asks

"Well, they had recruiters from various papers and print media organizations at school. I just went down the line and when I came to this paper's desk I saw no reason to pass it by. I mean, just because it's..."

"Colored?"

"Yeah. Just because it's colored. Besides I've always looked at this paper as more urban than colored anyway."

"Urban, huh? Didn't you notice all those times you were reading the paper coming up in your Westside, Mackenzie High neighborhood that all the pictures in this paper were of colored people?"

"Of course. But so what?"

"Let me ask you. When you were going down the line of recruiters at the school, did you notice the desks for Detroit's Jewish News and Polish News too? Did you apply there too, or was it just us who were so greatly blessed?"

"I talked to them too."

"And the Polack and the Jew were too smart to hire you, huh?"

"You know, Leon, I think you don't have much respect for minorities."

"I don't have respect for minorities? Goddamnit, boy, I'm the minority."

"I mean ethnic minorities like Polish and Jewish people."

"And Greeks, Germans, Chinese, Japanese, Lebanese, Maltese, Pekinese…," Harold calls over.

"Yeah, Germans. Why didn't you go to work for that Kraut newspaper? The Detroit…"

"The Detroit Abendpost," Bob says.

"The what?"

"The Abendpost."

"Yeah, the Over-roast. Why didn't you take a job with them?"

"Because I really don't speak German."

"Well, you really don't speak colored, either," Leon insists.

"Come on, Leon. Cut the boy some slack," Harold says.

"Shut up, Harold." Leon looks to Bob. "I respect those who respect me."

"I respect you. Like I said, I think you're a great writer," Bob maintains.

"You greasing me, boy?"

"Just telling the truth. In fact, your column - Tan Lines? I wrote a paper on it in college."

"You did? On my column? Did ya get an A?"

"I got a B."

"Then you didn't do me justice."

"If he'd written his paper on my column he would have been graduated summa cum laude," Harold laughs.

"I was summa cum laude."

"Big deal," Leon says. "Look, just put your stuff in here anywhere you want. Coffee's in the next room. The girls'll get it for you. Don't let Christine put your sugar in – do you take sugar?"

Bob nods.

"She'll have it all screwed up. Have Martha make your coffee or just tell Christine to bring you the sugar. She gets confused between teaspoons and tablespoons."

"Or I'll get my own coffee."

"Now don't be startin' any of that shit here. You white folks are all caught up in that Women's Lib but our colored gals ain't suddin' it."

"They ain't what?"

"They ain't suddin' it. Damn, and you're gonna be writin' for a colored newspaper!"

Harold translates again: "Ain't suddin': A colored colloquialism meaning paying it no mind to or ignoring something. Commonly used by ignorant colored men who are trying to put down a willing white worker."

Leon glares over at Harold.

"So, thanks for the help, Leon."

"Think nothing of it. Always glad to help a colleague."

Leon moves to his own desk.

Christine walks to Bob's desk. "Coffee, Bob?" she asks.

"No thanks, Christine," the young white man says. "I might get some later."

"Well, if you do, the sugar's in a bowl near the coffee maker and the cream's in a 'frig in there. There are cups on a shelf near the coffeemaker."

"Not the cup that has my name on it," Leon cautions. "Nor the one with Dr. King's picture on it."

"Any of the cups are fine," Harold says.

"Not mine and not the King cup."

"I have my own." Bob holds up a coffee cup.

"Whose picture's on that cup? Elvis?" Leon asks.

"No, mime. I had it made at the State Fair. Nice, huh?"

"At least it ain't Elvis," Leon offers.

Christine leans closer to Bob. "If you get your own coffee be careful about the spoons. Someone keeps mixing them up." She looks at Leon who looks away. "The small one's for sugar, not the big one."

Bob smiles. "Thank you, Christine." he says.

Christine returns to her desk. Bob finishes putting things away. Harold, Leon and Martha are working at their desks.

Leon looks back to Bob. "So, what do you drink?"

"Drink?" Bob asks back.

"Yeah, you know, as in throw down a few."

"Oh. Yeah. Why do you wanna know? You asking me out for a drink after work?"

"Hell no. I was just curious what you urban sophisticates are drinking these days."

"Bud, sometimes but mostly Stroh's. It's local."

"I know Stroh's is local. I've lived all my life in Detroit you know."

"Like me."

"No, not like you. Living in Detroit white and living in Detroit colored are two completely different things."

Bob ignores the remark. "So I drink Stroh's. What about you?"

"Yack," Leon answers.

"Huh?"

Once more, Harold translates for Bob. "Cognac. Colored men like Leon drink cognac on Fridays, Saturdays and Sundays."

"Then they drink Stroh's after their money runs out until they get paid again," Martha adds.

"I drink Yack all the time," Leon insists.

"And I drink beer, mostly Stroh's," Bob says.

"A real man of the people you are." Leon half turns his desk chair away from Bob's desk.

"Sometimes Goebel's."

"Goebel's?" Leon says, returning his chair to the position it had been in. "Damn I can't stand that stuff. You know what they can do with that Brooster, the Goebel Rooster."

"No. What?" Bob innocently asks.

Leon looks at Bob with scorn. He smiles. "And you're writing for this paper."

"What?"

"Pay him no mind," Harold says.

"Isn't Goebel's the beer they sell on the Bob-Lo boat?"

"No, that's Carlings Black Label," Bob says.

"Oh yeah - the Canadian Goebel's. Yech."

Christine smiles. "My boyfriend drinks anything. He's an alcoholic, you know."

Bob looks are Christine with a puzzled look.

"I'll tell you later, Bob," Martha says. She looks at Leon. "So, Leon. When are you gonna invite us all out for some cognac?"

Leon laughs. "You Christians don't drink. And Harold's too pussy to drink with and Christine's got her drunk-ass boyfriend."

"And?" Martha prompts.

Leon pauses as if to think. "Charles? Charles is my boss. You don't expect me to drink with my boss, do you?"

"You're leaving out someone."

Leon looks at Bob then at Martha. "The boy drinks Goebel's and he probably hangs out at a bar in Bloomfield Hills. You trying to get me lynched?"

"I don't go to Bloomfield Hills - too pricy. Mostly I hang around Wayne State."

"Good for you. You just keep throwing down Goebel's with your WSU friends and leave us coloreds to drink our Yack."

"Or Stroh's on Monday through Thursday, right?" Bob winks at Harold who winks back.

"So, you're really learning what it is to be colored, huh?"

"You're the one who asked what I drank."

"All part of the educational process, son." Leon returns to his work at his desk.

After a while, Martha gets up from her desk to collect various papers and takes them out of the office. She returns as the staff members keep at their work. Bob is reviewing a copy of the latest Observer that Charles had given him. As the young white man looks through the newspaper, Martha steps to his desk. "Bob, what are you doing for lunch. I can show you a nice place to get a burger near here," the black woman says.

Leon glares at Martha from his own desk.

"Thank you but I brought my lunch," Bob replies with a smile.

"Let me guess - sliced cheese on white bread with butter," Leon jumps in.

"How did you know?"

Leon laughs. "That's like the white national brown bag lunch, that's why. No meat. No mustard. Just plain cheese on white bread."

"With butter," Bob corrects.

"Oh, yeah. With butter."

Harold tosses a paper clip over at Leon's desk. It bounces off some papers the man has there. "So, pray tell, Mister Simmons," Harold asks. "How did you come by that piece of knowledge about the white folks?"

"The Army. I was in Korea, you know, after Truman integrated the Army. It's surprising what you learn from people when some Chink's trying to blow your head off."

"And you talked about favorite lunches?"

"And favorite bars; favorite women; favorite movies - anything to keep our minds off that Chink with the sniper rifle."

"So you know a lot about white people after all, huh?"

"I know. I know." Leon returns to his typing.

"The things you find out," Harold says.

"My boyfriend was in the Army for a couple months," Christine joins in.

"A couple months?" Harold asks.

"Yeah. They had to let him out because he was afraid of bullets."

Leon hits a stack of papers on his desk with a hand. "Christ!" he exclaims.

"He told them he was afraid of bullets and they let him go home."

"That's what he told you?" a newly concerned Martha asks.

"Yes."

"Be careful of that one, that's all I say."

Harold holds up a paper. "This needs to go to re-write," he says to Martha who goes to his desk and takes the paper from him.

"Your story on the end of Hastings Street." She looks it over.

"So sad. Hastings used to be the heart of the colored community. The clubs, the jazz places."

"The restaurants," Bob adds.

"What do you know about Hastings Street?" Leon asks.

"I read about Paradise Valley and what it was once."

"Before Urban Renewal," Harold says. "That's what they call moving colored businesses out to make way for expressways. To them it was Urban Renewal. To us it was Negro Removal."

"Expressways to get white folks to the suburbs, right?" Bob asks.

Harold smiles. "Right. That's exactly what they did to Hastings Street. Some city planner got a map of the city and drew a wide line right up Hastings. He said: 'This'll be a fine place to put the new expressway'."

Bob nodded. "The Chrysler."

"Right. They build that damn expressway right over the last of the colored businesses and then name it for a white man, Walter Chrysler."

Harold looks at Bob. "No offense, Bob."

"That's okay. I'm not a Chrysler. I'm a Weingard and I drive a Ford."

"Fine white man there," Leon leaps in. "Henry, 'know your place, nigger', Ford. Building those damn expressways was nothing more than a rip-off."

He looks at Bob to see if he reacts.

"A theft," the white man says.

"Yeah, a theft. A rip-off."

"Anyway," Harold continues, "I wrote a piece on what Hastings was and what it is now. Maybe, someday, the politicians will think twice before they destroy colored communities like they did there."

"Fat chance," Leon laughs.

"Fat chance," Bob echoes.

Martha smiles. "I remember Paradise Valley and the rest of the Black Bottom. Why, I was baptized in the fountain that used to be there at Clinton Street."

"Clinton Street?"

"Yeah, it was like Black Bottom's Main Street," Harold says. "There was this fountain there, where lots of local churches…"

"Colored Churches," Leon interjects.

Harold looks over at Leon. "Colored churches." He looks back at Bob.

"So, anyway," he continues, "these churches would have their baptisms in that fountain on Clinton Street with everyone looking on. It was quite the community event."

"I was all dressed in white, a long white robe, and I waded into the fountain with the others who were going to be baptized and the preacher put each of us down into that water. I remember going down how scared I was because I was afraid to get water up my nose. A sister standing there put my hand up to my face and had me pinch my nose. It was fine. I came up singing!"

"Singing?" Bob asks.

Martha smiles and sings: "'There is a fountain filled with blood, drawn from Emanuel's veins. Sinners plunged beneath that flood, lose all their guilty stains'." She smiles. "I remember how good I felt. And how that white robe clung to my wet body."

Leon laughs loudly. "That was one of the reasons so many of us heathens showed up to watch those baptisms - wet white clothes on a sister's wet body."

"Leon!" Martha chides.

"Just telling the truth." He looks over at Bob. "So, tell me, Bob, when you were baptized in that colored Church at Dexter and Davison, did your clothes stick to you?"

"I don't remember. I was a baby when I was baptized. And it wasn't a colored Church then. It was a Swedish Church then. I told you that."

"Just testin' your memory, boy."

"My church always baptizes adults and by emersion," Martha says. "Infant baptism just doesn't seem to get the job done to me."

"I was baptized as a baby," Christine reports. "I'm glad I didn't have to be dunked in a fountain like you were."

"If you ever change your mind and opt for immersion in a white dress, please invite me to the ceremony," Leon grins.

"Leon!" Martha says again.

"Watch that blasphemy around Martha, man," Harold cautions. "She's converted."

"I believe that it doesn't matter how something like that is done," Bob offers. "It's what in your heart that counts."

"Amen," Martha smiles. "Well, I'm happy you wrote this paper, Harold. I'll get it to re-write," she tells Harold.

Leon looks down and mutters, "It's what's in your heart that counts. Shit."

*

Bob Weingard begins working on his first actual assignment for the Detroit Chronicle. The publisher, Charles, hands the young white man some photos taken at the Michigan State Fair the year before and some information about the oldest continuing State Fair in the country. "Let's see what kinda slant you'll give this," the black man says.

Harold looks up from his typing and at no one in particular. "It's really raining out. You know, I sure hope the rain keeps up."

No one responds but Bob. "Why's that?" the young man asks.

"'cause if it keeps up, it won't come down," Leon says with a hearty laugh. "I can't believe you fell for that."

Bob smiles. "Funny. Is that an office joke?"

"Sure is and, you know what?" Harold asks.

"What?"

Harold motions toward Leon. "That's a good sign." The black man gets up from his desk and moves to Bob's desk. "Old Leon almost sounded like he accepts the fact that you work here now," he says to Bob.

Bob smiles and shrugs.

Harold looks down at Bob's work. "What ya working on?" he asks.

"A feature on the State Fair. Our photog's got good art and I'm doing the article."

Leon laughs. "Photog? Man, he talks like a journalism grad. See a lot of old newspaper movies, have you, boy?"

"Yeah. Front Page is my favorite."

"I figured. And you're Cary Grant, right?"

"Not 'til I'm as old as you."

Harold laughs. "Ouch!" he says.

"Leon's not old – just seasoned. Right, Leon?" Christine offers.

"Damn straight. I'm the one who brings maturity to this rag. You kids can write all you want about James Brown. I'm an Ellington fan."

"Duke Ellington?" Bob asks.

"No, King Ellington. Of course Duke Ellington, the greatest musician this country's ever produced. Bar none." He looks directly at Bob. "Bar none."

"I saw Ellington perform once."

"You did?" Leon asks with his skepticism dripping from his words.

"Yep. I went with my folks to Chicago and we saw him there."

"I like James Brown. He's so much of 1967," Christine says.

"Exactly. That's why I like the Duke," Leon explains.

Bob agrees. "Ever hear Ellington's The River? It's a great piece of music."

"It makes George Gershwin's shit pale."

"I like Gershwin, too."

"Yeah, Porgy and Bess." Leon sings in a raspy voice, 'I loves you Porgy'. Crap."

"I like lots else. But Ellington's great," Bob says, ignoring Leon's gratuitous critique of George Gershwin.

"Hey, you two are really on the same page, huh?" Harold grins.

"Like hell. I'm on the feature page and the boy's still on the society section."

"No, I'm writing 'bout the State Fair."

"He don't understand nothin'," Leon mutters. "Even when he's being put down. Hey, Bob what radio station is your favorite?"

"Right now? I suppose it's WKNR, Keener 13."

"See what I mean?"

"What?" Bob asks.

"Who's your all-time favorite DJ?"

"I don't know. I came up with Ed Mackenzie on XYZ, you know, 'Jack the Bellboy'? Then Mickey Shore and Tom

Clay before they left in all that payola stuff. But, I guess my favorite was Lee Allen on the horn."

"You didn't even mention the greatest disc jockey of all time."

Bob and Leon both say together: "Frantic Ernie Durham."

"You've heard of him?" Leon asks, genuinely surprised that the white boy knew of the famous black radio personality.

"Sure. When I was in high school my best friend, Todd, and I skipped school and went downtown to watch him do his show. We took the bus downtown and went up to the station's floor and watched Ernie through the glass. He waved at us. We spent the whole afternoon down there and tried to meet Frantic Ernie, but he didn't come out of the booth into the room where we were. Todd and I did stuff like that a lot".

"Yeah, sure you did. Tell me, where was his studio?" Leon asks.

"The David Brodwick Tower."

"Well that's right. So you did like the frantic one?"

"Are you kidding? Ernie Durhan was great. His patter. His rhymes. He was fantastic."

"And the music he played?"

"Great stuff."

"Colored music."

"I liked it. Mickey Shorr played a lot of R&B, black music. Mo-town, now. Just like Robin Seymour before him. I listened to Robin Seymour when WKNR was WKMH and he had that "Robin in the Morning" show. He played all kinds of music, white and colored."

"A real man of the world, aren't you?" Leon returns to his work.

"I like Martha Jean on WJLB," Christine says.

"The Queen," Bob smiles.

"Yes. Isn't she great. Martha Jean, the Queen, Steinberg, is from Memphis, Tennessee. When she came to Detroit a few years ago she really changed things. Now she's everywhere. She started on WCHB in Inkster and now - wow! She's making JLB a really big station. Do you know on the days the auto companies give out their bonuses Martha Jean announces it on her radio show so their wives'll know? Isn't that great?"

Leon lifts his head from his typing, again. "Yeah, great," he says. "Now, don't get me wrong. I like the Queen as well as anyone else, it's just when she starts crap like that – telling wives when their husbands get their Christmas bonuses – she's gonna get some Negro killed. The poor guy comes home and finds his wife with her hand out when he already lost the whole bonus check in a crap game or somethin'. There's gonna be violence."

"I've heard her show. She's got a great personality," Bob says.

"Maybe WKNR will hire her someday."

Harold goes to his desk. Martha comes back from the other office carrying a cup of coffee. She goes to Bob's desk. "One coffee, cream, little sugar, Bob," she says and she hands the cup to Bob.

"Thanks," the young white man says.

"You getting the boy coffee?" Leon asks. "What happened to that Women's Lib crap she preaches?"

"I was headed that way. What's it to you?" Martha looks down at Bob's work. "State Fair, huh?"

"Yeah, just a look at the Fair through the eyes of a Detroiter."

Leon holds up his glasses. "Wanna borrow my glasses?" he asks, sarcastically.

"Ignore him. He's ignorant. What's your hook?"

"I lead with a little girl looking at a pig."

"Close to home, huh?" Leon says, not looking up.

Martha steps between Bob's desk and Leon's desk to block the view. "Good idea. I like the way to tell about her being scared at first then being fascinated with the animal."

"A lot like here, right?" Harold asks, looking over at Leon.

Martha laughs and walks to her desk. Bob sips the coffee. Others type, or sort through papers on their desks. The rain continued outside the windowless room. There is quiet inside until Charles enters. The black man goes to Bob's desk. "How are things going so far, Bob?" he asks.

"Fine, sir. Just fine," Bob answers.

"Everyone making you feel at home?" Charles looks over at Leon.

"Sure. Everyone's been just grand."

"Just grand," Leon laughs quietly. Charles ignores him. "I like your idea 'bout the State Fair."

"Thanks. I've got it all blocked out and ready for rewrite."

"We'll run in on page one of our feature section."

Bob hands his copy to Charles who looks it over. "Looks good," Charles smiles. He purposely looks over at Leon. "Looks good," he repeats.

Charles hands the papers back to Bob and leaves the office, pausing briefly near Leon's desk before he continues. Martha walks to Bob's desk.

"Ready for rewrite?"

"Yep. Here you go. "Bob hands the papers to Martha. Martha prepares to exit with the papers.

Leon stops the woman. "If anyone's interested, I've got my column ready, too." He holds up a paper from his typewriter."

"I'll take it too, Leon," Martha tells him and she crosses to his desk and takes the paper from him. She looks at it. "'Tan Lines by Leon Simmons. Rethinking integration?'" Martha looks at Leon. "'Rethinking integration?'".

Leon smiles. "Yeah. I argue that maybe this integration stuff isn't all that it's cracked up to be." He looks over at Bob. "You know what I mean?"

"But just last week…"

"That was last week. This is this week. The Times They are a'Changin'. Bob Dylan, right?"

"Right, Dylan," Bob says.

"Bob Dylan. Born Robert Zimmerman and changed his name for his hero, Dylan Thomas. Folk singer who specializes in protest songs for the white youth of this country."

"Right on," Bob says. "You're a Dylan fan, Leon?"

"Right on," the black man laughs. "Yeah, I love a white boy who mumbles while he sings. Half the time I can't understand anything he's saying. He's no Nat King Cole. Now there's a man you can understand."

"You like Dylan or not?"

"Leon's just funnin' you, Bob," Martha explains. "Just like this column. It isn't serious."

"That column's as serious as a heart attack, girl," Leon insists. "Send it on down the line."

"Yeah, Charles'll love this," Martha says as she scans Leon's latest column. She leaves the office with Bob and Leon's work. In less than ten minutes Charles is at Leon's desk with the man's proposed column in his hands. "'Rethinking Integration?'"

Leon looks up at Charles. "Yeah, catching title, huh?"

"Are you serious?"

"Of course. It's my column. Run it".

Charles looks down at the paper and reads: "'The dream of Dr. Martin Luther King may, or may not, be an appropriate dream for all Negroes. There are those who call for black power – black separation'. Is this the Michigan Observer or a radical student newspaper like the Fifth Estate?"

"I'm serious about what I wrote. Integration may not be what it's cracked up to be. Do you think we'll be a better paper if every other employee is white?"

"I thought so. It's Bob, isn't it?" Charles asks, his voice now lowered so his new employee cannot hear him.

"No, it's me. Look, Charles. How much good is it if we get a few Negroes living in Dearborn or a couple of colored guys working at Ford Engineering if we lose what we have already? It's just like the story that Harold wrote on Hastings Street. Every time we got something, they figure out a way to take it away from us."

Charles looks over at Bob. "Bob's just here to write an occasional piece. He's no danger."

"Like hell. A fly in the ointment makes the whole batch stink."

Charles puts the paper back on Leon's desk. "Rewrite it, Leon. Think it over and rewrite it."

As Charles leaves the room Leon looks over his paper. "I'm thinking," he says. He looks over at Bob. "I'm thinking," he repeats.

*

A few days pass. Leon is at his desk. Bob is at his desk. Each has a copy of their newspaper. The two are alone in the office. Leon holds up the newspaper: "Tan Lines…looks good this week, doesn't it?" He looks over at Bob who is working at his desk. "Looks good, my column this week, doesn't it?"

Bob looks over at Leon. "Tan Lines?" He looks at his copy of the newspaper. "Interesting premise."

"Rethinking integration."

"It's a topic that should be explored. There are certainly people talking about it. Here and in New York there are the Black Muslims and in Chicago the Black Panthers. I read Stokely Carmichael's book, you know."

"Black Power. That one?"

"Yep. Interesting ideas. I don't agree, but interesting."

Leon rises and walks to Bob's desk. "My point is…" He pauses. "Why the hell am I talking to you about it? I know your position."

"You do?"

"Yeah, 'cause I know you. I've known you all my damned life."

Bob looks up at Leon with a puzzled look.

"Look, boy. You think you're unique. Well, you're not. You're just another liberal white boy who thinks he's gonna make his mark in the colored community. You think you can dance in here and write for a colored newspaper and be friends with us Negroes and drive back to your two-colored people neighborhood and tell all your friends how good you get along with us darkies. Well, it ain't gonna work here."

"That's not me, Leon."

"It's you. It's you in spades. In spades."

"Leon, you don't know me. You don't know ME. I'm Robert James Weingard, the son of Melvin and Ethel Weingard, who grew up in northwest Detroit and went to Mackenzie High. I'm not every white boy you've ever met. I'm me."

"Yeah, yeah, yeah. I believe you. You're unique. You're that rare creature – a caring white boy who doesn't judge coloreds by their race. You're totally devoid of racism. Yeah, right."

"I hope that's true, Leon."

"Can't be. Look, boy, you may really believe what you say 'bout yourself. But it ain't true. There's no such thing as a non-racist in this country - black or white. Race is the defining concern in America. It trumps everything else. It's like this: Thurgood Marshall's on the Supreme Court, but every time someone, anyone, white or black, refers to him it's always the Negro Supreme Court member. When Marian Anderson sings a concert she's "a credit to her race". – and they ain't talkin' 'bout the Human Race, neither. When you white people rave 'bout Nat King Cole and let him have a show on television it's 'cause he talks so good – that means talks white."

"You like Nat King Cole."

"That's beside the point. The point is that race matters more than anything else. I could work for the Detroit News or the Detroit Free Press and write great columns about politics and arts and when I die my obit would start – "Colored Writer Dead". They'd take my body to Cole's Funeral Home and when they write my name in the book at Elmwood Cemetery someone would write "Colored" next to it and I'd be colored even in the ground. Race is more important than anything else in this country, even death, and it always will be."

"There are those of us who want to change that."

"Never happen, boy. You're white and you'll always be white. That means you'll be at the front of every line, you'll be favored in everything, you'll never have anyone call you a nigger and you'll never be turned away from someplace because of your race."

"That still happens?"

"What still happens?"

"Being turned away?"

"Listen, "Leon says, "just last week I stopped by a restaurant over on Gratiot to get dinner. I parked out front and started walking to the door. The manager saw me coming and ran to lock the door before I got to it. I started running too and almost beat that son-of-a-bitch. I would have gotten there first if that bastard hadn't gotten a head start. But he got there first and locked that door right in my face."

"Maybe he was just closing at a certain time?"

"Yeah, at the time he saw my black ass heading his way. Get in the world, Robert James Weingard." Leon pauses and looks at Bob. "You're the stupidest son-of-a-bitch I've ever met. You're a danger, boy. You and those like you think you're gonna change the world and all you do is end up screwing things up. Like building the Chrysler Expressway through Paradise Valley. Like pinning all your hopes on someone like John Kennedy and when the son-of-a-bitch gets his head blown off – thinking that LBJ'll be the savior of the world. It's all bullshit, boy. Bullshit. Nothin's ever gonna change. Not really. As long as there's black people and white people and you can tell the difference – nothin's gonna change."

"I don't believe that, Leon. And that's not what you used to write before I got here. I remember your columns, like the one I wrote about in college. They were full of hope. They called for cooperation and looked to the future when things'll be better."

"Bullshit. I was shittin' my way to fame and fortune. I suppose I owe you thanks for pulling me out of that bullshit. Your presence here made me look at myself, at my column, at my world and, you know what? I saw it was all covered with bullshit. And you're standing right here, up to your hips in that stinking bullshit and you can't even see it, let alone smell it."

"I certainly don't see it that way and neither do people like Harold, Christine and Martha."

"Think not? Do you really think that they go home and think about that nice white boy they work with and tell their friends and family that they've seen the hope for a color-blind future? Bullshit. They're just like me. They just don't let it show, that's all."

"I know you're wrong about that."

Leon shakes his head. "You'll never learn. We're not your slaves anymore but we're not your friends. We can't be. You'll never learn."

Bob looks up at Leon. "I'll learn and, just maybe, you'll learn too."

"You want to learn? Here, I'll teach you something." Leon suddenly grabs Bob's head in a headlock and holds him as the young white man squirms to get free. Bob rises from his desk with Leon still holding his head.

"Let me go!" Bob says.

"Say it," Leon demands.

"Let me go! I mean it. This isn't funny." Bob twists but Leon has a good grip on his head and he cannot break free. The left side of his face is held hard to Leon's right side.

"Say it, honky," Leon insists.

"Let me go. I mean it, Leon."

Leon applies more pressure to Bob's head. "Say it. Say it. Say it, you stupid honky bastard." He rubs a hand on Bob's face. The struggling continues. Just then Christine, Harold, Martha and Charles come into the office. They stand, stunned by what they see.

"Say it!" Leon shouts.

"Let me go you damn nigger!" Bob demands.

Leon drops his headlock and grins. He looks at the others. "Questions?"

*

It is the same office a year later. During the year since Bob and Leon got into it in the Detroit Observer's office, Detroit suffered through America's worse riot. The eruption of violence that began on a hot night in July of 1967 at 12th Street and Claremont, left 43 dead, about 1200 injured and2000 buildings destroyed. Army and National Guard troops were called into the city by President Lyndon Johnson and Governor George Romney. It will be said that the city never really recovered from this uprising.

As our story restarts, the Detroit Tigers are on their way to win the 1968 World Series and pitcher Denny McLain was well on his way to win the Cy Young Award and be selected as the American League's Most Valuable Player.

Bob Weingard no longer works at the Observer. Christine, Harold, Martha and Leon remain. Charles continues to run the newspaper.

Leon Simmons is now wearing a dashiki and sporting a large Afro.

"Hey, Christine, turn on the radio," Harold calls over to the chesty, still blonde black woman. "I want to get the score of the Tiger game."

Christine reaches to a radio on her desk. "Is that cute Denny McLain pitching?"

"He ain't cute. He's white," Leon protests.

"He's a good pitcher, that's for sure," Harold maintains. "Nothing like Satchel Page was."

"Nobody is as good as Satchel Page was," Harold agrees.

"Who's Satchel Page?" Christine asks.

Leon winces. "Who's Satchel Page? Satchel Page was the greatest pitcher ever to pitch in the game. He was the star of the Negro League and if it weren't for white racism he would have played his whole career in the Bigs and have been the greatest baseball player of all time. Satchel Page pitched sixty-four straight scoreless innings. He had 21 straight wins one year. In 1933 his record was 31 and 4, for God's sake!"

"Satchel Page was something else, all right," Harold smiles.

"Did he ever play for a real team?" Christine asks.

Now Harold winces. "Don't go there, Christine. That'll only make Leon crazy."

"The Negro Leagues were REAL teams," Leon insists. "They had the best players and the most loyal fans. The only reason you don't know anything about them is because of white racism that made them play in cornfields instead of places like Briggs' Stadium. You know what happened when Satchel Page was finally called up to the Big Leagues?"

Christine shakes her head.

"The cigarette story?" Harold asks.

"Damn straight," Leon smiles. "Bill Veech, the owner of the Cleveland Indians, was in deep trouble. He needed a pitcher so he called on Satchel Page. But Veech didn't believe all the stories about how this old Negro's pitching ability so he tested him. What he did was he put a cigarette on the ground in place of home plate and had Satch stand on the mound. He told Page to pitch fast balls and, you know what?"

"What?"

"Satchel Page pitched five straight fast balls and only one of them didn't hit that cigarette."

"That's got to be hard to do."

"It's impossible to do. No one could have done it except the great Satchel Page."

Christine fiddles with her radio dials. "I don't think he's pitching today."

"What's wrong with that radio?" Leon asks.

Martha looks over. "Christine, I don't think it's plugged in," she says.

"Oh." Christine reaches under the desk to plug in the radio. "There."

The radio comes on with a newscast: "Mayor Cavanaugh has announced appointment of an independent commission to investigate the root causes of last month's riot…"

"Rebellion," Leon corrects.

"Governor Romney had appointed a state commission for the same purpose and the Mayor wants full cooperation with it".

"The score, huh," Leon prompts.

"Local Negro groups have demanded a federal investigation of what they are calling the Algiers Motel Murders in which black men were allegedly executed by police forces. The Detroit Police Department opposes such an investigation, saying that no improper actions occurred during that night of the riot."

"Rebellion," Leon repeats.

"Meanwhile, Tiger pitcher Denny McLain has been pulled in the fifth inning of today's game in Chicago."

"Ha!"

Christine turns off the radio. "There," she declares.

"Hey, the score?" Harold reminds.

Christine turns on the radio again.

"And, in other games, the Cleveland Indians lost to the…

Leon shrugs and looks over at Harold. Leon makes motions with his hands to indicate Christine's large breasts. "She can't help it," he grins.

Harold laughs. Christine turns off the radio.

"My church is raising money for the riot…" She looks over at Leon… "rebellion victims. Could one of you two great feature writers mention it in the paper?"

"Of course, Martha," Harold says. "Give me the information."

"It's just that so many people got their homes burned when the fire spread to them. The Fire Department couldn't do anything. Those people lost everything they had. After it started, I went to my church and helped those there who were setting up a shelter for the people who lost their homes or who were just too scared to stay in their homes. Those people looked so pitiful - so scared - especially the children. We're raising money for all the victims."

"We're all victims," Leon says.

"It didn't really get close to me," Christine joins in. "I stay near Wyoming and Joy, you know."

"It was close to all of us."

"You read Leon's series about it all, didn't you?" Harold asks Christine.

"Of course," Christine says. "But I can't understand the part about the riot being something so great. All I saw on TV was a lot of businesses and homes burned."

Leon looks over at the young woman. "What happened was a rebellion. I don't care if it began because it was too hot that night or the cops were manhandling a black woman or not. What it became was an outpouring of rage. All along Twelve Street, Grand River, Mack, and other places, blacks poured out their rage. The symbols of our oppression, the white owned stores, banks, and pawnshops were looted and burned. Men took up guns and fought back when the National Guard was sent in."

"I felt better when the Army came in," Christine recalls. "I was really scared."

"We all were scared," Martha says.

"Whitey was scared. And he still is," Leon says.

"I think the worst thing that happened was when that little boy was shot when he was standing with his father, or grandfather, looking out at the riot from their apartment window. The man lit a match to light his cigarette and a soldier thought it was a gun being fired. He shot and hit the little boy. That was awful."

"Those Guardsmen were killers, plain and simple."

"Those Guardsmen were plumbers and clerks and engineers and factory workers," Harold says. "What did they know about controlling rioters? They musta been scared too."

"Trained killers sent into our community to kill us."

"Some were black, you know."

"Do you really think things'll get better because of what happened?" Martha asks.

"Of course. The man's payin' attention to us now. There ain't nothin' that'll get a white man's attention more than a black man with a gun."

Harold smirked. "The theories of Leon X here aside, the riot did bring attention to certain complaints and needs of the colored community."

"We don't have complaints. We have demands."

Harold laughs. "Well, it was funny to watch Mayor Cavanaugh and Governor Romney at that news conference trying to explain how it wasn't their programs that set all that off. And Lyndon Johnson not sending in troops until George Romney publicly admitted that things were out of his control. Johnson was so afraid Romney was gonna be running against him this year. Everything is politics."

"Got that right, brother. And if everything is politics, it's important for us to be on the winning side. I loved watching those honkies squirming 'cause of us."

"'Us'? When the riot broke out you were sleeping at your crib and I was sitting on my porch trying to figure out what all that noise was down on Twelfth Street."

"Us, figuratively. Us, the whole of the African people in America."

Christine is confused. "I'm not African. I was born here."

"Call my mother an African and she'll cut your throat," Martha says. "Her great-great-grandfather came to Virginia before the American Revolution. She'll tell you that she's the most American person she knows."

"Her great-great grandfather may have come here before the American Revolution, but I'll guarantee you it wasn't on a vacation cruise," Leon says. "I don't think the old boy had a choice in his travel plans, do you?"

"He was a slave, but, thank God, his grandson was free. That's what he dreamed of, I bet. My mother told me stories about slaves who dreamed and prayed that their children would someday be free. She always told me that my ancestors suffered so I could be free and make something of myself and then help others to do the same. My great-great-grandfather dreamed about me and my freedom long before I was even born."

"He sure didn't dream up the Ghetto, I bet. His dreams have become our nightmares."

"Leon, you're so angry," Martha says.

"Anger is all they allow me."

Harold laughs. "Man, you're getting' radical in your old age."

"Radicalized," Leon corrects. "Made radical by the actions of others."

"I hope the Tigers win the World Series," Christine says, trying to change the subject.

"Some folks'll never get it," Leon says.

*

It is now a little later that day. Leon and Harold are at their desks. Christine is bringing Leon is bringing Leon coffee.

"Coffee, one sugar, black."

Leon holds up a hand without looking up and Christine hands the cup to him.

"Hot, sweet and black. Just like I like it." Leon ogles Christine as she returns to her desk.

"You still takin' those Red Rooster pills, Leon?" Martha laughs.

"Never you mind."

"What's that? Red Rooster pills?" Christine asks.

"They're pills to make old men feel like young men." Martha explains.

Leon looks over at Martha. "First of all, I'm not old and, even if I were, I won't need pills to get me to think young thoughts."

"I don't like black coffee. I like a little cream," Christine smiles.

"Speaking of that boyfriend of yours, you still seeing him?" Leon asks. "What's his name? Stewart?"

"No, I don't date him anymore. He was a drunk, you know."

"So I've heard."

"Good for you, girl," Harold smiles. "I was afraid you'd marry that one."

"Nope. He drank too much. It was fun for a while but then he hit me."

"He did?" Leon asks.

"Yes, he said he was sorry and he only did it 'cause he was drunk but I told him to leave. I mean if he's gonna be an alcoholic it seemed to me that he'd be drunk a lot and that means he could be hitting me a lot."

"Smart girl," Harold says.

"Yeah, smart girl," Leon agrees.

"I've got a new boyfriend now. He's not an alcoholic."

"That's nice to hear," Harold offers.

"He treats me nice, like a lady."

"As well he should."

"He wasn't in the Army was he?"

"No, until last year he was a college student so he was deterred."

"Deferred. He was deferred," Leon corrects.

"Right. Deferred."

"A college boy, huh?" Leon asks.

"Yes, he's real smart and he says that I'm real smart too but I gotta let it out."

"What college did he go to? Close Cover Before Striking U?"

Martha enters. She is closely followed by Bob Weingard. "Christine, someone to see you," the woman says with a smile.

Christine walks to Bob, smiles and takes one of his hands. "Everyone, you remember Bob, right?"

"Him?" a stunned Leon asks.

Christine looks at Bob. "Him," she says.

Bob smiles at Leon who scowls back. Leon rises and walked to the couple. "Are you nuts? Why on earth would you want to hook up with this racist?"

"He's not a racist. He's a Methodist."

Bob extends a hand toward Leon. "Good to see you again, Leon. I love your hair."

Leon ignores Bob. He looks at Christine. "You're shittin' me, right?"

Christine pauses and looks at Bob. She smiles and looks at Leon "Right. I am," she laughs.

"Sorry, man," Bob offers. "We're just pulling your chain." He releases Christine's hand.

"That ain't funny."

"And I'm not a racist."

"Sure you're not." Leon returns to his desk and sits there.

Martha laughs. "You two really had him going. I thought Leon was gonna bust a blood vessel or something."

"I was gonna bust something, that's for sure." Leon looks at Bob.

Christine and Martha go to their desks.

"So why are you here, other than to assassinate me with your wit?" Leon asks.

"Just stopping by to say hello. I was in the area."

"So say hello and leave. I'm sure whatever rag you're working for has something for you to do."

"The "rag" is this rag. I'm Charles' new assistant manager."

"Say what?" Leon stands up at his desk. Harold and Martha both rise from their chairs, too.

"I'm the new assistant manager here. Charles hired me last week."

Leon backs away from Bob. He shakes his head. "Uh, uh, uh. I knew Charles was over the edge but this is too much."

Leon returns to his desk and sits. "Son of a bitch. Just when I thought things around here were going to finally go in the right direction."

"But, at least Bob and I aren't going together," Christine maintains.

Leon glares over at Christine. "So that little act was just to soften the blow? We'll, it ain't soft." He looks at Bob. "Did he give you editorial say?"

"No. Mostly the business end of things. Leon, I'm not gonna change this paper's direction. I've been reading your stuff every week for the past year. I don't agree but I defend…"

"My right to say it? Well, thank you Mister Voltaire. When people say that do you know what that means? It means that they don't agree with what you say and as soon as they can they'll stop you from saying it."

"I'll have no editorial say here."

"Just business, right?"

"Right."

Leon laughs. "The editorial policy of a paper IS business. Even *you* must know that. As soon as you tell Charles that more people would advertise in this paper if we weren't too antagonistic to the white power structure, things'll be changed. You can bet on that."

"There are plenty of advertisers who want to target the colored community."

"Oh, I know all about black folks being targets. We've been targets ever since we were kidnapped in Africa and brought here. We were targets when we ran away from slavery. We were targets when we were in the army in the Civil War. We were targets for the Klu Klux Klan. We've been targets all the time we've been in America."

"You know what I meant. There are plenty of businesses, white and black, that want Negro customers."

"Negro money. They want Negro money. They don't care what color a person is as long as his money is green."

"In a way. And what's wrong with that? If people, white people, learn that doing business with black organizations, like this newspaper, helps them in the bottom line – that's progress."

"That's them taking over what we have. The bottom line is more money for whitey and less for us."

"What makes you so angry, Leon?" Bob asks.

Leon looks long and hard at Bob. "You really don't get it, do you?"

He pauses. "I was wrong about you. You're not a racist. You're just a damned fool." The black man looks away from the white man.

Harold walks to Bob and extends his hand. "Well, as far as I'm concerned you're welcome here." Harold and Bob shake hands. Bob slips the handshake into a black grip and both men laugh.

"He can't even get that right," Leon objects.

Martha stands from her desk, again, this time to face Leon. "Look, Leon. I've really had it with your ignorant attitude. You chased Bob away the last time he was here with all your black power crap…"

"Crap?"

"Crap. I'm all for improving things for the colored but that's not what you're about. You're just for getting back at whitey. All your talk and all your writing is nothing but a bunch of crap. It's about time we tried to figure out how we're going to make things better in Detroit…in America."

"They won't…"

"Listen to yourself, Leon! 'They won't.' It's always they. It ain't always about what THEY did but more about what WE will do. Ever since the riot – the riot – it was not a rebellion – ever since then, all I've heard from you and the others who talk like you is what THEY owe us. If they don't give us something, then we'll burn our own neighborhoods again. How ignorant is that! It's time for us to take charge of us. If you don't like white people – fine. Don't have nothin' to do with them. But stop holding your hand out to them too."

Charles enters the room but says nothing. He just stands and listens.

"I'm not begging from anyone," Leon insists. "All I want… all I demand, is what's ours."

"Then let him have what's his."

"This paper's not his," Leon said angrily.

Charles steps in a bit. "No it's mine," he declares. The black man crosses to stand beside Bob and puts an arm around Bob's shoulders. "And Bob is my new assistant manager. He's got the experience and the contacts now to do the job. Leon can write his column any way he wants. It's nothing to do with that."

Charles looks at Leon. "And if you don't want to write a column for a colored newspaper which has a white assistant manager, start your own damned newspaper but this one's mine."

"A newspaper belongs to the people who read it," Leon insists.

"It's belongs to me. I'm the publisher and editor. I write the checks to pay its bills. I'm the one whose livelihood is on the line if this paper fails. I know what you're saying, but, at the end of the very long day, it's my paper and what I say, goes."

"Well, maybe you can publish your newspapers without Tan Lines."

Charles moves closer to Leon. "Listen, Leon. I like you. I always have. You're a great writer and your column has a huge following in Detroit. You bring readership to the Observer; there's no doubt about that. But you're not the whole deal. If you think I can't publish this paper without your column, just test me. Over the years we've had good writers who have come and gone. Like Duff. He retired and although he was almost as popular as you are, if you ask our readers most wouldn't even remember his name. That's the nature of our business. What we write gets printed, read and cut up to be put on the bottom of a birdcage or used to pick up dog shit in the backyard.

I don't want to lose you, Leon, but, you know what? We'll survive."

Leon looks down at his desk "Do you really think they've forgotten Duff already?"

"Probably. That's the nature of the business. My father started this paper and was the sole publisher for years but ask anyone outside of the business who he was and you'll get a blank stare. That's the way things are."

"I remember him," Bob offered.

Leon looks over at Bob. "Good for you. I'm sure he's ecstatic."

"Think it over, Leon. Let me know your decision," Charles says. He leaves the office.

Bob approaches Leon. "Leon, I don't what to be the reason you leave this paper," he says.

"Good, then take a job with the News."

"I mean, I'll be working here but that shouldn't really affect your work. I'll be in the front office most of the time or on calls. I'll stay out of your hair."

"With that hair, that might be a problem," Harold laughs.

"Look, boy, you know how I feel about you. That's not it. I've got to figure out how I feel about myself."

*

Later the same day, Harold, Christine and Martha are at their desks. Leon is not. Martha looks at Leon's empty desk. "He gonna come back?"

"Oh, he'll be back, Martha. Tan Lines is his life. He ain't goin' nowhere," Harold assures.

"Anywhere. And you shouldn't say ain't," Christine interjected.

"Huh?" Harold says.

"My college professor says that we must speak well to be taken seriously."

"Your college professor?"

"Christine? When did this happen?" Martha asks.

"I'm taking a course at Wayne State. The TAAP program pays it for. If I get a good grade, they'll pay for more classes."

"Wayne State? Wayne State *University*?" Harold asks.

"Yes. I took a test." She looks at Harold. "Just because I have big breasts, doesn't mean I'm stupid, you know."

"I know that, Christine."

"That's not what you and Leon have been saying behind my back." She motions with her hands as Leon and Harold had.

Harold looks at Martha.

"Don't look at me. I didn't rat you out."

"People know when people are talking about them. So, anyway, you shouldn't say ain't and "ain't goin' nowhere" is a double negative."

Harold smiles. "Very good, girl. Charles'll be hiring you to write for the paper soon."

"So why did you say what you did in that manner?"

"You mean ain't and the double negative?"

Christine nods.

"Sometime educated, well-spoken people like myself, use the vernacular for emphases."

"Ven..?"

"Vernacular."

"We didn't study that yet. We're still in English," Christine reports.

Harold looks at Martha and both smile. All return to their work.

"Do you really think that Leon's coming back? It looked really mad when he left," Christine says.

Harold nods. "He'll be back, if not for us or for the paper – for himself. Despite how he talks or the dashiki he wears, Leon's a newspaperman. They used to say that a real newspaperman has ink flowing in his veins and, in Leon's case it's only black ink, but it's still ink. Leon was here when I started with the paper. So was Duff. They were friends – two birds of a feather. When Duff announced that he was going to retire and move to Mississippi, Leon when nuts. He called that old man everything but a child of God. You'd think that ole Duff had done something personal to Leon. I guess he did. He betrayed a code that Leon thought the two of them had set up. A real newspaperman dies at his desk, not in his bed on a farm in Mississippi. That's why Leon went nuts with Duff. Betrayal."

Martha agrees. "That's right. I was there. The two of them were in the coffee room and you could hear Leon shouting all the way out here. The things he called that old man."

"But, it was Duff's choice," Christine says. "He wanted to leave. He told me that he was born in Mississippi and he wanted to die in Mississippi."

"That didn't matter to Leon," Harold explains. "All he saw was a betrayal of the code. Real newspapermen die at their desks."

"And that's why you think Leon's coming back?"

"Yep. White Bob or not, this is still the newspaper Leon writes for and that desk of his will be the place where he lives, and if he's lucky, the first thing his face hits when he dies."

The three return to their work. Leon enters and slowly goes to his desk where he sits. Leon begins to type.

"He's back," Christine notes.

"I see," Harold says.

Leon looks over at them. "It isn't that I'm compromising, you know. I still have my principles."

"Don't we all," Martha says.

Leon looks down at his desk then looks back at his co-workers. "It's just that someone's gotta be here to keep that damn white boy from ruining our paper."

"Gotcha, man," Harold smiles.

Leon smiles, runs a hand lovingly over his desk and begins working again.

*

In 1968 the Detroit Tigers won the World Series, defeating the reigning world champion St. Louis Cardinals in seven games. Detroit pitcher Mickey Lolich, who won game seven over Negro pitcher Bob Gibson is the series MVP. Denny McLain, who pitched and won game six, is chosen 1968's MVP and wins the Cy Young Award. Following the Tiger's victory in St. Louis, thousands of Detroiters, black and white, pour into the streets to celebrate. There is no violence.

Detroit will never really recover from the damage done to it during the Riot of 1967 and will decline in population as both the white and black middle class flee to the suburbs.

Publisher Charles H. Webb will retire and hand over the operation of Detroit's only African-American owned newspaper to his sons who continue to publish the Detroit Observer.

Eventually widowed, Martha Adrian will marry a man she met at her church and later, with her husband, buy a house in Southfield, Michigan where the two will live out their lives.

Christine Johnson will go on to receive her Bachelor of Arts degree from Wayne State University and will start and run several successful businesses in Detroit.

In 1972, feature writer, Harold Williams will be killed in a drive-by shooting, as the man stands smoking a cigarette on his porch. He will be shot by gang members who mistake him for a rival drug dealer.

Bob Weingard will marry a black woman he will meet at the newspaper– no, not Christine – but a beautiful young file clerk named Holly. The couple will have a beautiful mixed race daughter and, later retire to California where the man will write a series of books and one play.

And Leon Simmons? Leon will begin wearing more conventional clothes and, after be begins losing his hair, will wear a hair piece - not an afro - and will, of course, die at his desk as he is writing his column, Tan Lines. In his final column he will argue that integration may not be a bad thing if it is properly controlled.

TERROR IN THE JUNGLE

It was the biggest damned gorilla I had ever seen and it was glaring out of the bush directly at me from only a few feet from where I stood. The animal's deep-set red eyes were filled with rage and they were fixed squarely upon my fear-frozen form. The huge beast was only waiting for me to move.

My wife had come to me two years earlier with the idea of visiting Uganda. With us being self-aware Black Americans she was, as she moved toward middle age, beginning to feel the need to explore our cultural roots. I tried to explain that our African ancestors, more likely than not, came from West Africa originating along the "slave coasts" of present day Nigeria or Liberia and not East Africa, but to my wife Africa is Africa and, besides, the travel agency with which she had talked was not running any special fares to West Africa.

So East Africa became "close enough" and she and I began planning our trip. It was a year after that lunatic, Idi Amin, was toppled from power by the invasion of Uganda by neighboring African states and before the terrible genocide that devastated that part of Africa in later years. It seemed, during that time of relative calm, to be a good time to go.

Uganda on Lake Victoria had always held some fascination for me. I had watched travel shows on television that had movies of other people's trips there and I loved the look of towering waterfalls and thick rain forests of this East-Central African country. And the thought of seeing all those wild animals in the vast preserves of Uganda and perhaps Kenya was also an incentive to vacation there. As I began to actively investigate the possibility of a trip to Uganda I began to think that my wife's idea was no bad thing after all.

To get to Uganda we could be routed through Kenya, seeing Nairobi and visiting the vast Serengeti Plain before going on to Entebbe and the dense bush of Uganda. At the time Doctor Leaky was promoting his *Australopithecus Africans*, "Lucy" as some kind of a universal ancestor of all humankind so, after all was said and done, my wife may not have been too far off the mark in the pursuit of our roots.

Anyway, we looked into scheduling a vacation in Uganda and soon she and I were both reading brochures and figuring travel costs. I would sit at my desk during slow times at work and figure and refigure the cost of traveling to East Africa.

"You know, honey," I finally said to my wife, "there is just no way we can afford this trip."

"That's the way I figure it too," my wife agreed. "The money'd be better spent on our children's' education.

So we did not go.

Oh, the gorilla? That was at the Detroit Zoo a year before Jim-Jim died of being overweight.

CHRISTMAS OF
THE MIND

"My father had a heart attack on Christmas Eve. I remember it well. But, of course, how could I forget my father havin' a heart attack on Christmas Eve?" The Captain looked across the table at me, directly into my eyes and he kind of winced as he awaited my reply to what I had mistakenly assumed to be a rhetorical question.

"I suppose you can't," I offered.

"Damned right you can't," he said, half smiling so that his stubbled face wrinkled. "My father jus' grabbed his chest and sank down in his chair. It was jus' after we ate and my father sat in that big chair o' his and he just grabbed his chest and sank down. Scared us kids somethin' fierce."

"I guess it would," I said, nor knowing if the grizzled man really wanted me to actively join his remembrance or not.

The Captain ignored me now and just went on. He recalled another Christmas when he got a toy car and went on in great detail about how that car sped across the wooden floor of his family's living room and bounced off the sofa. I just sat and listened and let the man run on. He told me all about that toy, how heavy it looked, how it was made of wood and metal, "not plastic like today's junk" and how important it was to him. I listened.

It was Christmas Eve, the year before I was graduated from college with a useless degree in anthropology, and two years before I left for Asia in that field trip that I was talked into by my "friend", Ralph. I was at a skid row mission, partly out of honestly held compassion for the down-and-outs who depended on the mission for food and shelter, and partly because I needed the community service credit in my course of study. The Captain was only one of the regular unfortunates who attended the mission; ate its hot meals; slept on its clean beds and returned each morning to the streets to drink from bottles wrapped in brown paper and held tightly in their hands, or to sell their blood to the plasma center, or to sleep in cold alleys or in deserted doorways. The Captain was, at least to my eyes, no more and no less "colorful" than were any of the street people who came to the mission that Christmas Eve.

"Colorful" - that is the way television sometimes portrays those people. They, according to popular wisdom, are philosopher/bums, the "knights of the road"; romanticized into something they are not and never were. They, according to this position, are the sacred homeless, quaint characters who are so pleasantly amusing.

The people who came into the mission that Christmas Eve when I was there were mostly the street people who haunted the near-downtown area. There were winos and bums who had not bathed in weeks. They were mostly men who could tell me about the good job they had lost but could not quite remember when that had been. They were the strongest of the weakest, the survivors of the streets, people who could never fit into what we call society but people who had developed and well defined society of their own.

Among these men, but apart from them, were the families: the ones left out of our abundant holiday season, the poorest of the poor whose food stamps never cover enough of the month, the occasionally employed who depend on the mission to feed their families on the occasions between employments. These people sat about the warm room, clustered in their family groups. They ate their dinners and edged away from those bums who came too close.

The Captain – that was the only name he gave and no one knew if it had been a real rank earned by some service to his country or on a job on the lake freighters which sailed on the Great Lakes or for some other reason – sat on the other side of the table from me and continued speaking of his Christmas memories. I had just finished my shift of serving meals to those who lined up to receive them and I was resting. I sipped at a cup of coffee and listened to the Captain go on.

"I was only eleven when my father died," the Captain told me. "It was just before Easter and he died in our living room right on that sofa that my toy car had banged into."

"I thought you said he died on Christmas Eve," I reminded, needlessly provoking the man.

"I said he had a heart attack on Christmas Eve. I didn't say he died," the Captain said over at me. His voice was impatient with my lack of understanding. "He died just before Easter. If you're gonna listen to me the least you can do is to understand what I'm sayin'." The Captain spoke as if he was doing me some kind of favor by letting me listen to his stories. The man placed one of his hands, lightly folded into a loose fist, along one side of his face. He kept it there as if his head was resting upon it but I could tell that there was no pressure placed on that hand. I looked across at the man's face. I tried to guess his age. It was difficult to accurately place an age to the man. Like so many of his fellow street people the captain had a darkened leathery complexion that, at first, appeared to be the result of tanning but was in reality more do to the constant ingestion of cheap liquor. His hands, both dirty, were quite wrinkled and callused as if that man had in his earlier years performed some type of heavy work. The Captain's hands perfectly matched his face that was rough as well. The man's greasy hair was unkempt and jutted from under a small cap which he wore as he ate.

But behind his puffy eyelids the Captain had beautiful eyes. The man's eyes were both blue and brown. Their irises were flecked with those and other colors. I tried to look beyond the man's leathery face to those beautiful eyes but my own eyes kept straying to his rough appearing countenance.

"Well?" the Captain asked, glaring at me. "Are you gonna listen or not?"

"Of course I'm going to listen," I assured him. "Go ahead."

"Well anyway, my father died at Easter time but it's the Christmases I remember the most." The Captain took a sip of his coffee and pushed a piece of white bread about his empty plate to pick up a few stray bits of gravy. He raised the bread to his lips and paused before popping it into his mouth. "Want some?" he asked. I think he was mocking me.

"No, thank you," I said. I really did not know if the man was serious or not. That was my main problem down there at the skid row mission. I never knew when I was being mocked. I am sure that my obvious suburban naiveté proved to be a constant source of amusement for the men to whom I served dinners once a week in the mission's dining room. One would say something to me using some street slang and when I responded with a "What?" or a "Huh?" he and everyone around him would have a good laugh. And why not? If intelligence is measured in terms of the ability to cope with one's culture, down there they were the geniuses and I was the idiot. It was still unnerving, however, to be the brunt of every joke when all I was doing was trying to help those unfortunates get a warm meal (and earn a few college credits while I was at it).

The Captain was talking and was well into his story about another Christmas when I realized that I was not listening to his words. I quickly refocused my attention upon what the man was saying.

"So with my father dead and my mother trying to get along the best she could we moved from place to place for a while. Then we settled down in this walk-up flat that had a lot of roaches but it was okay, I guess. I went to work, doin' whatever I could to bring in a little money. I remember one Christmas when all we had for presents was some fruit we got at the market. We kids wrapped up that fruit and gave it to each other. That way we all had somethin' to open up, even if it was only an apple."

The Captain looked at me and smiled. I figured he was making up all of this just to see if I was going to bite at his pathetic story.

"That's really sad, Captain," I said to the man. I felt I was saying what he wanted me to say.

"Ain't truth 'though," the man grinned, showing his lack of teeth as he did. "I never had no brothers or sisters. It was jus' me. I guess I was enough for my folks from the start." He grinned again and I did not ask why he had lied to me if he wanted me to pay attention to what he was telling me.

The Captain went on with another story about another Christmas and I listened, all the while trying to figure out if this one was true or not. I knew truth is a pretty tenuous thing. The bums and winos and other street people would have to tell so many lies just to get by each day that they, themselves, would forget what was the truth and begin believing their lies. Thus, the Captain may have actually had siblings as he lived with his widowed mother but it had simply served his purposes so many times to be an only child that he believed it to be the case by then.

His next story about living in Canada until his father's worst enemy died, I found to be equally farfetched. "That SOB woulda killed us all, if he had found my Pa and us before he died," he maintained. I let him go on, not challenging his recollections.

"That was before my father died," the Captain said. "We came back and he died not too much long after that." The man looked up at the room's tin ceiling. "I still miss the old man," he said.

By then my coffee cup was empty and I had a good excuse to leave the Captain's table. I held up the cup. "Well, it's time for me to get back to work."

"Your work's here, boy," the Captain said, looking directly into my eyes. "With me and with them."

"I've got to dish out the food again," I reminded the man.

"They need more than bread."

I settled back on the bench on the other side of the table from the Captain. We continued.

"You Cath'lic, boy?" he asked. I was taken aback by the question.

"No," I told him. "I'm Lutheran."

"Too bad. Cath'lics understand mysteries a whole lot better than you Lutherans. Can I tell you a mystery?"

"Sure," I said. I had no idea what to expect.

"We're not all gonna die. We'll be changed."

Where on earth, I thought, had the Captain run into Saint Paul's first letter to the Corinthians? *Behold, I show you a mystery. We shall not all sleep, but we shall be changed.*

134

Of course I recalled those words from my early Lutheran Bible study classes. Perhaps, this grizzled bum had been a church member in his youth too. Perhaps he still remembered through the fog of alcohol that clouded his brain the first lessons of his Sunday school or his catechism if he had been reared "Cath'lic" I smiled as I recognized what the man was saying.

"You've heard that before, have you?" the Captain asked. He seemed to already know my answer.

"Yes," I smiled. "That's in the Bible."

The Captain then smiled another of his toothless smiles. "Did you ever hear about a fellah called Saint Frances of Assisi?" he asked.

Even we Lutherans had at least a passing acquaintance with the *Lives of the Saints*. "Yes," I replied.

"Tell me about him."

I laughed slightly. "I know he loved animals and was a bishop or something," I offered. I was trying to hide my ignorance in this area.

"And he met Christ?"

"Oh yeah," I said. It was slowly coming back to me. The story was that St. Frances was on the road. He stopped to help a leper and later wrote that he realized that the leper was really Jesus. "Yes, as a leper," I said. I, being a good Lutheran, never believed that story was actually true but I understood its theological meaning.

The Captain placed the palms of both his hands on the table and slowly pushed himself up from the bench. All the while he did that he looked directly at me. The man smiled and slung one leg over the bench to leave the table. It was obvious the man was in pain.

"Can I help?" I asked.

"Yes, you can, boy," he answered. The man did not wait for any assistance from me but moved awkwardly away from my table as I rose to follow him. He held a hand to his left side and I thought I could see blood under it on his dirty shirt. "'Tis an old wound," he told me, noting my concern. He reached the door before I could join him because his position on the bench was closer than had been mine. When he got to the doorway the Captain stopped and turned back to me.

"Do you really want to help me?" he asked

I nodded.

"Feed my sheep," he said.

The Captain left the mission and although I quickly followed his exit I lost the sight of him in the blowing snow on the dark street.

I suppose that if I were a more religious man I would make more of this encounter with the Captain than I do. I might even, if given to be a mystic, maintain that this dirty alcoholic with beautiful eyes was really Jesus. I do not say that. I do not say anything about it. I just tell the story remembering the Lord's words, *"For I was hungered, and ye gave me meat; I was thirsty and ye gave me drink…In as much as ye have done it unto one of the least of these my brethren, ye have done it unto me."*

FIVE CHRISTMASES

I.

This Christmas would be different. This Christmas would be special. Kevin absentmindedly slid one of his fingers between two of his toes as he sat on the edge of his bed. It was the night before Christmas and, I suppose, if seven-year-old Kevin knew what a sugarplum was, sugar plum visions would be dancing in his head. He didn't and they weren't. A half an hour later when the little boy was asleep he was dreaming, instead, of Hot Wheels and Game Boys. A half an hour after he went to sleep little Kevin was dreaming about a Christmas that would be different, a Christmas that would be perfect.

Kevin's perfect Christmas arrived soon after dawn in what to the mind of the seven-year-old was only a second or two from the time he closed his eyes the night before. Kevin's perfect Christmas began with a flow of finally realized expectations. It poured out of the second floor bedroom and left behind a wall full of pennants that had mostly been collected by Kevin's father for him. It ignored the broken or scattered remains of last year's imperfect Christmas and it rushed through the hall and it poured down the stairs into the living room. This perfect Christmas met Daddy and Mommy and was finally resolved by the gloriously colorful packages that had been so artfully grouped under the family's Christmas tree. The lights on that Balsam fir were already lit and their light, reds and blues and yellows and greens, all filtered by the pine tree's branches, illuminated the gifts and added, in an immeasurable way, to their beauty.

Kevin stood still and silent before the glory of that tree and those presents. Then, as always, he was allowed to begin. There were choices to be made. Big or little packages first? Red or white paper next? Tradition ruled that the stocking that was filled with small presents would be emptied only after at least two of the large packages had been opened and tradition also ruled the Mommy and Daddy would wait to open their gifts until Kevin had opened all of his.

Choices were made and tradition was followed. The presents were opened and after all the paper was collected there were clothes to try on – no complaining about the scratchy tags – and Daddy drank coffee while Mommy sorted all the opened gifts under the tree. Kevin had a cup of hot chocolate with lots of whipped cream on top, just as he liked. By then, Mommy's sister was home. There were relatives to call – be sure to thank Grandma for the new coat – and there was the hollow feeling that began as soon as the last present was unwrapped. There was the hollow feeling that slowly grew throughout the rest of he day and finally proclaimed to Kevin that this Christmas was not the perfect Christmas. This Christmas had been no different. This Christmas was not special.

II.

Teri got up early on Christmas Day. The nineteen-year-old, still wearing her pajamas covered by her robe, unwrapped her presents with her family and watched her sister, her sister's husband and their seven-year-old son unwrap theirs. Before coffee and hot chocolate Teri went back to her room, dressed and left her sister's house.

Teri drove along Main Street past a nursing home in which an old man silently stared at a wall. She passed a pile of dirty snow mounded beside a fire hydrant that had a thick ice cycle hanging from one of its nozzles, and then passed rows and rows of stores, all of them closed for Christmas Day. Teri drove with the radio on and Christmas music filled her car. She neared her destination and as she pulled into the employees' section of the parking lot of the restaurant, she heard the host of the radio show she had on read a Christmas poem, and she turned off the radio wondering what a sugar plum would be.

Teri parked her car that had just gotten warmed by its heater, locked her doors and enter the restaurant through a rear door. The tall, dark haired girl tied an apron around her middle and with other young people got the restaurant ready to open for a heavily booked Christmas Day.

The Cornucopia Restaurant served turkey; ham and roast beef with mashed potatoes; peas; green beans; gravy and whole wheat bread stuffing. There was a salad bar with mounds of freshly cut vegetables, lettuce and a variety of dressings. There was a dessert bar with pies, cakes and puddings. There were no sugarplums at the Cornucopia Restaurant. That was good because Teri would not have known how to serve them if they were available.

III.

"'Twas the night before Christmas and all through the house…" Henry read from the large picture book to his son as he tried to settle down the boy to get him to sleep that evening before the Big Day. The man remembered how excited he used to be as Christmas neared and how difficult it was for him to get to sleep on Christmas Eve. Now he was a thirty-five-year- old man reading to his excited seven-year-old who kept talking about a "perfect Christmas". Here he was, middle-aged in his mind - if life expectancy is in the seventies, then thirty-five is in the middle – reading to his son who was too excited to sleep. "…While visions of sugarplums danced in their heads."

Henry's wife was already placing the wrapped packages under their beautiful balsam fir and after Henry finished reading his son to sleep he joined her in the inevitable task of last minute wrapping. By then all of their son's gifts had been wrapped in a variety of wrapping paper but there were a few things for others that still needed to be secured in Christmas paper.

"Who's this for?" Henry asked, holding up a blouse that until he picked it up had been carefully folded in a box.

"My sister," Henry's wife responded. Her voice betrayed a little exasperation at Henry for taking that gift out of its box. "You'd better let me refold it," she proposed.

"Okay. I'll wrap this other one. That's for her too, right?" Henry's wife nodded.

"Which paper?" Henry asked.

"The one with the purple blobs on it," his wife answered. She pointed to a roll of wrapping paper that was on the floor near to where Henry sat.

"Sugarplums," Henry said as he picked up the roll of paper.

"Huh?"

"Sugarplums. I think these things are supposed to be sugarplums."

"Think so?" his wife asked. "It's pretty ugly, isn't it?"

Henry looked at the paper. He pulled enough out to wrap the present he had and cut it with scissors. As his wife repacked the blouse they were to give his sister-in-law, Henry wrapped a sweater for the nineteen-year-old.

"Get that done before she comes home," Henry's wife urged.

"I like to take my time," Henry retorted. He carefully folded the paper to make a straight seem and then carefully taped it into place. "When do we have to be at your Mother's?" he asked.

"Any time after two, she said. We'll be stopping to see Dad on the way, you know."

"Sure. Want to take him something?"

"Like what?"

"Oh, I don't know. Maybe a piece of pumpkin bread or something."

"Yeah, okay," Henry's wife agreed. She looked down at the still unwrapped present that she had on her lap. "He won't like it," she offered.

"Maybe he won't," Henry said, "but let's make the attempt, okay?"

"Okay." The woman finished wrapping the blouse for her sister and placed it under the tree with the box that her husband had wrapped.

"Sugarplums, huh?" Henry's wife smiled as she looked at that awful wrapping paper.

Soon Henry's sister-in-law had returned from her shift at the restaurant to watch television in her room.

IV.

Linda sat across the dining table from her husband wrapping Christmas presents. She and he talked as they worked.

"Who's this for?" her husband asked, holding up a blouse that he pulled from its box.

"My sister," Linda reported. She tried not to sound upset that her husband had just yanked the gift from its box after she had just folded it in there. "You'd better let me refold it," she said.

As Linda rearranged the pretty blouse her husband began working on another unwrapped present. The man asked for some wrapping paper when there was a roll of it sitting on the floor right beside his chair. Linda pointed to it.

"Sugarplums," the woman's husband said when she asked what those awful purple blobs on that paper were.

The wrapping continued and Linda looked over at the wall clock. She knew that her sister would be home soon. "Get that done before she comes home," she told her husband. The man said that he liked to take his time wrapping presents and Linda wondered why bother. She was never one for fancy wrappings. Her parents had never done that. In her youth the woman was taught to wrap things nicely but she saw no purpose in overdoing it. The man she married, on the other hand, was a perfectionist when it came to Christmas present wrapping. He folded a careful line and taped the paper down. Linda folded her arms at looked over at him.

Linda and her husband finished wrapping the presents and made sure that their son's gifts were all under the tree together. Linda checked the boy's stocking and was satisfied that everything was done. Her husband checked the doors after Linda's sister came home to watch television in her room. He did that every night.

"So how does Santa get in?" Linda asked.

"The chimney. That's tradition, right. 'Placing his finger alongside of his nose' and all that, huh?" her husband answered.

Linda smiled.

V.

Harold sat silently staring at the wall of his room. With one turn of his head the sixty-seven-year-old man could have seen his daughter drive by but Harold did not turn his head. Instead of looking out of his room's window into the cold but sunny day beyond his room Harold simply stared at the wall.

Forty years before Harold lifted boxes onto a loading platform at the plant. Thirty years before Harold checked off names on a list he carried on a clipboard. Twenty years before Harold straightened his tie before a meeting. Ten years before Harold leaned back in his comfortable chair in his house's new den and smiled a bit at the dialogue of a television show. One year before Harold sat next to his wife at a matinee at the mall's movie house.

Now Harold sat alone in his room at the nursing home unable to speak since his stroke. Now Harold was staring at his wall as his nineteen-year-old daughter's car drove by on its way to the restaurant where its driver worked.

Harold's daughter, son-in-law and their child stopped by to see Harold on the way to where the man used to live. His wife had been by earlier. There was no pumpkin bread offered because, at the last minute, his son-in-law decided against bringing it. It would only make Harold's daughter upset to see her father reject it.

Harold hardly even looked at his daughter the entire time she and her family stayed with him. He stared at his wall and only briefly looked over at his daughter, son-in-law and grandson. Her heard their voices when they spoke to him and felt his daughter's hand in his when she held it, but the voices were impossible to understand and that hand did not seem real. When his daughter spoke to him it sounded as if she were speaking through a cloth, all muffled and garbled. Her hand felt like a foreign object. Nothing seemed real.

Harold tried to listen when his grandson spoke. Somehow, he thought, the seven-year-old's voice would be clearer to him but he could not understand anything he said either

Harold winced. That woman in his room asked him something. He wanted to tell the boy how Santa Claus got into a locked room when there was only an artificial fireplace and what the sugarplums tasted like when his mother made them for Christmas but these people in his room never asked.

THE LIVONIA RATS

"Living room," I said to Frank, one of my friends who were helping us move, and the man carried the lamp he had pulled out of our rented truck to our newly purchased house's front room.

"Kitchen," I told another friend who was toting a box.

It was moving day for us. My wife and I moved to Livonia, Michigan after living in Detroit all our lives. We moved from the city because my mother was living by herself in Livonia and we needed her to be with us. She sold her house; we sold ours and we bought a large home together.

"Mom's room," I directed and another box was carried upstairs to what was now my mother's room. My wife was at the bottom of the stairs to direct traffic. My mother was already planted in her new bedroom to be sure her collection of ceramic owls would survive the move and be placed just as she wanted them to be placed.

Livonia, Michigan was founded in the mid-1800s as a farming township. It was charted as a city in 1950 and for the next half-century had become a quiet, safe residential community known mostly because it was the city in America over the population of 100,000 with the smallest minority population. My wife and I, a white man and a black woman, added ever so slightly to the minority population when we moved in.

With my wife being the only black person living within a mile of our new home we were a bit concerned about our reception in our new neighborhood, but things went well. Neighbors from every side stopped over to welcome us and to introduce themselves. The fact that we had a backyard in-ground swimming pool, I was sure, helped them to be friendly with us, but most seemed genuinely nice.

One of our new next door neighbors actually came over with a long extension cord. "I don't know if you've had time to have the electricity turned on," she explained. He had but, what a great gesture!

As my wife, our friends and I unloaded the truck we had rented to move that last of our furnishings, other neighbors from the surrounding homes came to help. One woman brought a cake. We got to know our new neighbors quickly.

To one side of us were Buffie and her husband, Tommy – I called them Buffie and Jodie after the 70s TV show that featured children with those names. The first time I saw Tommy (Jodie to me), I was surveying the plants on the north side of my new house when I heard a voice call, "Hello neighbor". I looked up and saw the man sitting on his roof. He was adjusting his satellite dish. "Oh great," I said. "I bought a house next to the guy who sits on his roof!"

He and Buffy became friends and many afternoons after cutting my grass, I'd sit on their porch and sip lemonade.

Tommy looked like someone who lived in Burton Hollow; stocky with workman's hands. He told me that he was a plumber and if I ever needed his services I'd get the "good neighbor discount".

"Good neighbor discount?" I asked.

"Yeah, parts only. The labor's paid for with beer."

"Sounds good to me, Tommy," I smiled, trying not to call him Jodie.

The couple across the street from us, Fred and Kathy became Fred and Wilma for the Flintstones. Down the street were Ken and Carol whom I called Ken and Barbie, for the dolls. Bonnie and Phil, two doors away, to me were Bonnie and Clyde, for the bandits. I could not remember these neighbors' real names and really did not care to. The 1970s nicknames I gave them seemed good enough. My new neighborhood seemed to me to be a very 1970s neighborhood.

"You shouldn't refer to your neighbors like that," my daughter cautioned.

"Why not? It's just a joke," I told her.

We settled in. Our granddaughter was attending a Livonia school and we saw her a lot. Our new neighbors remained friendly and we began to feel at home in Livonia.

I wore a tie at home. People found that peculiar. I wore a tie because I didn't have to. I was retired and working part-time where no tie was required. But I was a rebel and every day, even when I mowed the lawn, I wore a tie. I enjoyed having people ask me why.

One day a neighbor, Dan, was over. I had yet to come up with a 1970's name from him but I was leaning toward "Danno" from Hawaii Five O but couldn't think of what to dub his wife, Fay. "McGarrett" didn't seem appropriate.

Dan and I sat out by the pool, talking and sipping drinks. Dan, like most of my new neighbors, liked to drink beer from a bottle and I accommodated him in that taste. I preferred a Manhattan cocktail from a stemmed cocktail glass.

Dan was a good-looking man in his late thirties, I guess, with jet black hair and a rather muscular build. He wore shorts, sandals and a very colorful short-sleeved shirt. No tie, of course.

Dan asked about my family and told me of his. We talked about hobbies and other interests.

Dan bowled and was a sports fan. I enjoyed neither of those recreations. I told him of my interests and activities.

Another beer, Dan?" I offered.

"Sure," the man smiled. He reached down to the cooler which I had stocked with bottled beer. He pulled out a Bud Light and twisted off its cap.

Sunlight filtered down on the two of us through the canopy formed by the trees on that side of my swimming pool. It was early July and getting humid as it often did during a Michigan summer. The partial shade of my backyard trees felt good. I was really happy that we had moved out of the city into this place of relative quiet and relaxation. Then it all changed.

"Bert," Dan said, looking over at me after a sip from his beer bottle, "don't take this wrong, but you guys really don't fit in here, do you?"

I know what Dan meant. My wife and I were Diamond Donors to the Detroit Repertory Theatre and members of the Michigan Opera Theatre Guide. We loved theater, opera, jazz and other more sophisticated relaxation. Our neighbors were mostly blue-collar working class people who drove trucks and enjoyed deer hunting, NASCAR and county music. They were affluent but not urbane.

Burton Hollow, the sub where we lived, was an upper income blue-collar enclave. Its homeowners were good people; hard-working skilled tradesmen and fire fighters with an occasional schoolteacher thrown in. They were good people but some neighbors sat in their garage on lawn chairs and drank beer from bottles. "The Garage People" we called them. One fellow always parked his truck the wrong way on the street in front of his house. "Wrong Way", I dubbed him.

I liked my neighbors but I knew what Dan he was saying.

"I know what you mean, Dan," I said back to my neighbor.

"It's not the race thing, you know," he included quickly.

"I know. I know what you mean. We've seen that too."

"I mean, come on – Manhattans?" Dan laughed.

I laughed too. Then I looked over at Dan and said it. I didn't know why I said it. Maybe it was just for fun. Maybe I meant to truly deceive him. But I said it.

"Dan, I'm going to tell you something but you've got to agree never to tell anyone else. Okay?"

"Okay," the man said.

"Dan, did you ever hear of the Witness Protection Program?"

The dark haired man's jaw dropped. His mouth stayed open. It was a bit of a mouth-breather anyway but this was more. "Yes," he said.

"Well…" I shrugged and took a sip of my cocktail. I was laughing inside but remained calm outside.

"You?"

"Yep," I said.

"What? Where?"

"Well, I can't say where. You understand."

Dan nodded.

"I was the money man, the financier, for a mob family. When things got hot I testified against my friends and here we are."

"You were in the mob, Bert?" Dan looked over my face looking for a sign that I was kidding him. I let none show.

"Yes. I started with friends and, like I said, I was the moneyman. I can't tell you how different things were then. We went to the best clubs and never had to stand in line. We spent money like it didn't matter, and it didn't. People respected us and feared us too."

I hoped Dan hadn't seen the movie, *Goodfellas*, recently because that was where I was getting my idea of what mob life was.

"I had the best women. You can't imagine what aphrodisiacs money and power are to some women. Most of us had wives but that didn't matter. It was all part of the life we were in. Then things fell apart. The FBI had a sting and got me. I could have gone to prison for life. Life, Dan! You know, all the years I was connected I never thought I could go to prison. I thought I could get killed. I feared my friends and my friends' competitors. But I never thought of going to prison, and certainly not for life. Come on."

I paused. My neighbor was eating this up!

"So I ratted out my friends and here we are."

"In the Witness Protection Program?"

"Yep," I said. I took another sip of my drink and was going to tell Dan I was just kidding when he spoke.

"I was with the Genovese Family," he said,

"What?" I asked, my drink dribbling down my chin. I looked down at the Manhattan cocktail puddle that was forming on my tie under my chin. Then I looked over at Dan.

"I'm in the program too," Dan said. "I wacked people for the Genoveses and when things got hot I turned rat, just like you did."

I looked back at Dan. "Really?" I asked.

"Yep," he said. "I'm surprised they put you here on the same block with me. Who's your handler?"

I swallowed hard. "Philip Harris," I said, making up a name.

"Don't know him. But he's not out of the New York Office, is he?"

"No, he's not," I said. My hands were cold and I put my drink down before I spilled it entirely.

"So, ain't this something?" Dan laughed.

"Yep," I said. "It sure is."

Dan went on to tell me some details of his mobbed up life. He had been a hit man for a New York crime family and now he was sitting in my backyard, drinking beer from a bottle. I was scared and tried hard not to show it. What would Dan do if he found out I had lied and now was privy to his secret? He was a HIT MAN, for God's sakes!

"And you know what, Bert," Dan continued. "Fred's in the program, too."

"Fred? You mean…" I motioned with a shaking hand toward "Fred and Wilma's" across the street.

"Yeah, he was with the Cleveland mob. Now he's here."

I desperately searched Dan's face for a sign that he was pulling my leg. There was still none there.

"And Tommy…"

"Jodie" to me.

"…he was with the mob out of Vegas."

"Come on," I said.

"No, it's true," Dan assured me. "He was a bag man. He knew too much and helped the Feds put some folks away. Here he is."

"But all here?"

"Yeah. That's why I was surprised when they put you here too. I mean, the block's just about full now."

"Sure seems to be," I said.

"We get together on Wednesdays at Denny's."

"Huh?"

"For breakfast. All of us. You're invited now."

"Denny's?"

"Yeah the one on Middlebelt. For breakfast."

"All of you?"

"Yeah. We eat breakfast and talk over old times."

"All of you?"

"Sure. Wednesday at nine. Okay?"

"Okay," I said. What else could I say.

So every Wednesday at nine in the morning I met with the other members of what we called the Livonia Rats for breakfast and old times. We talked about the old days and I became pretty adept at faking it. I had to.

I really did.

"Gentlemen," Dan said, raising his coffee cup as if he was proposing a toast. I drink to you and those who could not be with us."

"Here, here," Tommy answered with a raise of his coffee cup too. We all sipped Denny's coffee to ourselves and to those we had put away or had been killed. My hand shook just a little as I lifted my cup and put it to my lips. I sipped coffee and smiled around at the former killers and thugs with whom I shared our table. I put my cup back down and spilled a little coffee onto the table under it.

"Nervous, Bert?" Dan asked me.

"No, just old," I answered.

The former hit man laughed and slapped my on my back. We drank more coffee and soon were eating breakfast together.

This weekly meeting went on for months. I learned a lot about mob life that was not covered in *Goodfellas* and grew better and better at faking my bogus background.

Fred, the mobbed up man from Cleveland, was the titular head of our gathering. He was more my age than the others, mid-sixties, I guessed, with short-cropped salt and pepper hair and a bit of a scar on his lower lip I learned was from a knife fight he had won when he was much younger.

"You should see the other guy!" Fred laughed when he told me how he had come by his fight trophy.

"What, you left him alive?" Dan joined in.

"I didn't say that," Fred grinned.

I wiped my right palm on my pants and adjusted my tie. How could I get out of this?

"So, do we let Bert in on our plan or what?" Fred asked as he ate his omelet and one such meeting.

I looked over at the man.

"I don't know," Tommy said. "He was a money man and this plan ain't about money."

"But he's one of us now and I think we should give him a chance of refusal." Fred suggested.

"Yeah, Bert's okay," Dan agreed. He smiled over at me with a toothy smile.

"What's this all about?" I asked. I really didn't want to know but was afraid not to ask.

"The airport, Bert," Dan said. "Fred here is connected out there and there's a big shipment of furs coming in from New York next week. It's a piece of cake."

"Furs?"

"Yeah. Sable, mink, the whole nine." Fred took another bite of his omelet.

"And you want to steal them?"

"It won't be the first time, right?" the man smiled.

"But…" I desperately tried to think of an excuse not to participate.

Dan gave it to me.

"But, that's wasn't your bag, right, pal?" he offered.

"Right," I said. "Finances, that's me."

"It's okay, Bert," Tommy said. "Fred just thought you should be offered.

"Well, thanks," I said over at Fred. I went back to eating as my new associates planned the high jacking of the furs.

"This stuff's primo quality," Fred said. "It'll be a snap to unload and worth a lot."

"And security at the airport?" Dan asked.

"Everyone's looking for terrorists," Fred said. "As long as we're not trying to get on a plane healed, we're safe. Dan, we're talking about a fortune. You know that patio you want?

Dan smiled. "Right," he said.

The more I heard the less nervous I was in joining the plot. The shipment of furs was coming into Detroit's Metro Airport on a Saturday. The place would be packed with incoming and out-going passengers and a rented truck could easily be slipped into the cargo terminal and with Frank's advance work, we could steal the whole shipment and be well away long before anyone would know. It was foolproof.

I thought of the work that we needed to do on my house. I pictured my new kitchen and a finished basement. I imagined a professionally landscaped backyard.

"I'm in," I announced.

Over the next week the Livonia Rats rehearsed or plan. We arranged to rent a truck, using phone identification and credit information that Dan bought from an identity thief he knew from the old days. Tommy worked with Fred to make sure the timing was perfect. We made three practice runs to Metropolitan Airport outside Detroit. Fred stashed another truck in a park three miles from where the heist would take place so we could transfer the stolen furs and abandon the first truck there.

"Now Bert, just stay in the truck. We'll make the grab and be out with the goods in minutes." Fred instructed. "No sweat, right?"

"Right," I smiled.

I was glad that I was working with pros. They thought of everything. This was a fool-proof plan.

When the day came things, quickly fell apart. I found out the truth that every time someone comes up with a foolproof plan, someone comes up with a better fool.

"Move this truck," an airport security guard said to me as I parked near the freight terminal.

"I'll just be a minute, sir," I said to him. "Waiting for my boss to call me."

The young man looked at me, alone behind the wheel of our rented truck. He motioned and was quickly joined by another security guard. I was still trying to convince these two armed men that I was just waiting for instructions from my freight company when the rest of the Livonia Rats arrived with loaders filled with crates of high jacked furs. They all ran off to cars they had planted in case of trouble and I alone was caught.

"Look, pal, we know what happened," the Wayne County Sheriff Department sergeant who was interviewing me said. "You're just a regular guy who got caught up with the wrong people. "See that guy over there?" He looked over at a man in a suit. "He's with the U.S. Marshall Service and, guess what, it seems he knows some guys on your block."

The other man smiled. "Fred, Danny and Tommy, right?"

I knew that they knew. Both the fur company and the airline insisted on full charges. I had no choice so I ratted out my associates to get a lesser sentence and now I'm living with my family in Arizona in the Witness Protection Program.

Please don't ask me how I got here nor why we really don't fit in.

DEATH

THE COLONY

Sarah rose slowly. The large, good-looking female blinked and wiped the sleep from her large dark eyes. She stretched. She forced her neck back to work out the bit of pain that she found there. She stretched again and swung a leg out from under her one blanket to the floor of her tiny cell.

Sarah was a worker in the Colony's nursery, a large but gentle female who was bred from before her birth to nursery duties.

She rolled her neck around a little and smiled. The pain was gone. Soon Sarah was nibbling a sweet roll and her day had begun.

The corridor outside of Sarah's cell was crowded with workers. Members of the subterranean Colony scurried to their assignments. Those who had served during the night were returning to their cells. Sarah made her way down one corridor to another. Soon she was at her workstation in the Colony's nursery, picking out an embryo from containers to inject it with a variety of solutions.

Sarah worked as she did every day. She injected a red solution into one embryo to pre-select that one to be a worker in the nursery. That pre-born inhabitant of the

Colony would, like Sarah, be born with long sturdy legs, exacting eyes and a gentle touch.

The blue-tint solution made an embryo develop into a powerful male, a soldier and a defender of the Colony. The yellow one created tunnel diggers, large, strong workers with incredible endurance and sensitive eyes to see in the darkness of newly dug corridors. Other injections produced guards and other specialized colonists.

Each of those solutions, and others, were in injection implants before Sarah's workstation and the nursery worker deftly picked them out, often using two hands at once. The embryos were encased in small, tube-like structures through which Sarah could easily see them squirming in the fluid in which they lived. She injected the proper pre-selection fluid into each embryo case and then passed the future worker, soldier, tunnel digger, guard or leader to a worker to her left.

Sarah's day was long and tedious. There was only one rest period during which all the workers in the nursery ate a meal. Other workers who plied the corridors to feed the Colony provided the food for Sarah and her fellow workers. Those workers, pre-selected by Sarah or someone like her to this duty, were short but strong females who prepared and distributed the meals daily. The food was a blend of processed grains and molds that were grown underground in one end of the maze of corridors that made up the Colony. It tasted sweet as Sarah ate. She finished her meal and returned to work.

When her shift ended Sarah cleaned her work area and left the nursery. Hattie replaced her. Hattie looked exactly like Sarah, being bred, like Sarah, for this duty. Before she left Sarah showed her replacement where she had left off. Then she left the nursery.

Sarah returned to her cell for her rest period but she did not travel the same two corridors that had brought her to the nursery. Instead, the nursery worker purposely veered into a parallel corridor so she could pass him.

He was Harris, a guard whose station was along the corridor Sarah chose. He was black and was standing, strong and beautiful, at an intersection of corridors to protect and enforce.

"Move along," Harris urged as workers passed him. "Move along. Keep moving."

Sarah neared.

Harris' eyes fixed on Sarah. "Keep moving," he said. Then Harris smiled. That smile, fleeting and secret, was brief but Sarah saw it and it lasted long enough for her to know that Harris would visit her that rest period. The nursery worker passed the guard and Harris moved a leg forward just enough to have it brush one of Sarah's legs as she moved past him. The female fought back a smile as she felt her lover's touch.

"My God, Sarah, you are beautiful!" Harris grinned as he and the nursery worker lay together on her small sleeping platform that served as her bed. He had Sarah wrapped in his powerful, dark arms. The solder ran one of his hands over Sarah's pretty face. "You are my queen," he told her.

"One hour of forbidden love a week and I'm royalty?" the female smiled.

Harris slid his hand down to Sarah's thorax. He stroked her firm chest. "Yes," he answered. "A queen." Harris moved his hand down to Sarah's tight abdomen and held it there. He pressed his hard body to hers and the two kissed.

The lovers held each other for a while more. They talked some but mostly there was silence in Sarah's cell. They kissed and cuddled. They touched and smiled.

"I saw sunlight yesterday," Harris told Sarah after a long time of silence.

"Sunlight? How?"

"They had me in the new corridor on the North side of the Colony," Harris told Sarah.

"That's why you weren't at your station in the corridor yesterday? I was so afraid when I didn't see you there." Sarah stroked her lover's face.

"Yes. I was moved just for the day. There had been a cave-in and a couple of diggers were killed in it. They needed help for the day."

"Killed?" Sarah looked concerned.

Harris smiled. "I was just there for the one day," he said. "It was safe then. I just kept anyone from coming out to where it broke through."

"And you saw sunlight?"

"Yes," Harris said. "At the end, at the cave-in, it shown into the tunnel and gleamed in at us. I never got to the end to look outside but I saw the sunlight beaming in."

"And?"

"And it hurt my eyes," Harris said. "It was bright, brighter than the Great Hall during a mass meeting. I had to hold my hands in front of my eyes to keep from going blind."

"It was that bright?" Sarah and her lover, like all those who were the result of generations of subterranean genetic selective breading had extremely light sensitive eyes.

"Yes, and more."

"What?"

"The engineers who were directing the repair…"

"Yes?"

"They didn't have any radiation protectors. They just worked near the opening without any radiation protectors at all."

"Do you think it's safe up there now?"

"I don't know. They keep saying how dangerous it is but I saw them working at that opening with no protectors."

Sarah looked up at the ceiling of her cell. "I wonder," she mused. "I wonder what it's like up there."

"Destruction and death," Harris said. He was quoting what all the Colony inhabitants had been told over and over again.

"Destruction and death," Sarah repeated. "I wonder."

Days passed in tedious sameness. A quick nibble at a piece of food for breakfast; the short walk to her workstation; hours of injections; a food period; more work; the return to her cell for the rest period. It was too dangerous for Harris to come to Sarah's cell every rest period. Usually it was no more than once a week. Sometimes it was less, a few times more.

Harris and Sarah made love and talked. The lovers talked about their desires and hopes. Sarah, more than Harris, longed for a day when she and he could go to the surface where she could see sunlight and the two could walk together in air not filtered into the Colony's corridors through the complex's huge air scrubbing system. Harris was content with his occasional visits to Sarah's cell but held her with compassion as she went on about the outside and its fresh air and sunlight.

"Someday you and I will walk openly outside. We'll build our own dwelling place and live there together. And, my dear one," Sarah said with a smile and a touch to Harris's strong featured face," we'll have a child together."

Harris looked at Sarah. "Is that possible?" he asked. The only young born in the Colony were born in the community nursery where Sarah worked. The idea of having a child seemed alien to Harris.

"It could be," Sarah said. "Someday, it could be."

Harris kissed Sarah and the two held each other some more.

Sarah lay on her back on her sleeping platform, looking up at the ceiling of her cell with her large dark eyes. To have a child, she thought. To procreate with Harris! It was such a dream to her. She smiled and looked at her lover. "I love you," she said softly.

Harris only smiled. He held Sarah with one of his incredibly strong arms but ever so gently. He, like all those who served the Colony as guards, had been bred for body strength. That was one of Sarah's duties at the nursery – to inject the proper chemicals into the embryos that passed before her to create workers, guards, soldiers and the like. Each chemical mix would form a different body type. Each creation was carefully controlled by the Colony.

Sarah felt so protected in Harris' strong dark arm. She smiled up at her ceiling and briefly fell asleep.

Days passed in sameness. Weeks passed. Months passed, all the time without a glimmer of sunlight to differentiate day from night in the underground Colony. All was the same, then things changed.

One morning there was the smell of excitement in the air of the Colony. A mass meeting was called and workers, guards, overseers, and others all made their way to the Great Hall.

Sarah had been in the Great Hall before that day, but not often. Each time the nursery worker entered she was overwhelmed by the size of the cavern. Cut out of rock and soil, the Great Hall's vaulted ceiling could not be reached if twenty nursery workers were to stand one on top of the other to reach it. It was enormous and now, in its middle, stood the Book.

Harris had told Sarah of the Book. This huge volume of mystery had been uncovered during the digging of a new corridor to the south. Its massive size and unreadable printing had amazed the leaders of the Colony and every effort had been made to explain it. Now there it was, in the Great Hall with Denton, the General Overseer of the Colony, standing on a platform atop it.

Sarah formed up with other nursery workers. She looked around a nearby formation of guards to see if she could find Harris there. She could not. Then she looked to her right and there he was. The handsome guard was standing with some other guards. He was looking over at Sarah.

Sarah made a small movement with her head that was mimicked by Harris. The two dare not bring attention to themselves with anything more than that.

The inhabitants of the Colony assembled and Denton, a small-sized, but important leader, looked right, then left, then right again. All was hushed as he began to speak.

"Fellow Colonists," he said in a voice amplified by the walls and ceiling of the Great Hall, "This, as many of you know, is the Book. It was discovered a year ago during construction work in our Colony's outermost limits. It's huge size and strange markings gave us pause. We have studied it these many months and, finally can report on what it is and what it had taught us."

Denton paused and eyes from all over the Great Hall looked at him and the incredible book over which he stood. The huge tome was secured in place with great carved stones and heavy lines. It was closed, its time-damaged cover covered with strange markings. The General Overseer cleared his throat and continued.

"At first we thought this Book to be sent to earth by some space aliens, either just before or just after the Great War and Dying."

At the speaking of those words all eyes cast down. The Great War and Dying was the reason the Colony remained underground for so many generations. It was the reason the measures had been taken to organize the survivors in such a way as to keep life on earth from totally dying out. It was the unspeakable event that had changed everything.

"Blessed be the survivors," Denton intoned.

"Blessed be the survivors," thousands of voices said in low, respectful tones.

"This book, we have found predates that terrible time and, unlike what was assumed at first because of its huge size, was not sent here from another planet. It was here already." Denton paused again then continued.

"The great minds of the Colony have worked deciphering this book. We have learned much."

Denton looked around at the gathered inhabitants of the Colony. "We have learned," he continued, "that, unlike what we have assumed until now, it was not a war between us and the Reds which caused the horror from which we escaped. There was another life form here on Earth that caused it to happen. We have learned, from breaking the code of this Book, what they called themselves and what they called us.

"They were huge beings called humans and they called us….ants."

THE CRIMEAN HORRORS

Introduction

The Crimea is a mass of land that juts south below Preskop in the Ukraine into the Black Sea. One arm of this peninsula stretches almost to the Russian mainland and in doing so, forms the Sea of Azov. By the end of the Twentieth Century the Crimea became a resort area of the Republic of Ukraine that attracted many well-off vacationers from Moscow and St. Petersburg for good reason. The summers along the Black Sea coastline of the Crimea are pleasantly warm and each year bring sun seekers from Russia to its beaches, villages and hotels. In more recent times the peninsula was annexed by Russia, once more, by the actions of Valimir Putin. It remains a resort destination for well-connected Russians. In days long past, the Crimea was not a pleasant place to visit.

The descendants of the Ghingiz Khan conquered the Crimean peninsula and the Tartars ruled it, as they ruled was much of Russia, under the Khanate of the Golden Horde. Later, as the power of the Tartars waned, the area fell to the occupation of the Cossacks of the Dnieper, a group of a free-booters; escaped serfs; dislocated peasants and escaped criminals. These thugs, by more or less enforced neighborhood, formed into a people: the Cossacks. The

Cossacks developed strong armies of valiant horsemen that kept the drive of Russian society from reaching the Black Sea.

It was not until the sovereignty of Catherine the Great, that Russia was able to annex the Crimean peninsula and establish a port on the Black Sea to challenge the Turkish Empire at Russia's southern border. Much blood was let to suppress the Cossacks and establish a Russian rule of the area. A hundred years after Catherine, the Crimea once more became the center of violence. It was during this period that the Crimean Horrors began.

Russia went to war with Turkey, England and France in a conflict over the extent of influence Russia would exert in the Danube area and in the Balkans. The empire of the Turks, the Ottoman Empire, was in decline and Imperial Russia under Tsar Nicholas was expanding its power into areas ruled by it. England and France stood with Turkey in order to contain the ambitions of the Romanovs and to protect the power of the Western European countries in the region.

The details of this struggle do not matter to this story but some of the facts concerning the Crimean phase of the war are important. Following victories in the Danubian provinces the Allies decided to drive their victory home with an invasion of the Crimea. Combined forces of England and France landed at Euratoria in September of 1854 and it was only due to their general disorganization that they did not quickly drive on to take the Russian Black Sea naval base at Sevastopol. The Allies gave the Russians time to prepare an adequate defense and the war bogged down into mere killing and dying without the great sweeping victory by either side that could have ended it.

At Balaklava the British Light Brigade mounted its famous charge but its maneuver was more glorious than decisive. Most of the dying was the result of the insufficiency of supplies by both sides. The Allies were forced by logistics to bring their supplies by ship long distances through the Dardanelles to inadequate ports. The Russians, while fighting on their home ground and relatively close to their supplies of food and arms, failed to develop any reliable method of bringing those supplies to the front in any worthwhile regularity. Fraud by the contractors that were hired by the government was everywhere too common. There was no railroad to carry neither troops nor supplies. The men placed by Tsar Nicholas in command were, for the most part, incompetent. The war dragged on through a bitterly harsh Russian winter, past the death of the Tsar in 1855 until the new Tsar, Alexander II, mercifully agreed to peace in March of that same year.

Soldiers who had fought for the Tsar and for Russia reported the great resentment, the great anger they felt. Some think that it was this anger that gave birth to the Crimean Horrors. Others believe that these events grew from the general carnage that filled the area month after bloody month. Then, there are a few, just a few, who believe there is no such thing as the Crimean Horrors.

To this last group of people I say, read and believe!

I.

Vladimir Borkovsky walked with a limp that everyone assumed to be the result of a wound received during the Crimean War. No one could be sure of that. Borkovsky never talked about his war experiences. The retired infantry officer, who always stood erect as if attending a parade inspection, was by no means shy nor a recluse. Quite the opposite, in fact. He had traveled far and wide and prided himself on a wide range of friends. At the many parties he attended he even became loud while telling stories or recollections of his former times and adventures. At social gatherings the handsome middle aged man would often be surrounded by his peers as well as younger ladies and gentlemen as he went on with amusing or glorious details of an overseas trip, a local adventure or even a well prepared meal. It was just that these stories and recollections were never about the war.

Once, a fairly new acquaintance of Borkovsky asked how the man had come by his limp. "Painfully," was the man's reply before he changed the subject.

Nicholas Sergenov walked smartly with an unaffected gait. The former supply officer was employed in the War Office in a staff position in that time of relative peace. This employment offered him the opportunity to travel and to socialize. Sergenov was quite the popular fellow at parties both in Moscow and Saint Petersburg. For a time his presence was necessary to assure the success of any important gathering. Sergenov, unlike Borkovsky, talked at great length of his service in Tsar Nicholas' war against the Allies. He thrilled the young men and all the women with his tales of bravery and daring.

At one party while Sergenov went on and on telling his account of the action on the day of the Russian defeat at Alma, Borkovsky was overheard to repeat the old saying, "Those who know, do not say. Those who say, do not know."

A sudden hush spread over the room as Sergenov's eyes flashed toward Borkovsky. A couple of young men, both dressed in the uniform of fusiliers, stepped aside to allow these two men a better view of each other.

"Were you, perhaps sir, commenting upon my story?" Sergenov asked in slowly spoken words.

"Sir," Borkovsky replied, "I was commenting upon the words of all those who boast of things they never did."

"Again, sir," Sergenov said, "was it my story which prompted your words?"

Borkovsky looked at the former supply officer. He pictured the men of the Russian army starving for lack of food, freezing for lack of proper clothing or being slaughtered for lack of arms and ammunition. The man's eyes slightly narrowed. "Yes", he said.

Some people in the room gasped at that reply. Surely this meant a duel. One of the two men, or perhaps both of them, would die over this.

"No," a young woman pleaded Borkovsky. "Retract your words."

Borkovsky stood silent. He stared at Sergenov and waited that man's action. Sergenov slowly walked to Borkovsky. "I have never felt ill of you, Borkovsky," he said when he reached the other man's position in the large room, "but now I must kill you."

"If morning will suit you, sir," Borkovsky said and the duel was set. One would die, perhaps a causally of an ended war.

The following morning in Moscow was cold. It was the kind of damp cold that occurs often in Russia. The misty morning found the two combatants taken to the field with the respective supporters. The weapons, chosen by the challenged Borkovsky, were perfectly matched pistols each capable of firing but one shot. After the judge of the duel made his mandatory request that this question be settled without the loss of blood and was turned down by both parties, the distance was paced and Borkovsky and Sergenov both turned to face each other. The two men took aim.

"Fire!" the judge shouted. Sergenov's pistol fired first to be followed very quickly by Borkovsky's. For an instant both men were standing, but only for an instant. Borkovsky's bullet entered Sergenov's chest at a point just below the man's left breast. Its force shattered one of Sergenov's ribs and continued on to pierce the lower part of his heart. The bullet, doing its worst passed on through Sergenov's form to exit through the back of his jacket carrying a great spray of blood with it. Sergenov dropped to the damp ground as dead as any of those brave Russians who had died at Alma.

Borkovsky, unhurt, allowed his pistol to drop from his right hand and fall to the ground beside his feet. He turned to be joined by his friends. Then the uninjured man slowly walked from the field to his carriage. No one noticed the small hole that was in the front of the man's tunic or saw the equally small hole in the back of Borkovsky's coat.

II.

During the twenty years that followed the duel between Vladimir Borkovsky and Nicholas Sergenov, Russia moved from reform to reaction. Tsar Alexander II led the greatest of all Russian liberalizations, the emancipation of the serfs, then tried albeit vainly to halt the flow of Russian society to even greater reforms. The basically conservative but reforming emperor fought reactionary and revolutionary factions alike. Reforms met reaction. Reaction met resistance. The Russian Empire seemed to be in constant upheaval.

In 1881 Alexander was driving along the Catherine Canal in St. Petersburg when a nihilist threw a bomb toward the Tsar's carriage. The bomb detonated without harm to the emperor. Alexander got out of his carriage and while he was talking to some Cossacks guards who had sustained some damage to their persons, the assassin Grinevetsky threw a second bomb that exploded at the Tsar's feet. The force of that second explosion shredded Alexander's legs, tore open his stomach and ripped great hunks of flesh from the man's face. The Tsar, Emperor of all the Russias, muttered, "Home to the palace to die there," and collapsed.

The news of Alexander's assassination reached the Crimea and it found Vladimir Borkovsky there. The man, then sixty-five years of age, lived in a quiet retreat near Sevastopol. He was alone except for his three wolfhounds that were his constant companions. Alone, Borkovsky grieved for his emperor.

Borkovsky was no patriot in the imperial sense. Although he had no love for the ruling Romanov family, he had always respected Alexander. He had admired the Tsar's courage in directing his reforms and also in opposing those who would force Russia to reform more. Borkovsky poured himself a glass of wine and silently toasted a portrait of the dead Tsar that hung on one of his villa's walls. The man downed the wine and sent the empty glass crashing to the floor below Alexander's likeness.

The transformation of Vladimir Borkovsky from the popular socialite he once was to the recluse he had become had begun with his killing of Sergenov. A week after he dropped Sergenov onto the damp field outside of Moscow, Borkovsky packed and left the city. He traveled to St. Petersburg where he briefly stayed. From there the man traveled to Minsk where he lived almost a year. Finally he settled at his villa outside of Sevastopol in the Crimea.

As the great events of Russia occurred in the north, Borkovsky stayed to himself, making no friends, attending no receptions, receiving no visitors. This is not to say that the man met no one during these years in his Crimean retreat. He did. He met many people; people who after meeting Borkovsky met no one ever again.

Borkovsky met Boris Wycinsky, a shopkeeper, one dark and moonless night. That night was warm and it could have been pleasant except for the presence of a chill – no, not a chill but rather a feeling which resembled a chill. Boris, the shopkeeper, walked from his shop located on the outskirts of Sevastopol. He moved in the direction of his house. The middle-aged man's right hand, quite unconsciously, kept moving to the back of the man's neck as if to rub or massage away the uncomfortable feeling that was there. His left hand eased into a side pocket of his trousers to be sure his money was still there. It was there, but Wycinsky kept fondling anyway it with his fingertips.

The night seemed unusually dark to Boris Wycinsky as he walked toward his home. Deep within the darkened wood that paralleled one side of the road and stretched back for quite a distance, an owl screeched. The cautious movements of some hunting wolves had disturbed the bird's concentration. Farther away from the road a day-feeding bird readjusted its wings as it slept through the night. Nearby a mouse was foraging for food while trying to not be seen by the owl.

The sound of each animal's voice or each animal's movement blended with similar sounds to provide the constant sound of the night forest. Wycinsky heard this general background noise only when it stopped.

A sudden silence fell over the dark night and Boris' eyes vainly searched the edge of the wood for its cause. He felt strangeness without knowing its terrible reality. The man took a deep breath that was to be the last breath he drew and he felt the pressure of a man's hand upon one of his shoulders.

It is difficult, to say the least, to describe the sensations of Boris Wycinsky as he died. As oxygen stopped flowing to the man's brain a rushing feeling of light-headedness was what the shopkeeper felt first. Then the desire to call out along with the inability to do so struck him. This was followed by a sensation as if his life was a liquid that filled his form and that the liquid was now flowing up to his right shoulder and from him. Then true darkness followed a sudden and brilliant burst of incredibly bright light. Then there was nothing.

All of these things accrued to Boris Wycinsky within a matter of a passing second or two. Before the forest owl could screech once more, the man's fingers all curled into the palms of his hands, his arms and legs contorted and his face relaxed to show no sensation of pain. Boris' unseeing eyes stared into the dirt as Borkovsky walked slowly away from the shopkeeper's dead body and up the road toward his secluded villa.

Two days later Boris Wycinsky, a presumed victim of a heart attack, was buried as his widow cried and his neighbors and family members stood around his grave at their church's cemetery. Death was common in the Crimea in those days. Death was common everywhere.

Vladimir Borkovsky met Olga Taraskova while the young girl lay in her bed. The man moved slowly, limping ever so slightly as he moved. He eased himself to young

Olga's house, stopping just outside of a window that was between him and the child's bed. He silently gazed down at the sleeping girl. Olga's long blond hair covered the girl's pillow and flowed down to her bed. Her lips were closed but still stained by a small amount of blood her mother had not yet wiped from them. There also was blood on the small and frail child's pillow.

Borkovsky almost smiled as he reached a hand through the open window to touch Olga's pretty face. At the man's touch Olga made a sound in her throat that was not a word but more of a soft moan. Perhaps this sound was intended to be a word, but if it was it never had a chance to form upon Olga's dying lips. The eight-year-old girl never opened her eyes. Behind those closed eyes Olga saw a flash of bright light then saw nothing. Her ears heard a rushing sound almost like the sound she had heard when she and her mother had gone to the Black Sea to sit on the beach and listen to waves breaking upon the rocks before Olga got sick.

Then there was silence. Then there was stillness. The only sound was the soft sound of Borkovsky's exit. The only movement was the man's slightly limping slow retreat. After Borkovsky returned to his home there was only silence and stillness in little Olga Taraskova's room. There was only silence, stillness and the dead blond haired girl.

May is such a pretty month in the Crimea. Wild flowers spring into bloom to fill the rain-freshened air with their sweetness. The peasant spring festivals fill the same air with the sounds of music, laughter and joy. The hardworking people of the Crimea celebrate the end of their harsh winter the advent of the spring planting season with feasts and festivals. Bowls of *schav*, the ever popular sorrel and potato soup, are prepared by the women to be enjoyed by all. Men dress as *skomorokhs*, jesters and minstrels, and strum their *balalaikas* as children danced around them. The people eat *golubtsy*, their version of stuffed cabbage leaves, and dollop them with *Smetana*, the local sour cream. Great quantities of *drachona*, baked batter, is available to family, friends, neighbors and visitors. The people dress in their traditional *sarafan* outfits with their long colorful trapeze-shaped jumpers and dance their traditional dances.

The spring of year that Vladimir Borkovsky met Ivan Pskov was no exception. That May brought rebirth to the land of the Crimea. Peasants worked their fields to plant crops and to discourage weeds. Children played and worked. Young men were filled with hope and old men were filled with contentment.

Ivan Pskov was a young man who was filled with the hopes and ambitions of a young man. His father was a peasant and tied to the land. Ivan had left the farm, the seventh son of the family. He went to work in the city to earn wages. In Sevastopol, Ivan Pskov labored as a dockworker. He loaded and unloaded the many ships that berthed in the harbor. There were ships that plied only the Black Sea, locally trading in Russia and with the Ottoman Empire. There were larger ships that had come into the Black Sea from the Mediterranean and beyond. The grain of the Ukraine was being shipped to the hungry people of the world and manufactured goods were being brought into the Russian Empire from England, France and even America.

Ivan's work was not light but it paid well. Money was something that Ivan's father had seldom seen. Peasants raised crops, the surplus of which, if any, they could trade for those things they needed to see their families through the unproductive winters. Ivan was raising no crops. He earned wages that provided the young man with enough money not only to pay for his needs but also to save for travel or to invest. He had great dreams.

One day in the middle of the rebirth month of May, Ivan Pskov was unloading a ship with many other dockworkers. A rope slipped then was severed as the load it bore overwhelmed its tensile strength. The crate that the rope had supported fell where Ivan and a fellow worker were standing. The other man threw himself away from the crashing load. Ivan did not. The heavy crate caught Ivan at his right leg, crushing it and all but severing it from his body.

"God!" the young man cried out as his mangled leg spurted blood onto the ship's wooden deck. He looked up and his pale blue eyes were looking into the eyes of Vladimir Borkovsky. The older man smiled a gentle smile and he reached down to touch one of Ivan Pskov's arms. Ivan's lungs sucked in their last taste of air then stopped working. The young man's eyes rolled back and his lifeless form lay still on the blood-covered deck of the ship, still pinned to it under the crate.

III.

Igor Ivanovich Gorki met Vladimir Borkovsky in a very different way than did those many others in the Crimea. The young nobleman was visiting the port of Sevastopol in his office as confidante to the Tsar. Gorki was inspecting new fortifications near the naval base and, by proper etiquette, he was forced to call upon Borkovsky. Gorki's family and Borkovsky's family had been close in Moscow although Ivan had never met Vladimir. The day before he was to return to St. Petersburg Igor Gorki made his way to Borkovsky's villa and he met the man. The two dined together and talked.

Vladimir Borkovsky's years of relative seclusion had not managed to dim his fluent wit and charm. Gorki was taken with Borkovsky's ease of speech and his interesting way of telling stories. The man possessed details of Gorki's family that Igor had not heard and he expounded upon them at great length. Gorki listened in fascination as the older man talked.

Igor Gorki had been reared near to the intrigue of the Romanov court but he had allowed none of the cynicism that surrounded his upbringing to affect neither his manners nor beliefs. The highborn young man presented himself well with a confident manner and all the required politeness of his station. But, it was more than politeness. Gorki was inwardly good. He loved truth and hated falsehood. He glorified justice and opposed oppression. He admired bravery but was compassionate of the coward. When he met Vladimir Borkovsky he was fascinated with him.

Gorki was neither naïve nor inexperienced. He had traveled throughout the Russias in his service to the Tsar and had met many people. He had admired many men but there was something about Borkovsky that he found to be different and appealing. Borkovsky's remembrances were recalled vividly and with tender emotion. His smile was beautiful and infectious. His voice was soft yet manly.

After dinner the two men drank brandy in Borkovsky's drawing room and talked more. The light from the candles in his host's drawing room made Gorki's crystal brandy snifter sparkle with a brilliance that the younger man appreciated. He swirled his brandy and watched its auburn hue soften the sparkle of the cut glass. All seemed so gentile at this charming villa.

When Gorki left he promised to correspond with Borkovsky, a promised he tried to keep but found difficult to maintain. The young man's life and official duties kept him occupied to such an extent that he rarely was ever able to write Borkovsky. As he moved closer to the Tsar in his favor, five years had passed since that meeting with Borkovsky and at least four years since he and the man had been in touch.

The years between the first meeting between Gorki and Borkovsky and the second were filled with violence and death. The administration of justice in the Crimea was uneven at best. Peasants lost land due to false claimants. A growing working class became more and more restless. Administrators became wealthy while the poor became poorer. Crime grew in frequency. Murder became common. The Church was ignored. Parental authority was disregarded. Dry winters led to unproductive summers and sparse harvests. The peasants hardly had enough for themselves and never a surplus to sell. Despair came to the Crimea and it was in a time of deepest despair that Gorki heard from Borkovsky once more.

A messenger brought word from the south that Vladimir Borkovsky was in a hospital at Sevastopol. Moscow society was saddened. The word was that the man was dying. In St. Petersburg, Igor Gorki made immediate plans to go to the Crimea.

The main hospital in Sevastopol was grim with stonewalls and small windows. It seemed the very place in which to die. It was at that awful place that Gorki found Borkovsky. The man was an old-looking sixty-eight-year-old with mostly gray hair and hollowness to his face. He was alone in a small private room.

Because of his rank Gorki was escorted down the dimly lit hallway by a high-ranking hospital official to the wing of the hospital that contained Borkovsky's room and admitted to see the man.

"Leave us alone," Gorki said to the official who withdrew.

"So you find me here," Borkovsky said. He coughed as he spoke.

"What happened, my dear Borkovsky?" Gorki asked. He was shocked at the older man's debilitated appearance.

"My time had ended," Borkovsky stated. He looked down at the bloodstained handkerchief he held. Gorki looked concerned. "What I am going to tell you, dear Gorki, you will find all but impossible to believe. But hear my story through until you pronounce me a liar or a madman." The old man paused as if to catch his breath and gather his strength. He began once more. "It was not until after the War that I knew who, or rather, what I am."

Gorki made a motion as if he was about to interrupt Borkovsky but Borkovsky stopped him with a weak wave of his hand.

"You have heard of the duel between Nicholas Sergenov and myself?" Borkovsky asked.

Gorki nodded. Even after all these years that story was still being told in Moscow.

"And how my bullet killed Sergenov while his missed its target?"

Gorki nodded again.

"This is not true." Borkovsky paused to cough again. He held his cloth to his mouth and further stained it with blood.

"I shall get a doctor," Gorki said as he rose from the chair where he had sat.

"No." Borkovsky commanded. Gorki sat. "The bullet from Sergenov's pistol was fired first and true. It entered my body here," Borkovsky said as he pointed to his chest, "and passed through me to leave through my back."

"But..." Gorki began but was again stopped at a wave of Borkovsky's hand.

"That was the very moment that I knew what I was." Another blood-stained cough from Borkovsky gave Gorki a moment to speak.

"*What* you are, sir?" he reacted.

"Yes. Just as Jesus had been born a man to be reared as a human being in order to experience the life of a human being I was born into this human flesh to experience life as a human being only to learn on that field what I really am. I am death."

Gorki now knew that Borkovsky was insane. However, with pity showing upon his face, he allowed the madman to continue speaking.

"I have spent the last twenty-five years both experiencing and taking life," Borkovsky said. "Now, like the Christ, the time has come for me to experience death."

Gorki's face fell into his hands at the madness of this man he had so loved and respected.

"You do not believe me," Borkovsky said.

"No," Gorki answered. His face was still buried in his hands.

"You think me mad."

"Yes."

"Tell me, my friend, do you believe that Jesus Christ was born a human being but was God?"

"Of course," the devoutly Orthodox Christian Gorki replied.

"But, do you not see? It is the same with me. In Jesus, God had to experience life and death. Now, in me, death has experienced life and will experience death too." Borkovsky paused once more and for a moment the tiny hospital room was silent except for the rails of the old man's labored breaths. "Now," Borkovsky continued, "my time is over. I must die."

Gorki looked up from his hands slowly and sadly to shake his head. He could say nothing. He could do nothing.

"Let me tell you this," Borkovsky said. "There is a horror in this land. There is a horror which stalks the people and which brings tears and pain."

Gorki looked at the man, not knowing what to expect.

"This horror," Borkovsky continued, "I have seen and experienced. It is life. Robbery, fraud, lying, rape, incest, arson, disappointment, lost hope, lost love, starvation, pain and dishonor are here. I have seen it all. That is life. That is what your mortal lives achieve. Honor is overcome by falsehood. Peace is swallowed up in war. Hope is dashed and the criminal reigns supreme. This is what death has learned about life. 'Vanity of vanities. All is Vanity'".

Borkovsky paused and looked across the room at the grieving Gorki. "Now I go happily back to whence I have come. I am death. I die."

The old man was raving so that for the first time since he had entered the hospital room, Gorki feared for his safety. The younger man rose to his feet and reached out to subdue the madman who stood before him. As his hand touched Borkovsky's form the old man was no longer there. Alone in the hospital room Gorki screamed.

Unfortunately for him Igor Gorki chose to tell the story of what had happened in the hospital room at Sevastopol. As a result of that he spent a great deal of time in the lunatic asylum near Moscow. Only after he repented of his tale and the warden was sure he no longer believed what he had told about his last meeting with Borkovsky that Gorki was allowed to return to his still uneasy family.

So there it is: the revelation of Igor Ivanavich Gorki, confidante to the Tsar and highborn person of Russia. The ravings of a madman or the truth? Who knows? What is known is this: many years later, on his deathbed Gorki, then old and feeble, rose from his bed, stood erect and facing no one or no thing cried out "My Dear Borkovsky!" and dropped dead onto the floor.

THE CASTLE

I.

It was the year after I was graduated by Yale and I was seeking adventure. I left home on a steamship for England and from there, also by steamer, to the Adriatic port of Trieste that, in those days was a commercial city in the Austro-Hungarian Empire. From Trieste I went, partly by rail-road and partly by over-land stagecoach, through the province of Croatia and on into Hungary. I visited ancient cities along the way, spending an inordinate amount of time in Budapest on the Danube. My extended visit to the Buda side of the capitol of the Kingdom of Hungary was more due to my infatuation with a certain young lady of that town, but that is the subject of another story. Suffice it to say that my stay in the Hungarian capitol was cut short by the arrival of the young lady's fiancé, a man of great proportions and of whose existence I had been purposely left in the dark.

I fled Budapest in great haste, leaving behind one suitcase of clothing that, I am sure, proved to be an embarrassment to the lady in question. I traveled by coach into the Transylvanian highland, and area of immense beauty and overwhelming interest to me.

Yes, I had read that Bram Stoker book that told of the Life, or as it should be put, the *un*life of one Count Dracula as had any educated late Nineteenth Century young man. I was fascinated by Stoker's tale and I half expected to see the evil Count's castle looming above every hill my coach passed. Of course, there was none. There were castles but none, as far as I knew, that were inhabited by an undead count.

After a week on the road, staying at inns and taverns along the way I reached the quaint village of Malburg. I found Marburg, or Malik as the locals called it, to be a perfectly fine place in which to spend some time. It had a large inn that served good food and a wonderful local dark beer. It had a large town hall with a tower clock that chimed a pleasant chime each hour upon the hour. It boasted good hunting and had great fishing in a nearby cold water stream. It had a beautiful view of a large mountain and it had Maria, the innkeeper's daughter.

Maria Malsk was a strikingly beautiful girl with black hair and dark, dark eyes. She was of my age and could speak English in a manner that was passing but so beautifully accented by her native Magyar language to be almost lilting as she spoke it. It was Maria who brought me my first meal in Malburg. I checked into her family's inn, being greeted by her father, one Zoltan Malsk, a man of considerable size and obvious strength, and was assigned to a room on the tavern's second floor near to, but not right at the top of the stairs. I carried my own bags up the wooden staircase, as was the custom in local hotels and inns, and settled into my sparely furnished room.

I expected no comfort here. This was an inn in a small town far from the center of Austrian or even Hungarian culture. I was surprised to find a bed so comfortable that before even unpacking my suitcases I was asleep upon it, having sunk deeply into its feather mattress to get a much needed nap. It was Maria's rapping on my room's door that awakened me.

"Sir, Sir," she called into my room through that closed door. "Dinner is about to be served."

I rose and ran a hand over my clothes to smooth the wrinkles that had formed upon them. "I'll be right there," I called back to the innkeeper's daughter. "And thank you."

I was surprised to be called to my meal. I had assumed that meals here would be taken at my schedule, as was the case in most European hostels. In America meals would be included in a traveler's fee and, more likely than not, taken with all fellow travelers in a common dining room. In Europe the opposite was true. The room charge was only that, the charge for the room. Meals were extra and ordered at your convenience

As I made my way down to the inn's lower level I still did not know whether this meal to which I was called would be included in my already paid room charge or not. I had money to spend but, as I had been in Europe by then a total of two months and had not earned anything to add to what I had brought from America, my funds were far from being unlimited.

My doubts were dispelled when Maria sat me at a table, by myself. I was surprised to hear that the evening meal is always included with a traveler's overnight stay at her family's inn. "And ve offer vonderful fots, sir," the attractive young woman said in that wonderful accent of hers.

"I am sure you do," I smiled at her. The bosomy young woman leaned down toward me to put a saucer of a condiment on my table I let me look down the front of her blouse. I liked what I saw, and I am not talking about the spicy vegetable blend Maria had placed on my table.

She smiled and stood erect. Without a word she repaired to the kitchen to return with a platter of food. I dined that night as I had not dined for weeks. I was offered and accepted roasted chicken, perfectly done with a crispy dark skin and very tender juicy meat. As I cut into that bird its juices ran and I eagerly sopped them up with great pieces of dark, almost black, bread that Maria brought out too.

With the chicken came a bowl of small noodles, shimmering in a sauce of mostly fresh butter. I ate the noodles with the chicken and when Maria returned with a plate of tender beef stew I still had some noodles left to accompany this next course. The stew was heavily seasoned with a strong paprika and it had a thick and savory gravy. It included in addition to those large pieces of tasty beef, potatoes and onions as well. I consumed more bread with the stew.

For beverage there was only the beer. The dark potion was a hearty brew, heavy with hops and covered by a dark rich froth that never thinned. That froth left a mustache upon my mustache as I drank the beer and I was forever wiping my upper lip with the cloth napkin Maria had placed beside my plate before I had arrived.

My fork has but two tines and was perfect for stabbing and holding chunks of meat but little else. For the stew and the sauce I was forced to use my large spoon that accompanied my place setting. Those items were too good to waste by enforcing American culinary conventions in this foreign land. I scooped up large ladles of gravy and sauce and used my napkin to wipe them also from my mustache.

With the stew Maria carried out to me a bowl of roasted vegetables as if I required them. There were carrots, onions, turnips and a couple items I did not recognize. All had been roasted in the large fireplace that served as the main cooking point for the inn. They were a crusty caramelized brown on their exterior while being tender and moist within. Although I found the chicken and the beef stew to be quite adequate I tasted each of those vegetables, even those I did not recognize, and found them all superb in texture and taste.

More bread was brought to me and I ate it, having done with the meats and now concentrating on my beer. As I drained my glass Maria refilled it from a pitcher she had placed near my table. When the pitcher was emptied the girl had her father replenish it from the keg of beer he kept in a corner. Other men drank beer in the large room, too but as I looked around I perceived me to be the only one dining.

"No one else is hungry?" I asked Maria when she refilled my beer stein once more.

The dark haired girl looked around the room. "No vone else it staying here," she reported.

"No one?" I asked.

"No vone," she repeated.

I was surprised that such an establishment had no overnight guests but me. It was off the main road to Budapest but not so far back into the mountains as to go unnoticed by the traveling public. Besides, places like this one were routinely used by men on business. Traveling salesmen, itinerants, lawyers, judges, government official and the like stayed at inns as they did their rounds. Knife sharpeners, butchers, farm workers, and others would always be on hand. I had shared drinks and stories with plenty of them at other taverns and inns.

"Never. No vone," Maria said then she turned back to the kitchen. I continued to eat bread and drink beer. Then I reached into my waistcoat to draw out a cigar. The narrow smoke was no thicker than my index finger but was as long as two of my fingers together. I snipped its end and ran it under my nose to inhale its aroma. I smiled and put its end into my mouth, moistening the tobacco there. Before I could strike a match, there was one alit before my face. I looked up to see my host, Zoltan, Maria's father, standing there with a lit long match.

"Thank you," I smiled at the large man and put the tip of my cigar into the flame, rolling it in the flame a bit to toast its end before I drew in to ignite the cigar. After a few draws a beautiful smoke was filling my corner of the dining room.

"Iz da fot acceptable, young sir?" the innkeeper inquired.

"More than acceptable, sir," I answered. "All was wonderful."

The man nodded and blew out his match. He remained there without speaking.

"Join me?" I offered.

"No," he replied. The man adjusted the long white apron he wore. It was stained with beer and other things. He seemed to want to say something but remained silent. I assumed that his English was not up to the task.

"My daughter, Sir," Zoltan finally said.

"Yes?" I asked, looking up at him once more.

"She is a beauty, no?"

"Yes. Maria is beautiful," I told him.

The man smiled.

"And a virtuous girl as well," Maria's father announced.

I looked at him again. What was he saying? "Yes," I agreed.

The large man then leaned down to put his massive pock marked face directly in front of my young smooth skinned face. "And she vill stay virtuous," he said slowly.

"Yes, sir," I said, my mouth suddenly dry. When the man erected himself I grabbed for my beer and sipped it. He stood still for a moment more then returned to his other duties.

Having been duly warned I finished my beer only to have my glass refilled by the beautiful busty and virtuous Maria. I smiled at her and she returned the smile. I looked over at her father to see the large dark man glaring at me.

I picked up my beer as Maria cleared my table. I moved over at a table occupied by two locals. They were also drinking beer.

"English?" I asked as I did each time I wanted a conversation at a tavern like this one.

Each man shook his head.

"I speak English," a lone man at another table called over to me.

I smiled and joined him. "May I?" I asked.

"Of course," he replied and I sat with him.

"Clayton Marston" I offered, extending my right hand to the man.

The thick-handed Hungarian took my hand in his. "Tomas," he said, holding back his surname.

I sat and the two of us drank beer and talked. After a few minutes our beer steins were empty but instead of refilling them with the good dark ale we had been enjoying Maria came to our table with a round green bottle.

"Unicum,'" the attractive girl announced. "Zwack Unicum."

I looked puzzled at her. Then I looked over at my tablemate.

"Zwack Unicum," Tomas said. "A liquor. Very good."

Maria poured some of the liquid into two glasses, one for Tomas and the other for me. I raised mine to my lips and tasted its contents. The strong liquor was bitter in taste and herbal. It had the taste of a variety of herbs, more like the flavor of a roasted beef than a drink to my experience. I winced.

Tomas laughed and drowned his pour. Marie refilled the man's glass then left our table. I took a second sip of the liquor and found it less disgusting that the first. By the time I too had drained my glass, Zwack Unicum was my favorite libation.

"Jozseh Zwack has made this since 1840," Tomas told me, raising his glass before his round face. "It is made from a variety of herbs – good for the body and good for the soul."

I smiled. "So I can taste," I said. I finished a second glass of that strong Hungarian drink and poured a third from the bottle Maria had left on our table. Tomas and conversed as we drank although for the life of me I cannot remember a word of that conversation.

II.

All that followed the third glass of Zwack Unicom was a hazy blur of thoughts, sights and sounds. I awoke the next morning with a slight headache and a mouth that tasted as I had been chewing on my boot during the night. I washed up, using water brought to my room before I was awake, presumably by the innkeeper's still virtuous daughter. I rinsed out my mouth with warm water and went down to the first floor of the Inn.

Breakfast was offered by Zoltan and accepted by me. I began that day with sausages, eggs, breads toasted brown before the open hearth in the kitchen and beer. Yes, beer, the same beer I had enjoyed the evening before, was consumed by me for breakfast.

There was no one else in the dining room of the inn as I ate, something I found not at all unusual because no one else seemed to be staying at the hotel. I ate my food, served once more to me by Maria. The young woman brought out the foodstuffs in order of their preparation from the kitchen – boiled eggs first, then the roasted sausages accompanied by the toasted breads. Fish, in this case smoked fish, followed, then onions prepared with paprika in cream. I was surprised that there was anyone in the town of Malburg of normal girth if all ate in this manner.

I finished my abundant breakfast finding my headache relieved and my mouth no longer feeling poorly. I relaxed with a cup of very strong tea and a cigar before I prepared to walk about the town to see what could be seen.

"Are there castles in the region?" I asked Maria before I left. I still had such and interest.

The girl looked over at her father.

"Just one, young sir," Zoltan responded. "Half way up za mountain to the nort."

"Occupied?"

"One may say so," the man said.

I blew the last puff of smoke from my cigar into the air and put the stogie into a bowl supplied by Maria for my ashtray. "Cryptic," I said. "Is it the Castle Dracula, perhaps?" I smiled. He did not.

"If only the one who haunts Malik were but a vampire," the man said.

I looked over at him. "Then what?" I asked.

He looked away.

I shrugged and got up from the table. "I will be back for dinner," I proposed.

"Dinner is at three and supper at eight," Zoltan explained.

"Maybe supper then," I said.

"Vill you be needing a lunch?" the man asked. "I can have Maria prepare you something."

"Perhaps," I answered. "But not much. Your meals are enormous."

"Yes, young sir," the man said.

Maria prepared me a lunch that consisted of a large piece of meat, roasted and sauced, and an equally large piece of black bread. I carried this food in a sack that she supplied and left the Malsks' tavern to walk about the town of Malburg in the warm late Transylvanian summer.

Malburg, Malsk to its Hungarian inhabitants, was a town of a few hundred people, no more than a thousand, which sat in a small valley among a series of high craggy mountains. It had traditional architecture with dark woods and shuttered windows. I walked about the place greeting and being greeted by passersby. I tipped my hat to men and women and they nodded to me. Hardly anyone I met on the streets spoke English and when one did it was so broken and sporadic that any conversation was impossible.

I walked along the hard dirt road upon which the inn sat. It was Malburg's main road. I branched off onto side streets to view smaller, more humble homes. I moved on to more bucolic surroundings, seeing farms and their thatched roofed farmhouses. I moved on toward the rising mountain to the north of town. I was determined to see the castle that Malsk had told me was there. After two hours I was resting beside the road and enjoying the luncheon that Maria had prepared for me.

I bundled up the bag in which the food had been placed and stuffed it into one of my pockets. Then, straightening my outer coat, I rose and walked on. I first viewed the castle within a half an hour.

The castle that Zoltan had told me of was a large dark structure of obvious age situated upon a large rise at the crest of a ponderous hill. It was surrounded, entirely as much as I could determine, by a tall dark iron fence with only one gate that I reached after quite an effort. Slightly out of breath and a bit foot sore I stood before that locked gate and peered up at the castle beyond it. The gate was plain metal that bore a crest that featured a large letter M at its middle. A bird of some kind festooned one side and what looked to be a tree on its other.

Beyond the fence and the gate the castle looked all but deserted. Its parapets stood tall in the afternoon sun and they and the rest of the structure showed no sign of habitation. There was no smoke coming from any of the many chimneys that thrust from the slate shingled roof of the castle. I stood there and looked up at the unobtainable castle for a long time before I headed back down toward Malburg.

I reached Malburg just in time for supper. I joined Tomas at his table, the man having already started in on his evening meal. Maria brought me a plate and silver. She also brought out a glass into which I assumed she would pour beer. I was wrong. At this meal Maria Malsk brought Tomas and me a bottle of Tokay wine.

Tokay, Tokaji in her language, was a sweet and strong wine of dark color. It was full bodied and well accompanied our foods.

Tomas - Tomas Fernessi, I found after the man told me his surname – and I enjoyed what were leftovers from dinner, pork roasted in herbs, beef in paprika, more creamed onions and plenty of dark bread. We also drank large amounts of the deep golden colored wine and by the time our meal was over both of us were fast friends once more.

"You, my young American friend, are a remarkable fellow," Tomas grinned. One of his front teeth was missing and it gave the man's grin a peculiar look.

"Why do you say that?" I asked, his arm now draped over one of my shoulders.

"You are a remarkable young fellow," Tomas said, simply repeating his assertion.

He was drunk and I knew it. But, by then, so was I. He and I drank more wine and we talked some more. Then Tomas left and I was alone. I purposely ate more bread in order to have it soak up some of the alcohol I had so generously ingested and, to a degree, I was successful.

By the time Zoltan was extinguishing the candles and oil lamps that illuminated his inn's main room I was sober enough to realize that the man's daughter was smiling at me. I returned the attractive girl's smile and within an hour she had joined me in my room. The virtuous Maria proved to be quite the lover and she stayed with me in my bed most of the night.

III.

"I saw the castle yesterday while on my walk," I told Zoltan the next morning. The man looked at me with a suspicious look. I hoped he was thinking about my remark and not about his daughter sharing my bed the night before. I tried to look him directly in the eyes like an innocent man but I had to keep looking away. His suspicions grew.

"Did you meet anyone dare?" the man asked. I was relieved. He was concerned about my visit to the castle and obviously knew nothing about his daughter and me.

"No," I answered. "Is it occupied at all? It looked deserted to me."

"It iz well occupied, young sir, and you are more than fortunate that its inhabitant did not bid you to enter."

I smiled. "Come along, Zoltan," I prodded. "Enough of your Transylvanian cryptic remarks. I know of your Dracula story and I'm not scared of the ghost neither of Vlad the Impaler nor of any other Romanian or Hungarian specter. I may be young but I am not a fool. I am a graduate of Yale University, for God's sake."

"For God's sake," the man said, repeating my words. He looked down at a small golden cross he wore about his neck. "For God's sake," he intoned again.

I smiled. "The castle looks empty, but may not be," I said. "Perhaps I shall walk up there again today…if your daughter will prepare me another fine luncheon as she did yesterday."

"She shall, if you wish, young sir," Zoltan said.

"No warning about not going back to the castle?"

The large dark man shook his head.

I ate breakfast alone then was joined by a local man at my table for tea. This fellow, a tall, very slender black haired man named Lajos, spoke English enough for he and me to converse. He told me that he was a cooper, a maker of barrels, and with the coming festival his business has been brisk.

"Festival?" I asked.

"Yes, our annual festival," the man said. "On Sunday, of course."

"Of course," I smiled, having no knowledge of this upcoming event.

"To celebrate what?"

"To celebrate?" the man asked back.

"To mark, to honor. Why is the festival held? A religious holiday? A feast day of your local patron saint."

At the words, patron saint, Lajos' eyes widened and the man smiled. "Patron," he said with a nod. "To honor, to cel-e-brate, our patron." He pronounced celebrate slowly as if learning a new word.

"And that would be?"

He looked back blankly.

"Your patron saint," I prompted. "Which of the saints do you honor with your festival?"

"Saint, no. Patron, yes," he answered.

I was confused and knew my confusion would not be resolved by any more conversation with this man. I sipped the last of my tea from its cup and prepared to leave the table. Maria appeared to clear the dishes. She and I exchanged knowing smiles and the girl looked down. She moved closer and bent forward to allow me to recall her ample bosoms as she picked up the dirty dishes and empty teacups. I smiled again and so did she.

"Beautiful girl, is she not?" Lajos smiled as Maria walked away from our shared table.

"Very," I agreed.

"And a virtuous one as well," the man offered.

"So I hear," I responded.

I walked about that day but did not go up to the castle again. Instead I ate the food that Maria had carefully packed into a sack for me along the road that led down from the highlands and across the small valley in which Malburg sat. I ate cheese and dark bread and watched sheep grazing in a nearby field. It was late summer and I knew that my European adventure would soon end. I had to be home by autumn in order to accept a position my father had secured for me at his bank. He was an officer there and wanted me to start as a cashier to learn the business from a practical level. I acquiesced. After all, he had paid my tuition to Yale. I owed him at least that much.

I would have rather stayed on in Transylvania to see the snows come and to spend the winter with Zoltan Malsk and his young daughter but, obligations being obligations, I knew that was not to be.

A sheep came near to the wooden fence that separated me from its flock. The animal made a low sound that caught my attention.

"You don't eat cheese, my good man," I said, not recognizing a ewe when I saw one. Then the sheep turned enough for me to see its prominent utter. "I am sorry, madam," I smiled at the beast with a tip of my hat. "But I still have nothing here to your taste."

The ewe returned to the other sheep and I finished my luncheon. After I was done I folded the empty sack in which had been contained my food and placed it in one of my pockets. I got up, brushed grass from my trousers and continued down the peaceful valley. When I returned to the inn there was a message awaiting me.

"You are invited to the castle, young sir," Zoltan told me, his large round face showing excitement at this news. "Da Count has heard of your presence and wishes you to dine with him this evening."

"The Count?"

"Lord Malak," the man said. "Our patron."

"Your patron?" I asked.

"Yes, sir. He rules over all these parts in the name of the Emperor Franz Josef."

"I thought Vienna extends its influence into the countryside through administrators, not the aristocracy."

"Not here," Zoltan said. "Here iz different. Here our patron sees to our needs."

"How quaint," I smiled. "I certain would be please to meet this Count of yours."

"And yours, young sir," Zoltan added to include me into the rule of this mysterious Count.

That night I dressed and was picked up by a coach sent down for me from the castle. The coach was black and bore on its doors the crest that I had seen on the formidable iron gate when I visited the castle a day before.

As the driver drove the team of four black horses along Malburg's dirt road and on up into the hills I thought how perfect this was. I was Renfield, in the book, *Dracula*, being delivered to the evil undead Count Dracula. I laughed. Fiction is fiction. This was real.

The black coach entered the castle grounds through the same gate that I had studied on the prior day. It rumbled up a narrow path to the main entrance to the massive stone structure. There the driver dismounted and opened the coach's door for me. He looked quite normal to my eyes, certainly not one of the tormented undead.

Nor did Count Malak. The man was rather light in complexion, especially when compared to the swarthy townspeople of Malburg and had blue-green eyes that seemed kind. He greeted me with a polite handshake and I bowed ever so slightly from the waist. I was an American after all and not one to engage in European formalities.

"Your name is Clayton Marston, iz it not?" the man asked before I could introduce myself.

"Yes, sir, it is." I was stunned that he knew that.

"Velcome to my home, Mister Marston," Count Malak offered in a very slight accent that sounded nothing like what readers assumed Stoker's count to sound like.

"Thank you, sir. It was so kind of you to invite me here."

"I observed you looking over my castle yesterday and looked into your presence. Ve don't get many visitors from America here."

"I thought the place was deserted," I said. "There seemed to be no life about it when I was at your gate yesterday."

"Life? The 'place' is full of life," Malak laughed, emphasizing my Americanism as if he found its use amusing. "I vas a bit indisposed yesterday, that was all. Othervise I would have invited you in at that time. I love showing off our heritage to visitors."

"I certain am grateful for this invitation, sir," I responded.

"Let me show you around, young gentleman," the count offered. He was dressed in a business suit of a brown color that made him look more like an associate of my father than an undead monster. He led me through several rooms of his dwelling and the beauty I found there impressed me. The count possessed a remarkable collection of framed art, oils by the masters including Rafael and Rembrandt. He showed me a Renaissance sculpture that I just stood and studied for quite some time.

"Beautiful, is it not?" the man asked me.

"Quite," I answered. I moved to one side then the other to view the piece of marble. It was exquisite - two lovers locked in an embrace while reclining on a lounge. I was thrilled that the count allowed me to touch it.

"Beautiful," I smiled as I ran my fingers along the cold stone.

"Love, you know," Malak smiled.

"Yes," I responded with my fingers still touching that statue.

I saw other treasures there - paintings, tapestries and other statuary then my host sat me at a small table and he and I were served a fine, but not formal, dinner by a bald-headed servant who flawlessly performed his duties. If not for the surroundings, I would have felt I was dining at a Paris restaurant.

We ate roasted beef with sauce and boiled potatoes with bread. He offered me Eger Bikaver, a strong and delicious liquor that burned on the way down my throat and warmed my chest.

"Dis iz a liquor of the town of Eger," my host explained as he poured a second taste for me. "Its name literally means 'Bull's Blood of Eger'. It is a national treasure."

"So I can tell, sir," I smiled as I watched the man refill my glass. I sipped the liquor this time instead of swallowing it all as I had the first one.

Count Malak smiled, holding his glass up before his handsome face. He said something in his language I could not understand. He translated. "Iz better than medicine. He who drinks shall live 'til he dies."

I smiled and took another sip of the drink.

"Do you smoke?" the count asked after his butler had cleared our table. The man offered me a cigar that I accepted. He and I left the table, carrying our drinks, to sit before a large fireplace and talk. The butler clipped our cigars with a scissor-like cigar clipper and we lit our cigars from a long taper. My host and I blew smoke into the air to watch it sucked into the draft of the fireplace before which he and I sat.

The food had been good. The cigar was quite good and the conversation excellent. Count Malak asked me many questions about America and answered many questions about his homeland.

"For many years all of Transylvania has been a battlefield," the man told me, "a contention between the Ottoman Turks and the Christian Austrians. Now we are part of Austria, ruled through Hungary, but we have our own identity."

"Romanian," I proposed.

"Transylvanian," he corrected. "While we have affinity to Romania we remain our own people. And Malik iz an example of that."

"Malik?" I asked. "You use the local name for the town, I see."

The count smiled. "They may call it Malburg in Vienna but here it is Malik, a form of my own name, Malak."

"I see," I said. I puffed on my shirking cigar and flipped it toward the open fireplace to flick its long ash into the flames. I took another sip of the Bikaver and asked the count about his politics. "If you don't mind, sir," I proposed, "are you in support of Austria's stand against Prussian expansion?" All of Europe was abuzz with rumors of war that seemed possible between those two German speaking countries."

Count Malak looked at me. His blue-green eyes narrowed. "War is unthinkable," he said.

"Some have said that it's inevitable."

"Nothing except death is inevitable," the man corrected me.

"And taxes," I added. I looked at his puzzlement. "Our Benjamin Franklin said that the only things in life that are certain are death and taxes."

"How true. How true," the count smiled.

We talked some more, mostly of art and music, two subjects of which both he and I were knowledgeable. Then our conversation turned to philosophy. "Tell me, Mister Marston," the count said, leaning a bit more toward my chair. "Do you believe in the existence of a god?"

"I'm a Christian," I said, thinking that I was answering the man's question.

He smiled. "Yes, but do you believe in the existence of a god?"

I was puzzled. I presupposed my adherence to the faith of my fathers answered the man's poser. "Yes," I said. "How else could everything be made?"

"How else indeed," Count Malak said. He blew another puff of smoke toward the fireplace and watched it drawn into it. "But is this god of yours a personal one or just the creator of the universe?"

I really didn't feel comfortable talking about this subject. I squirmed a bit in my seat. "Personal," I replied, "although I am not one for too much religion."

"Too much religion?"

"Yes, you know, the Bible thumping preacher and his ilk." After all, I thought, I was a graduate of Yale.

The count smiled. "Yes, I know of what you speak. But if God is a personal being to you, how can you ignore him?"

"I don't believe that I am, sir," I said. "I believe in God but I make it a practice of allowing others to have their beliefs and to live my life in peace with them as much as I can."

"I see." The count raised his glass to his lips but drank not from it. "Do you believe in justice?" he asked me.

"I suppose. You mean judgment and redemption and that sort of thing?"

The man nodded and took that sip from his glass that he had postponed.

"Yes. As a Christian I am obligated to accept that Christ died for my sins and for my redemption." How often had I heard those words at chapel service at school and from my family's pastor when we attended church services together at home.

"And that means?"

"Salvation through Christ," I supposed.

"Salvation from what?"

"Damnation, you know, hell and all of that. The wages of sin."

The count smiled once more. "The wages of sin is?"

"Death," I said, completing Saint Paul's quotation from a book of the Bible that at the time I could not identify.

"Death?" the good-looking man looked over at me. "You fear death?"

"Don't we all?"

"I suppose we all do," the count said. "And when death comes – your Benjamin Franklin said it must, correct?"

I nodded.

"Vhat then?"

"Heaven or hell."

The count laughed. "Heaven or Hell," he repeated my words. "And vill hell be so bad?"

"That's what they say."

"I don't care vhat they say. Vhat do you say, Clayton Marston?" The kindly looking man looked a little less kindly as he spoke now.

"I don't know," I answered. "I suppose hell will be bad for those who go to it. It's supposed to be a place of punishment."

The count looked directly at me with those beautiful eyes of his. He smiled a gentle smile and I was, once more, impressed by what a beautiful man he was. His eyes were captivating and his skin smooth. His hair, a shiny shade of brown, fell over his ears and over the back of his collar. He was a trim man who appeared athletic. He was compelling and I had no interest in offending him. "Sir," I said, "I really don't know much of theology. I attended church with my family and was required to attend chapel at school. I feel comfortable in my beliefs, that what they are, but I certainly am no expert about such things."

"Comfortable about you beliefs," Malak said. "Good. A man should be comfortable in his beliefs, I feel. I hope that my conversation in this area did not make you feel uncomfortable. That would be an unforgivable breach of hospitality on my account."

205

"Not in the least," I said, lying about my comfort level. "I am most comfortable talking about anything with you."

"And I wit you, young sir," the count smiled. The count changed the subject and we again conversed about art and music. He loved Wagner and went on at length about that great composer's music.

"More theology," I laughed when the count expressed his love of Wagner's Ring Cycle operas.

The man laughed too. "The opposite, in fact," he proposed. "At the end of Gotterdammerung, the age of the gods ends and the age of man begins. No more theology."

"I suppose you could look at it that way. But it's the music I really enjoy."

"Uplifting, isn't it?"

"Certainly."

We talked about Wagner some more, then Chopin and other composers. I was so glad I had taken that music appreciation class during my college career.

Our intercourse lasted for an hour then he called for the carriage and I was returned to the inn.

"I hope to see you again, sir, before I leave for home," I said.

The count smiled. "You may *count* on it," he replied.

On the way back to the village I wondered if the man had intended that as a pun. I had not laughed at his remark in case he did not.

IV.

The next morning was overcast and bleak looking. Maria had slipped into my room after I returned from my visit with Count Malak and we had made love. In the morning she was no place to be found. Zoltan brought me my food; again sausages and breads. When I inquired about his daughter's absence the man gave me the most curious reply.

"Daughter? I have no daughter," he said.

I looked up at him as he put the platter of food upon my table. Had he discovered Maria's indiscretion with me and had read her out of his family. I really did not dare to ask so I let the man's remark pass unchallenged.

The food, with or without Maria's presence, was as good as it had been on prior morns and I ate it with beer and tea. After my meal I walked about, disappointed that I had no lunch prepared for me by the daughter my host no longer acknowledged. I hoped he had not harmed the girl on my account.

As I moved about Malik I stopped at a tiny tavern that featured tables and chairs placed outside its front door. I sat there with a townsman named Janos and his friend, Bela. The two were already drinking and a waiter brought me a glass for sharing from their bottle.

"Szilva Palinka", Janos offered, raising his glass after he poured into mine.

I had no idea what he was saying but took a drink from my glass anyway." Slivovitz!" I declared. I instantly recognized the taste of that fiery plum brandy that kept most of Eastern Europe from being sober.

"Szilva Palinka," the man grinned, nodding at my word. He, Bela and I drank the whole bottle. Then, each of us staggering some, we walked together down the main street of Malik to see the preparations for the upcoming festival.

"Da Count and hiz vife will be here," Janos proposed in very broken English."

"His wife? I didn't know the count was married." I assumed the man to be a bachelor. He certainly hadn't mentioned his wife during our long visit together.

"Hiz vife," the man repeated. I shrugged and went on with him and his companion.

That night I dined alone at the table I normally used. I was all by myself in the large dining room of Zoltan Malsk's inn and was served by the innkeeper himself. Maria? Not to be seen nor, as I found by asking her father about her, to be acknowledged either.

Zoltan Malsk said nothing that would lead me to believe that he was punishing Maria for her two visits to my room nor did the man mention the subject to me. I certainly did not press him in that regard. After dinner I drank Unicum and had a cigar. After waiting for a while to see if Maria would make an appearance I retired and slept that night quite alone in my soft feather bed.

The next morning was Sunday, the day of the scheduled festival. I rose and had breakfast, once more served to me by Zoltan alone. As I ate I noticed something I took to be peculiar. There were no church bells. It was Sunday morning and there was not the ringing of church bells as I had heard in every other Eastern European town I had visited. There were people on the street, going this way and that, but no church bells. I thought about it. I could not remember seeing a church.

That was odd, I thought. Every European city or town I had seen was dominated by at least one church. From the smallest village to the great cities of Vienna or Budapest, churches were prominent. They overlooked the town and those who dwelt therein. On Sunday they were packed with worshippers. The church building was always the most ornate building in town and was the center of city life.

But in Malik there was no church. How odd.

I finished my meal and went out into the bright sunlight of the streets. My eyes narrowed at its brightness. I looked to my right then to my left. Hundreds of people crowded the streets, lining the main road on both sides for as far as I could see. Great throngs of people, most obviously dressed in their best clothes milled about as if waiting for something important to happen. I asked several about the festival only to get blank stares from them in return.

I took a place along a wall not far from the inn and waited, I knew not for what. There certainly was an air of anticipation in the crowd and I was interested in finding out why it was.

After some wait a cheer arose from the crowd farther up the road from where I stood and I craned to see its cause. There was nothing at first then I saw it. A coach, a black coach that I instantly recognized to be that of Count Malak, slowly made its way up the road. It was pulled, as it had been when I rode in it, by four large black horses, each sporting black feather plumes on their heads. The carriage neared and I could see the kindly face of my former host, the count therein. But the count was not alone in his coach. Beside him, and plainly to be seen by me as the vehicle neared, was a young woman with long blond hair that was piled upon her head in the most elegant fashion. I looked at that young woman and my eyes widened. It was Maria Malsk!

The count's companion had yellow hair but she was undoubtedly Zoltan Malsk's daughter, Maria. I knew her face. I knew her dark eyes. I had no doubt.

Zoltan had stepped out of his inn to see the coach's approach.

"It's Maria," I told the man.

"She is the count's wife," the man said. "The Countess Malak."

"Maria, your daughter." I insisted.

"I have no daughter, young man," the man said. "She is the Countess Malak, wife to the Count.

"Impossible," I said, staring into the passing coach. The carriage stopped before me. Its driver held the leads of its four horses in his hands, the reins draped between his fingers. He stared straight ahead. The count looked out at me from inside the coach.

"Ve meet again, young sir," he smiled. I began to smile back but something stopped me. A cold chill formed in my spine and I looked back at the man's eyes. This was the same Count Malak with whom I had supped but those were not his same eyes. The count I remembered, the kindly, well-spoken, gentile Count Malak had beautiful kindly blue –green eyes while now he looked at me with eyes of flame. What should have been white was red, deep red, and his gaze burned a hole into my soul.

I froze, unable to move. I saw the woman who sat beside the Count; the beauty that I had known as Maria, nod and the man beside her, the red-eyed one, man stretched a hand out in my direction.

"Down!" Zoltan, who had taken a position beside me, yelled. He pushed at me just in time to push me aside from what appeared to be a lightning bolt that came from the Count's fingers. That terrifying charge lashed out and struck the wall behind where I had been standing. A great blackened and smoking hole appeared where it had struck.

"Fool!" the Count said and a bolt of lightning was directed at Zoltan who was instantly destroyed by it. I fell to the ground then scampered along the street, seeking shelter behind those who had lined the way. Another lightning bolt passed within inches of me, making my hair stand out from my head and burning my right arm. I fell again. I looked up from the ground to see those around me move away. When the carriage came into view I rolled to one side to avoid yet another lightning strike then scurried down the road to get between two buildings.

The ground shook. The building around me began to shake.

"Hail, Prince of Darkness!" all in the crowd shouted.

The ground quivered, knocking me off my feet. Debris fell about me, one piece of wood striking me hard enough upon my head so as to draw blood.

"Hail, Satan!" all but me yelled.

The bell in the town hall's tower clock began to chime. It was high noon and the bell chimed twelve times. When the sound of its twelfth proclamation was still resounding, I looked up to see the building around me rising from the earth. I clung to the very ground upon which I had fallen and saw the entire town of Malik, building, fences, fence posts, lamps and lamp posts sucked up into the air to be held in the sky above me. Over me too were the coach, its horses, its driver and its two passengers. A horrible smell of sulfur filled my nostrils and I gagged at the rotten egg taste it put into my mouth.

I looked to my left to see the castle I had visited two days before, rise up from the high hill upon which it had rested and take wing like some gigantic horrible black bird and soar up into the sky.

I watched in horror as the castle, the town and the coach joined together in the air under a huge black cloud that had suddenly formed in the hitherto cloudless sky. I trembled without control over my body. I stared up at that terrible sight.

Then it was gone. All of it. The entire village of Malik, Maria, the Count, the townspeople, and the buildings the horses and sheep, all swept out of sight into that black cloud that itself simply dissipated. All that was left was the bare ground and I, lying still on the ground with wet pants and a trembling body.

I walked around the site of where Malik had been for hours that day. All I found of any remembrance of the place was the tiny gold cross that Zoltan Malsk had worn around his neck the first day I had met him. That and nothing else. Just before dark I was picked up by an overland coach whose driver, although he had traveled this same route daily for years, said that he knew nothing of the town of Malberg or Malik.

I returned to America and entered banking with my father. I still have that gold cross and the terrible memories of my visit to the Transylvanian highland, memories that wake me almost every night in trembling sweats and the inability to breathe.

I have long thought upon what message I could garner from this incredible experience and have come to few conclusions. I know, however, more that most that evil exists. I have looked into the eyes of evil to see what appeared to be kindness and as gentle spirit. Evil cloaks itself in beauty.

This is the testament of Clayton Marston, late of Yale University and sworn before witnesses. All that I experienced is included. I have left out nothing. I tell this tale as a warning to those who read it in the fervent hope that you may understand what I learned that terrible day in the Transylvanian highlands - that evil cloaks itself in understanding and beauty and that evil must be exposed.

TO MAKE THEMSELVES
A HOME

Demons haunt the spot,
For the nobles now are gone;
There no kingdom proclaimed,
The princes are no more;

Thorns thrive, where once where palaces,
Nettles and thistles fill the forts;
There jackals prowl,
There quarter ostriches,

Wild cats hunt with hyenas,
And demon calls to demon;
There vampires settle,
To make themselves a home.

Isaiah 34: 12 – 16

I.

I had never been much of a Bible reading person although anyone educated at a classical school was given a general knowledge of that Book. It was because of my relative ignorance of Old Testament scripture that I did not know what to expect upon seeing Thorncastle. The warning words of the prophet Isaiah remained unknown to me as I walked with my wife through the partly broken and dirt encrusted gates. I was fully ignorant of the danger as I mounted the steps and pressed my advance into the house itself.

Before I can adequately retell the story of that awful place I need to explain a little about myself and the curious string of partly connected events that had brought me from London, to my former country home, to London, once more, then to Thorncastle.

I am Paul Robinson Smithe, the second son of a London merchant of moderate success in business. Moderate is the word we use to convey a sense of propriety. We say that a friend drinks but moderately when if it were anyone other than a friend we were discussing we would say that he was a lush. Or, we say that I am a person of moderate means instead of saying that I am poor, or not poor, as is the case and the relative prosperity of the listener may be. So I say that my father was moderately successful in his occupation in London that is to say that half of our associates found him to be ostentatiously rich while the other half pitied us for our poverty.

I was reared into manhood in London, attending a moderately respected school, met and married my wife and acquired Thorncastle. But I still am not ready to continue the narrative already begun without relating more of my situation in order that the true impact of my experience may be appreciated.

I met my wife, Marlene, at a party that was given to celebrate some alleged success, such as a birthday or an anniversary. It has always amused me that some people seem so pleased with themselves that they have been able to go one more year without dying or without killing their wives that they feel compelled to mark this non-event with a party at which their friends and acquaintances drink and eat to excess so as to hasten their own deaths.

It was at one such party that I danced with Marlene. Redheaded women had always attracted my attention. So did large-chested women. In Marlene Worthington-Jones I found both. The female's large and well-formed breasts brushed softly at me as we danced and her red tresses gleamed like fire in the bright ballroom light and I knew that I had to have her. I knew that I would do anything to have her and I did. I committed the most horrible act that a happy and popular bachelor could do to have this large-chested redhead. I married her.

I suppose I could, at this point go on a great length concerning my abhorrence to the institution of marriage but those views are widely known and so widely shared by my friends that I need not waste time nor space to expand upon them. Suffice it to say that my marriage to Marlene – to the large-chested, red-haired, smooth-skinned, loving and lovely Marlene – did nothing to alter my opinion of marriage.

The only good that came from this union was that, thank God, we did not produce children. No whimpering, snot-nosed children follow me calling me Papa, or worse, Daddy. No son to support through school. No daughter to provide with a dowry. At least I was spared those terrors.

Marlene and I settled into the country home with which her family provided us. It was a rather pleasant place that was situated upon ample grounds but it was not all that I had hoped it to be. It did have a stable but I was expected to supply the horses to occupy those quarters. It had a goodly spread of farmland but I was forced to pay the farm workers. Managing such an agricultural enterprise was outside my experience and well beyond my desires. I had been reared with the singular talent to enjoy life. I had learned at school to tell the difference by taste alone between a Chateauneuf-du-Pape and a Cote-du-Rhone. I had learned to indulge the Saxon part of my English character by downing great quantities of ale without appearing drunk. I knew that I was ready to take my place in proper English society at the head of my wife's family's London business. Now I was planted well into the country with empty stables and unplowed fiends far from my true lifestyle.

Marlene's large breasts and red hair could never compensate me for that.

I am forced to pause, once more, to provide an insight that I am sure will be missed without me noting it. It is that I am neither the bounder nor the cad that some might assume me to be by reading the proceeding. That is to say that, although I hold strong beliefs concerning marriage and country living, my positions are matters of personal privileges. I do not challenge the idiosyncrasies of others. I expect to be accepted as a gentleman despite mine. Beside, one would not know my true opinions unless I tell them and I pray I not be judged harshly for my honesty.

After all is said and done, Marlene, who was forced by convention to live as my loving wife every day, seemed not to mind her habitation with me at our country estate.

I suffered at the country house as much as I could. That turned out to be two years. Then I could stand it no more. I raised all the money that I could, leased the country estate to a fellow who was willing to waste his life as a country gentleman farmer and I invested in a proper London business.

London, in those days, was the thriving centre of European commerce that we English had created it to be after the defeat of Spain's Armada and before the rise of American economic imperialism. Somewhere in town Charles Dickens was writing one of his novels and the streets of the city were filled with Tiny Tims, Oliver Twists and David Copperfields. Good Queen Victoria sat upon the throne of England and her German cousin, Albert, stood by her side. Somewhere in a dark and cold garret Karl Marx brooded about the failure of 1848 European revolutions, and crazy Charles Darwin was writing about monkeys becoming men.

London was the beating heart of all England and I was there. There was money to be made and I was there.

The business into which I bought my way was one of import and export. We brought in shiploads of goods from the Continent to sell them in bulk to wholesaling concerns in London or to be transshipped to the Americas. Much of our business involved the importation of wine from France and, as earlier stated, this was part of my calling. I knew fine wines and I used that knowledge to make a great deal of money. When he had first moved to London, Marlene and I had taken a "moderate" home. Now my success demanded more. It demanded Thorncastle.

II.

Perhaps I am now ready to tell the story of our arrival at Thorncastle. Maybe I am not. Perhaps, it would serve to better illuminate this tale to tell more of Marlene since my wife figures so prominently in this story.

Marlene Worthington-Jones was born into a family whose success was hardly moderate. The Worthington-Joneses were well known for their commercial prominence as well as their social and political successes. Amoung them were several millionaires; many social lions; three members of Parliament and two members of the House of Lords. Marlene was the daughter of Lord Worthington-Jones, The Earl of Rockingham and the head of the House of Worthington-Jones, the brokerage house I had hoped to head.

Marlene was well-schooled in the social graces and, as I assumed that I alone knew, she was in bed, a tiger. Marlene Worthington-Jones Smithe was my greatest asset in the early development of my London business. I used her family's brokerage firm and her family's considerable connections to advance the cause of my house. My wife also provided me with a great deal of love and encouragement for which I will be always grateful.

However, in all modesty, the subsequent success of my business was due more to my ability and ambition than to anything that Marlene brought to me. When I am placed in the proper position and circumstance, I am not at all lazy and in my business I applied my talents and energy well. Within a year of assuming the presidency of the concern I had doubled its profits, froze out my partners and doubled the profits again. I was amazing and all London society recognized it.

It was in this newly found position of success and business leadership that I became aware of Thorncastle's availability.

Thorncastle – the very name appealed to me. It was part Saxon and part Norman – much like we English. It was regal. It was mysterious. I had to have it.

A friend, or rather a business associate of mine, had come by rather devious means to own Thorncastle. All I cared about was that this man legally held the title and that he was willing to sell it to me. He and I bargained without me ever seeing the estate I was buying. That was unusual for me. I did not get to be rich and respected by buying a pig in a poke but Thorncastle was different. If I had not moved quickly someone else could have purchased it before me. Besides, everyone in London knew Thorncastle. The old place was a former royal residence and had recently been owned by an embarrassingly poor earl who was forced by his poverty to sell the place to avoid its seizure for his debts. Thorncastle passed through several hands before coming to me. I knew that it had stood vacant for years and it would require a great deal of money to make it livable but I did not care. It did not matter. All that mattered was that I, Paul Robinson Smithe, owned Thorncastle, an estate that had once housed a king!

The ride to Thorncastle was a long one from our leased London home that first time, neither in actual distance nor in actual time but in perceived time, the stuff of which life is made. Hours passed for me as minutes actually elapsed. Our coach rattled over the hard surface roads from center London to its outskirts and my attention was only on what lay ahead of us. I am afraid that I was of little company to Marlene with my eyes fixed out of the carriage's window to see the streets change to lanes and the lanes to a pike. She remained characteristically silent as I looked to see my first glimpse of Thorncastle.

Then we were there. The coach stopped before the poorly maintained gates of the estate and my wife and I dismounted. The driver held out his hand to steady our descent. Marlene took it. I did not. Once to the ground we walked through the gate and to the house's huge front doors. I pushed at the massive oak doors, forcing them open before us. My wife and I stepped into our newly purchased house.

It was dusty within. Very dusty. The floors, although covered with dust, seemed sound as I trod them in careful steps. The walls were dirty but intact and the place spacious.

I almost shouted as I stood there. I looked over at Marlene and for a brief moment I thought that I could detect the same level of excitement in the woman's eyes. Marlene, as always, hid her emotion, if there was really any in her. She did that most of the time with the greatly appreciated exception, as I stated earlier, of when she and I were in bed.

She and I walked from room to dusty room. We surveyed. We inspected. We planned. I would restore this place to its former beauty and then more. With the money that came into my then sole-owned business, I could do just about anything that I wanted to dress up Thorncastle. The lack of money could no longer hold me from my due place in English society. Only my reach bound me, and my imagination, and neither of them was restricted.

A full description of Thorncastle is unneeded. Trust me that the estate was a magnificent one. It had large rooms with high ceilings and thick plaster. It was well placed upon large grounds and no part of those grounds was put to farming. All were intended for gardens and for play. This was no country estate with agricultural needs. It was a palace for a king. Once it was restored it would impress the Royal Family itself, a goal of mine that would include getting the Queen to visit Thorncastle.

Together Marlene and I explored our new home. We made careful note of what repairs would be required and we began to plan how those repairs would be accomplished. As we moved through the rooms of Thorncastle we paid little note of its vast cellar. How I wish now that Marlene and I had made a more complete inspection of those quarters. But, be that as it may, she and I completed our inspection to return to London and begin the implementation of our plans.

On the way back Marlene, if excited by all of this, kept that excitement hidden. She was mostly quiet as I boiled with anticipation. I did not resent this quietude on Marlene's part. In fact, I was grateful for it. I compared her quiet demeanour to that of my friends' wives and I knew I had the advantage over those men. I had no chattering magpie. Although Marlene, as would any female, had times of mindless babbling, she was, for the most part, a quiet one. Sometimes I could pretend she was not there.

Despite what slanders that would later be told, I loved my wife,

III.

Now, at last, I believe to be ready, with the proper and needed foundation laid, to tell the story of what happened to Marlene and me at Thorncastle and how those events forever and irrevocably changed my life. The following words are true. They may be difficult to believe – many have come to that position – but they are, nonetheless, true. All of the events that I shall relate happened exactly as I shall tell them. I will add nothing. I will take nothing away. Judge then, the tale:

The restoration of Thorncastle was more labourious and more costly than I had originally anticipated. The project took most of the profits from my still thriving business to complete the heavy work and left little with which Marlene would use to purchase the needed furnishings. We had expenses to pay on out London apartments as well as the expense of Thorncastle. Because it would have been unthinkable to go into Thorncastle with the place only partially furnished, I was forced to borrow the needed funds. At last it was done and Marlene and I occupied our new home.

From the first night, if my eyes and ears had not been closed by my love of the place, I should have known something was amiss. Sights and sounds went unseen and unheard, at least by me. Marlene, of course, suspected something from the first but, quite like her nature, kept it to herself. At night whilst she and I were in bed, whether sleeping or not, she would hear something the sound of which was at the same time familiar and strange.

She said nothing of those sounds and she continued to say nothing when, during times when I was away at the office in London or on an inspection of an incoming ship on the Thames, she thought she perceived a shape, usually out of a corner of her eye, that would be gone the second she looked over at it. Of these occurrences and others, Marlene said nothing.

It was not until we had been living at Thorncastle for over four months that we began to admit, first to ourselves, then to each other, that things were not right. "It happened again," Marlene would say as I walked into our house after a difficult day at the business. I would know what she meant.

I would be treated to a tale of a disappearing form or a mysteriously moved piece of furniture. Soon Marlene and I were referring, partly in jest, to "our ghost". How I wish that we were correct in that description!

Allow me to pause, once more, in order to give one more piece of background information that I feel must be presented. If it were left only to me I certainly would not bring into this account the name of Sarah Tillsbury but others have already injected that name into the scenario that will follow. After slandering the lady, those who called forth her name have crawled back into anonymity to leave me alone to defend what truly needs no defense. Quite reluctantly, then, I say the following:

I met Sarah Tillsbury in London a year or so after I married. The young woman was as talkative as was my wife silent. She was as outgoing as my wife was shy. And, I am pressed to say in a most ungentlemanly fashion, that she was as active in bed as was Marlene.

Those scoundrels who rushed charges into popular knowledge have already published all of this. Because they are widely known I attest to them as facts and I attest to these facts only. The rest: the lies about Sarah's supposed Gypsy heritage; the lies about her alleged interest in witchcraft; the lies about her unnatural influence upon me and my subsequent behavior on its account, all of these and other untruths, no matter how often told and how widely accepted as true, remain lies.

Here is the truth:

I loved Sarah Tillsbury in a carnal way without allowing that passion in any way to interfere with the love I maintained for my wife. Sarah Tillsbury, and I assure the reader that this is true, never had any influence over me except as one would expect as a lover. She knew nothing of the supernatural and she led me toward no evil. The full and complete extent of our relationship was one of a passionate nature and, in that way, was no different that those of most of my friends and their mistresses.

Now I can return to the tale.

One night, whilst I was in the arms of Sarah and my wife was alone at Thorncastle, Marlene slept, believing me to be working late. That night she was first visited. Marlene slept. Her eyes never opened. A mist filled the darkened bed chambre and with just a few breaths of it the sleeping woman sank into deep and unnatural sleep. A dark figure neared. The gown that Marlene wore was swept back from the sleeping female's throat and a pair of pale lips pressed to my wife's neck. There were no two small punctures that have been described by fiction writers. This was no fable written to frighten and fascinate women and children. This was brutal reality.

With sudden force and violence teeth bit into soft flesh and the still unconscious woman's form began to twist in reaction. Blood was not drawn nearly from her veins. It was lapped up from a wound that was large as a Sovereign in Marlene's throat. The jagged gash gushed blood up into the mouth that devoured it. The recipient's teeth reddened, its tongue thickened as more and more of my wife's very life was taken from her unconscious form.

This horror began in violence and continued in violence until it abruptly ended. The dark intruder quickly fled through the bed chambre's door to leave my then awake wife screaming as she held a hand to her still bleeding throat. Blood covered her hand, her neck, her upper chest and the top of our bed. She continued screaming.

The doctor and several friends were already at Thorncastle when I arrived home. There seemed to be a great deal of confusion as to what had actually occurred. I rushed to my wife's side and attempted to comfort her. I had never before seen Marlene so terrified. The frightened woman's blood covered body trembled in my arms and she sobbed as I held her. All the emotion that she had never shown me poured out of her in heaving cries of anguish.

Marlene's wound, although deep and gory, was not fatal. The doctor bound it and gave his patient some laudanum to ease her pain and panic. The opiate worked and Marlene was limp in my arms.

A complete search of Thorncastle found nothing to be amiss. My friends, the doctor and locals searched the grounds, finding nothing. My associate, Roger Williamson, a large and powerful man, offered to spend the night outside out bedroom and I accepted his offer. After abandoning the gore-covered bed in which my wife had been attacked and washing her body and slipping a clean gown onto her, I carried Marlene into another bedroom where she and I spend a restless night. Roger sat on a chair just outside our door.

Even at those precautions it took Marlene a long time to regain sleep. I am not ashamed to admit that sleep was difficult for me to obtain as well. But we did sleep and as we did, Roger Williamson died.

IV.

Please permit me to pause, once again, in my narrative in order to tell something of Roger Williamson and how the man came to be in our house on the last night of his life.

Roger was five years my junior and quite a handsome fellow. He was rich, having both inherited wealth and earned income from his wise investments. Against this good and honourable man who was both a friend and business associate to me, have, in recent months, been circulated the most reprehensible and despicable rumours concerning the existence of a supposed liaison between him and my dear wife. These rumours, as most of the unattributed lies concerning the events at Thorncastle, are unworthy of a gentleman's reply. I only need to say that there was nothing of an intimate nature between that gentleman, or in fact, any gentleman other than myself, and my wife. I was as distressed as was anyone over Roger Williamson's murder. It was this friend who had advanced me the money I had so needed to complete the restoration of my beloved Thorncastle. It had been his trust and generosity that made my lifestyle possible and, although it had been erroneously told so, he never pressed me for the repayment of the debt.

As Marlene and I slept, Roger Williamson met his death in the hallway just outside our bed chambre's door. I wish that I had not slept so soundly so as not to have heard the attack. I would have sprung up from my bed to the defense of my friend and benefactor even if that action had meant my own death. I was that close to Roger. Unfortunately, I did sleep soundly and Roger died alone.

We found the young man the next morning lying in the hallway, covered with his own blood, his handsome face distorted by the pain and horror he experience at the last. Great chunks of flesh had been ripped from Roger's neck and also from his arms. These pieces of human flesh were never found and we all suspected the worst. The members of the local constabulary were aghast at the sight. None of them had seen anything as bad as this before that night. All who saw that grisly sight were horrified by it. None could bear to look long at the blood-spattered walls of the hallway or at the mutilated corpse of Roger Williamson.

Marlene would remain in our home only after the police were persuaded to provide a constant presence of protection. Another complete search of the premises found nothing. I, myself, helped in that search and it was then that I began to feel what was happening.

There was no ghost at Thorncastle. I felt a strange and damp feeling when I walked alone down the wooden steps and into the cellars. I looked about the various rooms there and felt the presence of someone not seen. I turned sharply and my eyes were looking directly into the eyes of a creature, the description of which sounds insane. I only saw it for a moment. In an instant it faded into nothingness but I will never be able to forget its eyes. Those horrible eyes were large and catlike in appearance. Their irises were vertical slits, much like a cat's. The parts of the eye that should have been white, instead were yellow, a dark yellow.

I blinked and the creature was gone. A strange haze remained for a moment then it was gone too and I was standing quite alone in my cellar. I knew that I had found the source of Thorncastle's terror and I also knew that no one would believe me. I searched the cellar by the light of several candles I held in their holder. I desperately looked for a clue, some solid evidence of what I had just seen. There was none. I returned to the others in the hopes that the creature that had revealed itself to me also had appeared elsewhere in the house. This hope was in vain. I alone had seen it.

That night I was all for leaving Thorncastle to stay elsewhere and I told Marlene so. For some reason, perhaps in a misguided effort to please me, my wife insisted that we stay in our home. She and I argued about this and it was this muffled quarrel that the police constable heard through our closed door. Later the man would testify that he heard only voices and did not hear the words we spoke. Marlene was adamant in her position to stay and I finally acquiesced to her wishes. How I wish I had forced her to leave with me.

The mist filled the room two hours after Marlene and I retired to our bed. I awoke but I could neither speak nor move. I watched in wide-eyed horror as the mist came together near our bed to form the shape of a human being. This shape was concentrated together until it was the figure of a dark man and when it was it came toward my wife and me. Marlene's eyes, those beautiful pale blue eyes, were open but it was obvious to me that she could not move. I could see her nightgowned form struggling for motion but she remained on the bed as if tied to it. Then I saw the creature's eyes. This time they glowed red, crimson red, and not yellow. Those horrible red eyes stared down at my wife as the beast's face lowered to her neck.

I tried to scream but could not. I tried to reach out toward Marlene but I was held in place as if bound there. The creature's mouth, now dripping a foul smelling fluid, moved steadily down toward my wife's body. Then in a sudden lunge the beast thrust its teeth into Marlene's throat and at the same time it ripped at her nightgown with its clawed hands. It tore at that garment and caused deep gashes in the woman's large breasts. Blood gushed from under the horrible beast's face and splattered the creature and splattered over me. With each and every beat of my wife's heart, more blood was shot up over the two of us, the creature and me. Then the beast lapped blood from my wife limp and lifeless form.

I knew Marlene was dead because her blood was no longer pumping from her neck wound. That precious fluid only pooled there. The creature, its eyes glowing red, looked at me. It was a sight beyond my power to describe. The red eyed and pale skinned being's face was covered with blood and a great deal of it dripped from its chin. It almost smiled at me. Then it simply vanished, leaving nothing behind but my frozen form and my dead wife.

I was found the next morning in a state of shook. I was lying beside my dead wife, covered with her blood and unable to describe what I had witnessed.

As is well known, I was arrested to be charged and tried for the murders of both my wife and of Roger Williamson. I feel no animosity for those people involved in my trial. I would, if not knowing what I had seen, have voted to convict as did each man of my jury. I do, however, abhor those writers, both in and out of the press, who have printed lies and rumours without foundation in this matter solely for their own enrichment.

I was found guilty and I expected to be hanged. However, luckily or not, I was spared the rope to be sent to this merciless asylum where I write these words so that my case may be fairly judged. Here I am and here I shall remain until I join my sweet wife in death. Whether I am believed or not, I assure everyone that in the cellars of Thorncastle, the creature still lives! Whether I am believed or not – it lives.

THE CONNOISSEUR

God, I hate him! Barbara thought as she looked across the table at her husband. David was inspecting his wineglass for water spots again. The woman wished him dead.

David Grant and Barbara Williamson were married in a large church wedding and treated to a lavish reception. Her family was rich, very rich, and she had already been given a huge trust fund the proceeds of which would fund David's extravagances. The principal of that fund could not be touched until the woman's fiftieth birthday or her death, but the investment income was available for use and that income proved to be substantial.

The couple, both in their thirties, moved into a large home and David continued as an executive in his wife's family firm, although with a larger office. They seemed happy but Barbara soon was not. She saw her attentive fiancé quickly become an overbearing bore. David had always had airs. Barbara's family didn't like him much. He was competent at the office but much too pretentious for family gatherings. The Williamsons were third generation money. David was first. His parents were middle class. He had been educated at a private school and was well behaved but not comfortable in the moneyed set like his in-laws.

The Williamsons were the kind of rich people that working class people liked. They seemed to be "regular people" to those who worked for them. They were not condescending nor stuck up. David Grant was both.

No one really liked David Grant. Barbara Williamson loved him, at least for a while, but she never liked him. He was always talking down to someone whether it was a waiter at a restaurant or a typist at his office. There was always only one way to do things and that way was David's way. Barbara soon found out that the man's way of demanding perfection extended to the home.

"Good," David declared after he finished inspecting his wineglass. The man looked at each piece of his silverware and his wife was relieved to find that they had passed his muster too. "Aperitif?" David offered, looking across the dining table at Barbara.

"Yes, thank you," the woman responded and she lifted her wineglass toward David. It was exactly one-third filled by the man who then poured the before meal wine into his own glass. David swirled the glass in front of his face to observe the legs the wine left on the inside of the glass. He smiled, put the glass to his nose and inhaled the almond aroma from it.

God, I hate him, Barbara thought again as she watched her husband sip his aperitif wine. He seemed so pretentious, so pompous.

A nod from David allowed Barbara to taste her drink. She sipped it and awaited her husband's next directive.

Barbara Williamson Grant had been plotting her husband's murder for several months. She planned to kill the man at home, preferably by poison, and then at night take the body to one of her family's mills to incinerate it in the furnace. He was a man of slight build and Barbara knew that she could transport his lifeless body with a little effort. She had access to a door that led directly to the furnace and had practiced dumping blanketed pieces of old furniture into its all-consuming heat. She had not been seen doing that nor did she have fears that she would be. The only concern of Barbara was exactly how to do it. She had to do in David with a poison the man would not suspect. He was, after all, such a stickler for tastes.

Poison in his food seemed a good idea but David always oversaw the preparation of each meal that Barbara prepared when the cook was not on duty. He could suspect something. Besides, Barbara was afraid that cooking could destroy the full power of a poison or dilute it enough just to make David ill and not dead.

No, the poison for this job must be fast acting and discrete. Poisoning David's food would not work but poisoning his wine would be not only more effective but also much more poetic. It was David fawning over the wine at dinner that rankled Barbara the most. The man, after reading just about every book on the subject of wine, considered himself to be an expert. He made such a show of tasting each wine when they ate, whether they were eating in or out. Barbara was embarrassed by it. At restaurants her husband would make such a show of his wine authority, sniffing and sipping his freshly poured glass. He would hold the glass to the light, preferably a candle, and explain in boring detail to Barbara, their dinner guests and to the waiter, how the wine was made; from what grapes it had been created; it's history; its ownership and how it differed from similar wines. Barbara knew that David had become sources of bemusement by the staff of certain restaurants and by her friends.

Waiters and bussers called David not a connoisseur but rather the "kind-of-a-sewer" behind his back and made fun of his affectations. More than a few times dinner guests smiled into their hands as the pretentious man went on.

Poison in David's wine seemed so right.

But which poison? Which wine?

A strong tasting poison like the rat poison that Barbara had purchased for the job was ruled out after she dissolved a large quantity into a glass of wine as a test and found the wine's bouquet to be so altered as to immediately give away its presence. David always made such a show of sniffing his wine for the subtleties of his fragrance that any poison would have to be subtle as well.

Ground glass sounded interesting at first. Barbara read how slaves used to kill their masters by putting ground glass into the food they prepared for them. Too slow, she decided. Besides, in modern time, a doctor with the proper test certainly could diagnose internal bleeding before it could kill David. No, poisoned wine still was the best idea.

Then, as David went on and on about a newly purchased sherry, Barbara knew her problem was solved. Sherry, first a fortified wine made from a Spanish grape and then a brandy that was made from the wine would be perfect.

"Almonds," is the word from David that clinched it. Barbara, after doing a lot of reading on the Internet had learned that arsenic had a bitter almond taste and, if added to a sherry, she supposed, would be undetectable.

"Almonds?" Barbara asked.

"Yes, a fresh, smoky almond aroma," David said in that haughty tone of his when he was pontificating on wine.

Perfect, his wife thought behind her smile.

Barbara waited until David purchased a new bottle of Sherry. At dinner she uncorked the fortified wine and decanted it. To be sure that David suspected nothing; the woman put the poison she had obtained, once more from an Internet purchase, into the entire bottle of decanted wine. She swirled the glass decanter to mix in the poison before she brought it to the table.

David was already there. He was standing at his end of the table, awaiting his wife. When Barbara put the decanter of sherry in front of him the man poured two glasses. He handed one to Barbara who took it to her seat at the table across from him. She sat. So did he.

"Now, Barbara," David began, looking at the sherry glass. He picked up that glass and gave it a gentle swirl. "Legs," he smiled.

Drink it! Barbara inwardly shouted as she remained outwardly quiet and calm. But David did not drink. He put the glass down then looked over at his wife. He just looked at her for a moment and during that moment Barbara was afraid the jig was up. He must have detected something in the poisoned sherry.

"It the sherry all right?" Barbara asked.

"Oh, yes. I'm sure it'll be fine. But there's something…"

"Yes Dear?" the woman inquired.

"The books at the office."

"Yes?"

"There's a problem and I need a large amount of money to make things right. You'll have to give it to me or I'm going to jail."

Barbara looked over at David, not knowing what to say. All her trust fund proceeds went into an account that David managed. She had no extra money to give him.

"I don't have any money other than what we have."

"Yes you do," David said. "Your trust fund."

"You have that money," Barbara reminded her husband.

"The earnings, not the principal. I need it all."

"But the trust can't be used until I'm fifty," Barbara protested.

"Or dead," her husband added. The man reached under himself to pull out a pistol he had hidden on his chair. "Someone broke in on us while we were eating. I resisted and you were shot. Sorry." With that the man pointed the gun at his rich wife and pulled the trigger.

The force of the 36-caliber slug sent in through Barbara and into the floor. The woman was dead as soon as the bullet passed through her. David looked across at what he had done. The man smiled. He knew he would have to create evidence of a break-in and a struggle but he had time. First…

The man picked up his glass of what he expected to be an excellent sherry and drained it into his mouth. "Very good," he smiled as he tasted the hint of bitter almonds.

RUSSELL SCHOOL

The first of the deaths at Russell School occurred almost exactly twenty years before the 1917 addition was built. In the spring of 1897 when the buds of nearby elm and maple trees were preparing to bring forth leaves, Samuel Fournier died.

The final construction work was completed on Russell School on a crisp and clear day in 1887. The new school building that towered three stories in the bright October sunlight looked over the surrounding streets of wooden houses and wooden barns. The newly constructed Eastern Farmer's Market, the lynch pin of Detroit's Eastside development, could be seen from the flat roof of the new brick school building. In an area that had once been a forest; then a meadow above the long and narrow French farms that had stretched up from the Detroit River; then plowed fields; then cemeteries, farm sites and rural homes, the school and its soon to be completed neighboring firehouse were built to complete the northernmost part of the new Market area and the newly built homes about it. Detroit, once a fur-trading center, in 1887 was nearing the coming of the Twentieth Century with growing industrialization. By then heavy manufacturing was occurring in the city. The rich red clay down river from

Detroit was being made into fine bricks. Cast iron stoves were forged and assembled in the former fur-trading town. Immigrant women and children worked in cigar factories to make the highly prized Detroit Cigar. Great warehouses lined the Detroit River. Those warehouses were filled with goods to be shipped west to Chicago or north into the heart of the Wolverine State.

Russell School was a symbol of the city's progress. It stood huge on the Eastside with its heavy Detroit brick giving the structure a substantial look. Soon children, the children of those who made bricks and the children of those who assembled stoves, would attend elementary school classes in the beautiful brick building. Soon Russell School would be given more than form. It would be given life. With that life also came death.

Mr. Fournier, Sam to everyone at Russell School, had been the janitor at the building ever since the school board opened it. Sam was a quiet and reclusive sort of a fellow and lived in a small second floor room in the center of Detroit not far from the newly constructed J. L. Hudson's building on Woodward Avenue. Sam walked to work every day even when Detroit's streets and sidewalks were obliterated by snow. He plowed his way through the snow from downtown Detroit to the Eastern Market where Sam would buy an apple or two that would be his lunch that day at work.

Sam Fournier got to the Russell School long before the students or any of the teachers arrived. He had to. He was the janitor and part of his duties was to stoke up the huge coal-burning furnace in Russell School's basement to get heat up to the classrooms and the offices before the beginning of each school day. Despite his long walk from his residence to the place of his employment, Sam had the boiler hot every school day for ten years except one.

One day the teachers arrived at Russell School to find the building cold. They all knew something was terribly wrong. Sam Fournier had never missed a day of work and had never before failed in his job. A quick search of the school building's brick walled basement found the answer: Sam Fournier, the faithful janitor of Russell School, was dead. The man's body, still dressed in his warm winter coat, was found in a corner of one of the many basement rooms. The man's neck, crushed and blackened by some awful and violent force, bore witness to the meek janitor's murder.

No murderer was found to condemn for Sam Fournier's murder. No one was sent to the state prison in Jackson for this crime. Sam was buried in Elmwood Cemetery and the school board hired a new janitor. After a year or two people stopped asking about Sam and his murder and he and the event were not mentioned except to a new employee who was getting a tour of the site. "And this is where a janitor was found murdered," someone would say as he conducted a walk through the basement. He was strangled. His name was Sam something-or-other."

That was it. That was it, until the next person died in the basement of Russell School.

Another October day began with a bright red eastern sky that slowing faded into blue as the sun rose to illuminate the city. The air was cool and brisk after being unseasonably warm. It slapped the faces of those who left their warm, coal-heated homes for their jobs.

She was there again. For fifteen straight sixths of October, without missing one, the woman who this year was dressed in a closed cloth coat and a dark shawl that was pulled over her dark hair, stood for an hour or so, silently looking at the Russell School building. This year, 1902, she stood as she always stood on the southeast corner of Russell and Eliot Streets and she silently looked at the red brick school building.

Once someone had asked her what she was doing there and her only answer was, "Looking" without adding more information. But this October the Sixth, 1902, she would answer more.

"I'm going out to talk to her," Mary Maxwell, the assistant principal of Russell School said. She looked out of her office window at the lone female figure standing silently on the corner.

"Good luck," Principal Ralph Simpson offered.

Without further comment Miss Maxwell slipped on her coat and left the school building. She walked directly to the mysterious woman. "Excuse me," Mary said as she approached the woman, "but I've seen you out here every October the Sixth for years..."

"Fifteen years," the woman said.

"May I ask…?"

"Why I come?"

"Yes. Please tell me." By then Mary was standing in front of the woman. This mysterious visitor appeared to be old but as Mary studied her face she reassessed that notion. Her appearance was old but she was no more than forty-year-old age. She had more of a tired look about her than age.

The woman looked at Mary. Her eyes moved over the school administrator's rather attractive face for a moment then she began her tale.

"I have come here every October Sixth because of a promise I made to my husband," she said.

Mary must have looked puzzled because the woman smiled a fleeting smile at her.

"Let me explain. Jim, my husband, was a workman. He was more than a workman. He was a skilled bricklayer, a mason. He worked on many buildings in Detroit."

"This building was among them?" Mary assumed.

"Certainly," the woman said. It was here that Jim died." The woman briefly paused. Her dark eyes moved to look over at Russell School. "Jim was one of many masons working on that building fifteen years ago. And he died here while laying brick at its completion."

"And that is why you come here each year?"

"Yes, to look for him."

"To look for him?" Mary was puzzled anew.

"I'm not crazy, the woman said, answering Mary Maxwell's unspoken thoughts. "Jim was working on the top floor of that building, laying brick near the crown. Up there." She pointed to the upper roofline on the north side of Russell School. Mary turned and looked.

"He fell and was gone."

"How terrible," Mary said. Her face showed pity for this woman's loss.

"I don't think you fully understand, Miss," the woman said. Mary looked back at her. "He was gone. They never found his body."

Mary's face showed that look of puzzlement once more. "But how is that possible?" she asked. The assistant principal looked back at the school building.

"It isn't," the woman said in a matter-of-fact tone of voice. "That's why I come here every year on the anniversary of Jim's death. I come to find him." But he has not come to me."

"But if he's dead…"

"So I will no longer come back," the woman said, now ignoring Mary's words. "I promised Jim fifteen years ago I'd do this and this is the end of it."

"Have you children?" Mary asked, her voice quivering as she spoke.

"Jim was a musician, you know," the woman said, unable to hear Mary. "His powerful hands that laid bricks by day would tenderly hold a violin at night. He would play that violin of his like you've never heard. Sweet music. Bold music. He would play…" the woman's voice trailed off as she looked up at the third floor of the Russell School building.

Mary silently stood with the woman for a few more minutes before she walked back across the street to the school.

"Well? What's her story?" Principal Richardson asked as soon as Mary returned to the office. "Did she speak to you?"

"I'll tell you later. Later," Mary replied as she wiped a tear from one of her eyes.

Eastern Market expanded northward along Russell Street toward the school and sheds were built upon old cemetery grounds. Rumors soon were circulating of ghosts roaming the market, poor disinterred spirits, ever restless. No thinking person ever believed such rubbish.

Soon the market had reached the place where the old army barricades had once stood. Wholesale buildings and warehouses were constructed where Lt. U.S. Grant had commanded the Provost Guard during his duty in Detroit prior to the Civil War. Here had stood the officers' quarters and the horse sheds. Here men lived and some had died.

Russell School was expanded with a beautiful addition to its south side in 1917. More emigrant families had moved into the neighborhood of the school and more classroom space was needed to teach their children the Three R's. The new addition was completed the very year that Detroit young men were shipped off to France to "hang the Kaiser". It connected the original Russell School to the old firehouse that stood on the next corner. With this new addition, Russell School dominated the entire block on Russell from Eliot to Rivard Streets. The deaths continued.

Jason Tweeny was a teacher at Russell School for only four months before his body was found in the building's basement. His neck had been crushed by some powerful source. The Detroit Police Department still carries that murder in its open file. The file, marked, "Finny, J. – 1921 Unsolved", is stuffed into a drawer with similar unsolved murders at the Police Department's archived cases that are located in the basement of the Police Headquarters building.

In 1936 when the old Russell School was showing its age, the body of Leroy Phillips was discovered under a pile of cardboard boxes in the basement of the school building. At first it was thought that Leroy was just another hobo who had died in the basement while he was seeking shelter from another depression winter. Then someone noticed the horrible condition of the old man's neck and another file in the police building was marked "murder".

Every few years a murdered human being would be found in the basement of the Russell School. This continued even after the building was condemned for further use by the school board and given to the Detroit Water Department to be used by its Maintenance and Repair Division. Workers came to the old Russell School to work there and go home. Paul Lybeer served as superintendent of the Maintenance and Repair Division until he retired. William Herrscher followed him. Clerks Vivian Adrian and Art Tattlebaum staffed desks in what had been the Russell School's kindergarten room, as did Stan Urbanek and Chris Christopholis. The sons and the daughters of those who had attended school there now worked at Russell School. Fred Parks supervised an office. Sam Johnson and Joe Ancona followed Mr. Parks after his retirement. Clerks, typists and field workers came and went. They worked, were transferred, quit, retired and were fired while working there. Only a few died at Russell School.

During the terrible riot in Detroit during July of 1967 in which the hopes for racial healing in the Motor City were both burned and born in the flames of arson, another body was found in the basement of Russell School. This death, like that of Leroy Phillips, was at first misunderstood. Another riot death, it was thought to be. Then, about a year later, the file on that murder was transferred from one section to another second at police headquarters and the murder of John Rauch was carried as unsolved and unexplained.

The next person to die was Jim Grant, a clerk who had an occasional romantic meeting with a co-worker in the basement of the former school building. On the last day of his life Jim went on ahead to scout the basement to locate a secluded place while his "friend" slipped away from her desk. By the time that woman got to the basement Jim's lifeless form was sprawled atop some discarded cardboard boxes.

In 1982 the Detroit Water Department, after years of planning, abandoned Russell School to move its Maintenance and Repair operations to another location. At first only the clerical workers left. The field workers followed them when a new facility was built on Huber Street. After standing on Russell Street almost a hundred years, the old Russell School was slated for demolition.

As workers sorted through the rotting basement of the old red brick school building an old mystery was solved and a new mystery was begun. As the bricks of a non-loadbearing wall were removed for salvage the remains of a man's body were found. In exactly where it would be if it had fallen from the crown of the building almost a hundred years before, was the skeleton of an adult human male. That discovery solved one mystery. What began the other mystery was that although the bones of that ancient skeleton were powdery and rotted, the skeleton possessed a pair of perfectly preserved and powerful hands!

A DEATH WITH DIGNITY

Emily Martin stared at the single capsule she was holding in her fingers. The 50-year-old woman slowly rolled the red and green capsule between her pointer finger and her thumb, looking at it intensely. It looked like so many other pieces of medicine she had taken before but Emily knew this was different. This capsule was not intended to cure any disease; it was intended to cure all disease.

"You have a large tumor at your liver," Emily's family doctor told her following the MRI. "I'm going to refer you to an oncologist."

"Cancer?" Emily asked. "Liver cancer?"

"Not exactly. Cancer, most probably, but not in the liver. It seems to be in the lymph system near the liver. The oncologist can tell you more. There is a very good one in Farmington, not far from where you live. I'll make the referral."

Emily was confused. If she had cancer, why was the doctor being so matter-of-factly about it? How could she just say it that way? Didn't the doctor know that Emily had come in perfectly healthy in her mind and not was told that she had cancer? Cancer!

The oncologist verified the diagnoses. "Lymphoma at the liver," the man said. "We can treat it with chemotherapy. This seems to be a kind of cancer that responds well to chemo."

"Chemotherapy? My God!"

The oncologist put a hand on top of one of Emily's hands. "We'll do it here, in the office. Twice a week for, maybe, three months. Eat well, exercise and let it work."

The consultation continued. Is there someone to drive Emily to her therapy? Yes, her brother. To help her at home? Yes, her daughter.

"How old is she?"

"Seventeen," Emily said then she began to cry. "She's seventeen," she repeated, realizing what she was going to put her daughter through.

Emily and her daughter, Karyn, had moved to their new state after Emily's divorce from Karyn's father. They wanted a new start and Emily had been offered a job that seemed perfect. Her salary would be high and she's have full medical benefits. She would be working in a field she loved and there were great schools for Karyn to attend.

Then there was that pain in Emily's belly. At first the woman thought it was indigestion and then, when it got worse, food poisoning. After a week, she went to the doctor and was sent to the hospital for the MRI.

"Can you cure it, doctor?" Emily asked the oncologist, the woman holding a hand to her stomach.

"This type of cancer responds very well to the medicine," the oncologist answered, without answering.

*

Ray Owen was diagnosed with lung cancer just after his fifty-fifth birthday. The retired firefighter had a chromic cough, but, as a cigarette smoker, he was used to a bit of that. It was the presence of blood in the product of his cough that sent him to the doctor.

"Here," the doctor said, showing Ray the position of his lung tumor on the X-ray.

"What do we do?" Ray asked.

"Surgery, radiation and chemotherapy," the doctor answered.

"A chance?"

"A good chance, Ray. Not one-hundred percent. More like seventy."

"To be cured?"

"To go into remission following treatment. That may buy you a year, or two or ten. It's impossible to tell."

"Let's do it, doc." Ray was a firefighter with the emphases on fighter.

*

Emily and Ray met in Doctor Collins' treatment room. It was Emily's second treatment and Ray's first. They sat in comfortable longue chairs placed in front of a bank of windows that looked out on a pond. The day was sunny and warm and there were birds pausing to drink from the pond and hummingbirds hovering just outside those windows.

"First time?" Emily asked after the nurse installed Ray's IV in the man's right wrist.

"Yeah," Ray smiled, looking over at the woman. "You?"

"Second."

Ray nodded. He and Emily continued to talk and they were joined by one, then two of the other chemo patients there who were sitting side-by-side in the long row of lounge chairs that looked out over the pond. One, a woman of maybe thirty years, was bald. The other, another woman, was older, more Ray and Emily's age. She was bald, too, but wore a well-made wig that made it all but impossible to tell.

"Second month, the bald one said. "I'm responding well."

"Doctor Collins is really good," the wigged one offered. "My tumor's almost gone. Smaller every time."

"That's great news," Emily smiled. She looked at the woman. There was no outward sign of the disease that she and she fought. That gave Emily hope.

"We need men's magazines here," Ray observed as he looked through a group of magazines beside his chair. "These are all fashion and family."

"I'll get you something," a nearby nurse said and she went out to the waiting room to return with a Sports Illustrated."

"Thanks," Ray said. He took the magazine from the nurse. He looked through the issue as the women continued to talk.

Twice a week, Emily Martin and Ray Owen sat near each other in the treatment room, each receiving a dose of chemo drugs through an IV. By the end of the first month Ray no longer had that mop of auburn hair that so identified the man and, completely bald, looked older than his years. Emily, too, was hairless but wore a wig or a scarf. The two talked, with each other and with others there. They talked about their progress; their families; their faith; their hopes; what they were going to have for dinner: everything but their fears.

By the end of the three months, Emily and Ray were happily talking about their "cures".

"One-hundred percent gone," Emily smiled.

"Me, too. Can't find anymore cancer," Ray reported.

Both cancers returned after about a year.

*

There was little to be done. Emily's lymphoma had metastasized into several locations as had Ray's lung cancer. Ray entered the hospital, then hospice. Emily saw her doctor and asked about ending her life.

The days were difficult. The nights were all but unbearable. During the days there were distractions. There was television to watch; books to read; crossword puzzles to do and people to talk to. Ray had his wife. The childless couple was close the way many childless couples are. All they had, in their minds, was each other. They had friends, but their friends were *their* friends. Since his retirement, Ray Owen had less and less interaction with his former fellow firefighters. Close as family while on the job, they no longer had their job in common and, although he attended retirement parties and an occasional bowling outing, Ray had less and less to do with his former colleagues.

Ray and his wife, Martha, grew closer and Martha spent most of her time at the hospital and, later at hospice. As her husband grew weaker, she grew stronger. Ray had always been in charge of finances and, now, Martha had to learn to follow the household budget and manage the investment portfolio that was financing Ray's care. She'd hold her husband's hand and proudly tell him how she managed to get a lower rate on their car insurance by changing insurers or how she transferred funds from one investment to another after consulting with their financial advisor. Ray squeezed her hand and told Martha how proud he was of her.

Martha never cried in front of Ray. She kept that activity until later when she was alone at their apartment.

Emily's brother helped a lot. He visited his sister and his niece as often as he could and drove Emily to her doctor's appointments. He helped the woman with her finances as best he could but she was not about the business of securing things as much as the man would have wanted. She had turned inward: to far inwards as to exclude her daughter from her pain and her doubts.

Karyn did her best to comfort her mother but her mother resisted her comforting. In Emily's mind it was her job to care for her daughter, not her daughter's job to care for her. She told her doctor about that and asked about ending her life herself.

"We're one of a few states that allow me to help you, Emily," the doctor said. "If that is your real desire; it can be done."

"It's the pain, doctor," Emily said.

"There is medicine for that. If what I've prescribed isn't doing it; I can prescribe something else."

"I don't want to be all doped up, doctor. I just want to get it over with."

"Have you discussed this with your family?"

"No." Emily looked hard at the man. "I don't want them to know."

There was more consultation, as the law required; then the doctor provided what his patient wanted.

Emily Martin swallowed the capsule she fondled for about a half an hour before she took it. She lay back on her bed and went to sleep, never to waken. Her daughter found her like that.

*

"How are you today, Hon?" Martha asked as she sat on the edge of her husband's bed.

"Good," Ray answered. He half smiled. "There's another firefighter here and he came in to see me this morning."

"From your house?"

"No. He was with another department; up north. He was a captain and we talked about the job. It was nice to talk to someone who speaks the same language."

Martha knew what Ray meant. Firefighters, cops and military all have their shared experiences that were unique to them.

"You sleeping okay?"

"Sure. That shot they give me is terrific. No pain and I sleep well." The man squeezed his wife hand. "You know, Hon, when I really retire I'd like to be in a place like this. They really take good care of people here."

Martha looked at Ray. Had her husband forgotten? He smiled. "It's gonna be okay, Hon," he assured her.

"Of course it will."

"Let me tell you about the old lady."

"The old lady?"

"Yeah. They got this old lady who volunteers here. She comes in each night just before I get my shot so I can sleep. She talks to me a little and holds my hand then, just before I get my shot, she leans down and kisses me on my forehead."

Ray paused. "You know, I don't care for that much, but the old lady gets so much out of it, I don't say anything."

A tear formed in the corner of one of Martha's eyes and the woman was careful to wipe it away without her husband seeing. Here Ray was, dying but ministering to the hospice volunteer – so typical of the firefighter.

Ray Owen died in hospice care and his body was cremated. His ashes were kept in an urn at the apartment he had shared with his wife on the mantel next to a photo of him in his uniform along with the photo of him and Martha taken at their wedding.

LAUGHTER

BEANWACKER
AND DUDLEY

"Mister Dudley?" my secretary called into my office through the open door.

"Yes, Miss Chapman?" I called back.

"There's a call for you on line two."

"Miss Chapman, if you press the intercom key…" I thought a moment. "Never mind," I called to the young woman. Jennifer Chapman had never been able to master the use of our office intercom in the more than two years she worked for us. I knew it was too late.

"Thank you, Miss Chapman," I picked up line two on my desk phone. "Beanwacker and Dudley, Dudley speaking."

I had been a partner in the law firm of Beanwacker and Dudley for five years. Harvey J. Beanwacker, my partner, and I had started the firm as soon as we both got out of law school and passed the bar. We started slow and built the practice into a moderately successful enterprise. We had our own office suite in a moderately priced office building in which the elevators usually worked. We had one employee, the secretary, Miss Jennifer Chapman, whom Harvey Beanwacker had hired so, no matter how incompetent she was, I couldn't fire her. We had desks and file cabinets. We had a few steady clients but depended mostly on referrals and responses to our meager advertisements.

The practice had grown enough to allow my partner, Harvey J. Beanwacker to totally avoid work. That had always been Harvey's dream. When he and I were in college together Harvey did as little actual work as possible. It worked out to Harvey's advantage to have me as his friend and roommate. I was the bright one, the one who could complete Harvey's assignments and get him through his exams. Harvey offered me a partnership in his then nonexistent firm while we were still both in law school and the law firm of Beanwacker and Dudley was created.

I created relative wealth that allowed Harvey not to work at all.

"No, Mister Beanwacker isn't available," I said to the phone caller, a prospective client who wanted to do business with the partner whose name was first on the door, "but, I'm available and quite competent." I talked to the caller and made an appointment for him to come in.

"Miss Chapman," I called out through the open door of my office. "There'll be a James Johnson coming in tomorrow at one. Okay?"

"Johnson. Johnson," I heard through the doorway. "A, B, C, D, E, F, G…H, I, J." Miss Chapman was filing a card for our new client.

I did some work on another client's file before Jennifer Chapman came into my office.

"Mister Dudley," the shapely brunette said, "I have an idea."

I couldn't wait to hear it. "Yes?" I asked.

"Well, you know I've been having some trouble with my filing and all…"

Boy, did I know that! I was surprised whenever I found a client's file where it should be. But, of course, Jennifer's talent was not in her knowledge of the alphabet.

"I think I came up with a way to solve my problem."

"And what would that be?"

"We can have our clients come in in alphabetical order. The first one would be Adams, then Brown, then Collins and so forth. Vale and Wellman would be at the end of the day. Get it?"

I smiled and nodded. "But, wouldn't that be difficult for our clients?" I asked.

"They'll have to adapt," the secretary said. "It just makes so much sense."

I took in a deep breath and expelled it. I knew there was no arguing with Miss Chapman's logic. The young woman turned and walked toward my office's door. She turned back. "So, I'll reschedule Mister Johnson for noon, okay?"

"Okay," I said.

Jennifer left and I settled back into my chair. I was so happy our filing problem had been solved.

Jennifer Chapman had obtained her formal secretarial training at the Chix-n-Flix club where my partner had met her. Day after day, Harvey went into the porn palace with a bag of quarters. Hour after hour, he sat in the chair that faced the tiny stage where Jennifer, then known as "Jen the Bend", performed her strip and pose act while her client fed quarters into a slot to keep open the partition between them. The two got to know each other that way and chatted for hours as Jen posed and Harvey poured quarters into the slot near his chair.

"But I can't date clients," Jen told the fat man who sat in the chair in front of her small stage. "It's against the rules."

"Do you know the alphabet?" Harvey asked the performer as she stretched a leg behind the back of her neck.

"The what?"

"The alphabet. You, know, the ABCs"

"Oh, yeah, I know them…sorta."

"Sorta's good enough for me," Harvey smiled as Jen the Bend looked back at him from between her legs. "I got a job for you at my law firm."

"Your…?"

"My law firm. The business I own."

"You own a business?"

"I sure do." Harvey popped another quarter into the slot beside him just in time to keep the partition between him and Jennifer from closing. "I'm a lawyer and I own a law practice," my partner said without mentioning me. "I could use a secretary."

"Would there be a lot of the ABCs?" Jennifer asked.

"Not much and we got a guy named Dudley who'll help you with it. Okay?"

"Okay," our soon-to-be secretary agreed.

So, because Miss Jennifer Chapman had been hired under these professional conditions without the requirement to fully know the alphabet, I had little choice but to agree to Jennifer's idea of scheduling our clients in alphabetical order.

Later that day *she* walked into my life. She was tall and slender with a Mary Astor look about her. Instantly I was Philip Marlow. I looked at her and at Jennifer who was quickly following behind.

"I'm sorry. Mister Dudley," my secretary/file clerk apologized. "She just walked by me."

"It's okay, Miss Chapman," I said without looking at my employee. I was still staring at the woman who had so abruptly entered my office. Jennifer turned and left for her desk. "Can I help you?" I asked the beauty.

"Are you Mister Beanwacker?" she asked.

"No, I'm Dudley," I told her.

"I'm sorry but I'd rather keep this on a last name basis," She assumed, as did so many, that my first named was Dudley.

I was Dudley all my life. In grade school when other kids were Jimmy or Johnny or Butch, I was Dudley, even to teachers. It seemed natural, I guess. In high school I tried to be "Moon" because of the roundness of my face. I figured Moon was better than Dudley. That's how desperate I was. It didn't work. I remained Dudley all through the twelfth grade.

Then there was college and a new chance to be Moon, or Keg and Butch or anything other than Dudley. It was my friend, Harvey Beanwacker, who kept my last name as my only name.

"Dudley, it fits you, pal," the heavyset nineteen-year-old grinned and I was Dudley forever.

"No, I'm Dudley. You know, Beanwacker and Dudley?" I offered.

She looked at me with a rather puzzled look.

"How may I help you?" I asked her. She was beautiful with brown hair pulled up under her pillbox hat that sported a bit of a black veil. She was wearing a trim suit and black shoes. She really looked like Mary Astor in the Maltese Falcon.

"I'm an actress," she told me as she stepped in front of my desk. "We're shooting a movie down the block and they've got me dressed up like Mary Astor. It'll ruin my career." She spread her arms to display her look; a look I found to be attractive.

"And?" I asked, motioning with a hand for her to sit. She did.

"I want you to get me out of my contract," she said.

"And you chose this firm because..."

"Because you were the first law firm in the building," she said. "I came in to get a doughnut in the lobby and there you were."

"Fate," I smiled.

"No, jelly," she insisted.

I got her out of the contract and she paid the fee. Three months later, after a lot of lunches, then dinners, then weekends in the country, we were engaged. I asked her to dress up like Mary Astor sometimes and she understood.

"You're getting married, huh Dudley?" Harvey J. Beanwacker asked me when he called from Acapulco. My law partner was spending some time in Mexico so he could spend the proceeds of our practice on his luxury. I pictured the now very fat lawyer lying on the beach surrounded by school-teachers on vacation like some overfed bull seal and his harem. I heard Harvey sipping at a drink as we talked.

"Yeah, Harvey. How 'bout that?"

"That's great, kid," Harvey said. "Let me know when the wedding date is."

"It's November 12," I told him.

"November...November," Harvey said as he flipped through his ever present pocket calendar. "No, the twelfth is bad for me. Surf will be just right for watching the broads at Waikiki. Can't we make it some other day?"

"It's Joyce's choice."

"Well then..." Harvey paused to take a sip of his drink. I assumed he moved the little umbrella aside to do so. Harvey loved drinks with little umbrellas. "Let me talk to Jenny. I'll send you two something nice."

I knew that meant that my partner would be drawing money from our office fund to buy us a wedding gift. "Thanks, Harvey," I said before I transferred the called back to our receptionist.

If Harvey wasn't interested in my impending wedding, Jennifer Chapman was. My secretary/file clerk announced that she was going to be our maid-of-honor. My finance soon learned she had no say in the matter with Miss Chapman being hired by Harvey Beanwacker and all, so it was settled. I tried to explain to Jennifer that we intended to get married by a judge I was trying to schmooze but that didn't matter. This was her chance to wear a maid-of- honor dress and walk down the aisle in front of us.

"There won't really be an aisle," I told her.

"That doesn't matter, Mister Dudley," Jenny said.

"It'll be in the judge's chambers."

"I don't care."

She didn't care. When the big day came Joyce and I stood before Judge Gillmore in the man's chambers and Jennifer Chapman, wearing a god-awful pink dress and a huge floppy hat, walked down the non-existent aisle, heel-toe, heel-toe to the music only she could hear.

Joyce and I really didn't honeymoon. I had to be in the office because the surf was perfect in Hawaii for broad watching and someone needed to make the money that Harvey needed for his considerable expenses. Joyce and I spent the night together in a nice downtown hotel and enjoyed the complimentary breakfast before I returned to the office.

When I came in, Jennifer, my secretary/file clerk/maid of honor, was still wearing the hat.

It was that very night that my new wife's neck became "out of bounds".

"Dudley, don't!" she said as I tried to kiss her there.

"What?" I asked.

"Don't kiss my neck."

"Why not?"

"It's just that I don't like to be kissed there. I think a person's neck should be out of bounds for such things."

That was okay with me. Joyce had a pretty neck, but she had even prettier other parts. Then her arms were out of bounds too.

"Your arms?" I asked.

"Yes, and my knee caps. It just seems I should have some private parts"

"What does Howard Stern have to do with this?" I asked.

"Huh?" Joyce had not read the radioman's autobiography. "It's just I want to keep those things private."

"So it's neck, arms and kneecaps? That's all?"

"Yes, that's all," Joyce said with a pretty smile. We made love with me carefully avoiding my wife's neck, arms and kneecaps.

Elbows were next. That took a week. Following elbows in order of restriction were calves, stomach, middle of back, left shoulder, ankles and wrists. Until then, wrists and hands had not been included in arms. Then they were.

"Hon," I said ever so carefully, "maybe we should talk to someone about this?"

"About what?"

"About your private parts."

"If my private parts are private, how can we talk to someone about them?"

Joyce's logic was impeccable and the list grew.

"What's left?" I asked in frustration the night my wife's breasts were added to the list of her private parts.

Joyce smiled and looked down herself. "That's not private," she said of her privates.

Then it was.

I worked longer hours. I had to and I wanted to. My wife's whole body with the exception of her forehead and the back of one knee was off limits to me. I made the most of those two spots but my imagination in that area was limited. There wasn't much I could do so I worked in the office as much as I could.

As I said before, a lot of our business was the result of referrals. I had doctors, dentists and other professionals referring people to me. I passed out my cards everywhere I could and I'd get an occasional referral from another lawyer.

"Beanwacker and Dudley. Dudley speaking," I said into the phone and I was talking to J. Howard Harris of J. Howard Harris, P.C.

Howie and I had been in law school together. He liked me because I was no threat to his ambition to lay all the girls in our class. He was successful in that quest and held me as partially responsible. Every once in a while my friend would throw me a case, usually something too small for his rapidly growing law firm to take.

"I got one for you if you can squeeze her in," J. Howard Harris said. "She's small potatoes but you might like taking on her case."

"Let me check," I said as I pretended to look through an appointment book. "What's her name?"

"Her name? Why does that matter?" Howie asked.

"It's out filing system," I said as if that made sense. "Her last name?"

"Hillyard. Two l's and a Y."

"That would be about eleven in the morning," I said.

"I'll let her know," my friend said with a chuckle in his voice.

When Grace Hillyard walked into my office I recognized a "dame in trouble". If Joyce reminded me of Mary Astor, Grace was Veronica Lake. Her long blond hair hung over one of her beautiful blue eyes and her red lipstick glistened on her full, sexy lips. Instantly I was Bogart again.

All she needed was some routine legal work but within a week we were in bed together and I found out that she had no private parts at all. None.

I was thrilled. Until I married Joyce I could not have what I wanted the most – an affair. A single man could be having sex with a woman but, in my mind anyway, it was not really an affair because the man wasn't married. How could it really be an affair if I wasn't cheating on someone? Now, there I was, in bed with this luscious creature committing adultery. Finally.

My mother had always said – "When are you ever going to be an adult?" Now I was. I was an official adulterer.

Joyce suspected something when she put her forehead off limits and I didn't whine. She hired a private detective. I had no idea. After all of my wife's body, with the singular exception of the back of one of her knees, was entirely off limits to me, how could Joyce be upset that I was touching someone else's elbows or arms?

But my wife was jealous and her private detective easily caught Grace and me having a romp in my office when Jennifer was at lunch. He got pictures. I later offered him a few hundred for copies but he said, by law, they belonged to Joyce and that, as a lawyer, I should have known that.

Joyce divorced me and got as her alimony a portion of the meager part of the law firm's income that Harvey Beanwacker allowed me to have. My friend, J. Howard Harris, represented her.

"Hey, pal," the successful lawyer said with an arm around my shoulders. "I could have wiped you out, if I had wanted." Howie laughed. I did not.

It wasn't all that bad, though, because now I was free to marry Grace.

I proposed and she accepted. She and I married before Judge Grant – I didn't want Judge Gillmore to know – and Jennifer was a maid-of-honor again. Harvey Beanwacker couldn't attend. That had something to do with Beaujolais Nouveau being released.

Within a month my new wife's arms and wrists became private and I started sleeping with my ex-wife. Joyce had decided that when we were no longer married and we were committing adultery, we should be adult about having sex and there would be no private parts.

Harvey J. Beanwacker remains abroad.

THE HITCHHIKER

"Let me tell you a story, son:"

"Splashdown!"

The television network reporter on board the United States aircraft carrier, *Abraham Lincoln,* was looking out over the blue Atlantic Ocean a few hundred miles from America's East coast and described the recovery of the Mars probe. In earlier days this event - the return of such an extensive unmanned mission to Mars - would have been broadcast live and worldwide but in the days when space exploration had become so common with shuttles and an international space station, this sort of thing almost went unreported.

In earlier days most Americans knew the names of its country's astronauts. Now few really cared.

The Mars probe was recovered and hoisted about the *Abraham Lincoln* with the reporter covering the story on tape. Helicopters moved overhead, trained service personnel did their important jobs and nobody really cared. The space probe's capsule remained in quarantine in a specially designed compartment below the aircraft carrier's deck. It was inspected and investigated. It was opened and data was recovered. The samples it had taken of Martian soils and rocks were studied. No one could see the water molecule that was so radically changed in the water where the probe had come down.

"Doctor," a reporter asked at a briefing once, "Could you comment on the fears some people have about bringing back some kind of alien life-form in returning space probes."

The scientist chuckled. "You mean like in the movie *Alien*?" he asked. "Not a real problem. We have substantial safeguards in that area. The capsules are sanitized, sterilized and are, in fact, completely safe. The contents are contained when inspected and we certainly would be interested to find any signs of life in them, but so far, we have not. Our larger concern is contaminating anything we may indeed bring back with Earth's air or with our bacteria. We would seek to protect any life form from damage by them."

As the *Abraham Lincoln* made its way to port to unload its cargo, a mass of jelly-like substance was floating in the Atlantic Ocean five hundred yards from where the aircraft carrier's personnel had picked up the space probe. The blue-green and semitransparent form drifted with the ocean's current. It grew larger as it merged with the surrounding seawater.

The splashdown of the Mars probe occurred in July. By August 10, an eastbound freighter reported sighting what appeared to be a very large jellyfish in the general vicinity of the former splashdown site.

On August 15 a frantic radio message from a Russian trawler was cut short. No further contact was recorded. A search of the area proved futile. It was one hundred miles from the splashdown site.

It was raining in Fishkill, New York. It had been raining for three days. The quaint Hudson River community was soaked and the city manager was considering CSO's.

"If we throw the switch we'll divert our sanitary sewerage system into the Hudson," the water department's director explained. "That'll relieve the pressure on our sanitary sewers and stop the basement flooding in the north part of town. My people recommend it."

"Another Combined Sewer Overflow and there will be hell to pay with the EPA and the environmentalists," Phil Coleman inserted. Phil was the city manager's deputy and chief political advisor. He wore two hats and he seemed always at odds with himself.

"Damn it, Phil," Hal Morris, the city manager said. "You're the one who warned me about letting that flooding continue."

"Sure. Those folks on the north side will be pissed. I mean, three, four feet of shit in your basement – come on."

"And if we divert?"

"It'll stop the flooding and prevent more," the water department director said.

"And dump all that waste right into the Hudson River," Hal offered.

"Yes. But we've done it before."

"I know and after that last time I issued the order to refrain from doing it again without my approval. I mean, the river smelled like a toilet for days and the bacteria level went through the roof. There were dead fish everywhere. The papers called it the 'Fishkill Fish Kill' for godsake."

"The sewage level's about three feet in basements now," Phil reminded. "And those people are voters."

"What side are you on?" Hal demanded of his deputy.

"Yours, Hal," Phil answered. He put an arm around his boss' shoulders. "You can't win either way. Just do what's least damaging to your reelection."

"And that would be?"

"Open the valves," Phil recommended. "The damn fish don't vote."

Richard Henson left port, outbound early on a Monday morning. His ship's fishnets hung high over each rail of his fishing boat. The *Mary Ann* chugged under power seaward as the sun swept up over the disappearing shoreline.

"Hold that course," Richard said to his coxswain, a young man the captain had hired earlier in the year. "Due west for five miles then we'll sweep south and deploy our nets."

"Aye-Aye, sir," the young man at the helm answered.

Richard Henson laughed. "This ain't the Navy, son," he said.

"Yes, sir," the young man said.

"Just keep west."

"Aye…" The 21-year-old college dropout cut his answer short. He looked ahead at the broad ocean and then down at the compass stand beside the wheel he held. He kept the indicator steady on the west marker and the *Mary Ann* continued its westerly course.

The morning air was damp and chilly, but as the sun rose it warmed quickly. Richard Henson's small fishing boat powered on then turned south where Richard and his five-man crew deployed their nets. They were fishing a hundred miles from where the Mars probe had landed in the Atlantic but were on a collision course with the unplanned result of that splashdown.

"What the hell's that?" Richard said as he looked ahead and slightly to port through a pair of binoculars. The man's blue eyes studied what appeared to be a huge jellyfish. "Take a look, Mack," he said, handing his glasses to a shipmate.

The other man looked at the object. "Too big for a jellyfish," he said. "Debris?"

"Give," Henson said, holding out his hand. He took back the binoculars. "It looks uniform and large – very large."

"How far is it?" one of the other crewmembers asked. He and all his shipmates were looking out at the distant object.

"Half a mile?" Richard offered.

"Can't be and be that big. It's got to be closer."

"Half a mile, at least," the captain insisted. "It must be huge."

"A mile across?"

"It may be," Henson said as he swept his binoculars from one side of the glimmering object to the other. "Steer more west," he ordered and the young wheelman steered to starboard. Richard Henson intended to avoid this unknown object. The *Mary Ann* moved through the water, its prow cutting through the low waves. Richard Henson continued to observe the object and it seemed to be getting closer.

"The tide's carrying it in," he said. "Tim, get on the radio and report it. Someone's gotta get out here and take a look"

Tim Philips radioed the Coast Guard that took the information on the sighting. They recorded latitude and longitude and in the time that it took to make the report the object closed within a few hundred yards of the *Mary Ann.*

"It's not just being carried by the tide or currents," Phil said. "I think that damn thing's chasing us."

"Chasing us?" Mack asked. He looked out toward the mass. "What the hell is it?" As he and his shipmates stared out at the approaching jelly-like object a long and thick tentacle from it squirmed below the ocean's surface to stretch under their boat.

The crewmembers felt their small fishing boat quiver as if it had struck something. Then it came to a full stop, an action that tossed all aboard to the deck.

"What the..." Henson asked, looking up from his wooden deck.

He looked up to see a shimmering mass overwhelming his boat.

A Coast Guard Cutter arrived at the location reported by the *Mary Ann* to find some floating debris, some life jackets, wooden planks, fishing gear and other flotsam, but no sign of the jelly mass reported by the doomed fishing boat. It swept the area and found nothing. The object of its search had moved on.

The jelly-like mass was now two miles wide at its narrowest point and moving against the tide toward the New York coast. Inside its shimmering slimy bulk Martian molecules merged with Earth's seawater molecules to form a new substance, a substance requiring more feeding. The bodies of the members of the *Mary Ann's* crew had long since dissolved and their molecules had been blended with the mass.

"The valves are open full, Your Honor," Phil Coleman told his boss. The water department director reports that the shit level in the north side homes is receding.

"Good news," Mayor Hal Morris said. He was happy at that news but he was not smiling. "What about the Hudson?"

"A toilet," his deputy answered. "There'll be crap from here to the Big Apple for days."

"Fine," Hal frowned. "'Fishkill Kills Fish'" again.

"You did the right thing, Hal," Phil assured his superior. "You had no choice. It's still rainy and you couldn't just let the north side flood. We'll start the water department working on an EPA report." He looked at the mayor. "And something for the newspapers too," he added.

It finally stopped raining in lower New York State and the Fishkill CSO worked its way down the Hudson River toward New York City and the Atlantic. Warnings were issued about higher than normal bacteria levels but no one swam in the Hudson anyway. It just smelled worse than normal. By then the jelly mass had been sighted of the New York coast and investigated by the United States Coast Guard, then by other authorities.

"It's definitely extra-terrestrial, sir," a NASA liaison to the White House told the president.

"How could this have happened? I was assured there were the proper safeguards."

"Well, with the recent funding cut and other things..."

The president dismissed the man with a frustrated wave of a hand. "What do the Joint Chiefs say?" he asked the Chairman of the Joint Chiefs of Staff.

"It seems to be a problem that the Scientists should handle, Mister President," the general offered. "We've tried bombing and napalm. We've shelled it with naval gunfire. No effect. We've got to be given the tools by the science boys. If we had the funding ourselves..."

Another hand wave from the president shut off that discussion. He turned to the NASA man. "What can we do?"

"I don't know, sir," was the reply. "We don't even know what this thing really is. All we know is that it's now five miles wide and headed straight for New York City."

The president was still in conference when the first of the Martian-Earth mass reached landfall. Slashing ashore at Fire Island it quickly devoured the few people who had not evacuated the island when the general notice was given. The mass enveloped the entire island and soon covered it. Its shinny appearance could plainly be seen from nearby settlements.

There was no way that the millions of people on Manhattan Island could ever be effectively moved out of the danger. The tunnels and bridges were clogged with panicked people all trying to flee the approaching doom. Boats made hurried trips to the Jersey coast carrying as many terrified New Yorkers as they could.

The mass reached the East River then stretched around to the Hudson. It moved up the "pointy end" of Manhattan Island, killing as it went. Fulton's Fish Market was enveloped. Ellis Island was covered. Liberty Island had the mass up to the knees of the Statue of Liberty. All life it encountered was included into its molecular structure. Dogs, cats, rats, pigeons, sea birds, fish – all swallowed up and absorbed. And people too.

Then the slimy shimmering mass of ooze extended itself up the Hudson side of Manhattan Island toward the George Washington Bridge. There it encountered result of the Fishkill Combined Sewer Overflow. At once it solidified and began to sink. Its very nature changed from being a fluid to being a solid - a gray-black, heavy and inert solid. Its leading edge sank into the Hudson. The rest of it either sank into whatever water in which it had been floating or, if already ashore, it just solidified into a harmless lump.

It took several months for the Parks Service to chip the Martian mass from the feet and calves of the Statue of Liberty. It took longer for the New York authorities to clean it from the streets of lower Manhattan. The Army Corps of Engineers helped plan the removal of the sunken debris that had obscured navigation. The only thing that got done in a hurry was to honor Mayor Hal Morris of Fishkill, New York for saving humanity by opening those CSO valves. He still has a framed copy of the New York Times over his desk with its banner headline:

FISHFILL SAVES NEW YORK!
Rest of world saved too

"So that's how the Combined Sewer Overflow from Fishkill, New York saved the world. What do you think of my story, son?"

"I think it's a lot of crap, dad."

MY AUNT RUTH

Ruth Clift was born in 1915 in Detroit and died in 1992 at my mother's house in Livonia, Michigan. She was my mom's maternal aunt, the sister of my grandmother. Ruth married her childhood sweetheart, Ray Cliff, who became publisher of a suburban Detroit newspaper chain and she lived with him in Belleville, Michigan until her husband's death. At that point in her life Ruth moved in with my mother, her niece, temporarily. That stay lasted the ten years until her death.

Ruth was a remarkable lady who often defied logic while living her life. At her funeral her nephews and nieces gathered and shared their "Ruth Stories" Here are mine:

Sunrise...Sunset

Aunt Ruth owned a cottage at Spider Lake, near Traverse City, Michigan. She worked as a secretary at Elwell School in Belleville so she had the summers off. She and my mother would spend much time at that cottage, especially after my mother retired from her job as assistant manager for the National Bank of Detroit. The two aging women would sit out on the front porch of that cottage, looking out at Spider

Lake. Ruth would think how fortunate her niece, Isabel, was to have an aunt with such a nice cottage. My mom would try to count the days until Ruth's vacation was over.

It was not my mother's favorite place to spend an entire summer. Ruth dominated my mother's life. When they were at my mother's house in Livonia, Ruth felt no need to help with the payment of utilities because as she said, "You'll have to have electric and heat whether I'm here or not, Iz."

The food was different. The two women split the cost. Ruth would buy her blackberries in February at $5.00 a pint and mom would pay for half of the cost. But that was fair because Ruth would chip in half toward mom's corn flakes.

At the cottage things were about the same, except Ruth paid the utilities.

My aunt invited my wife, Armaine, and me up to her cottage and we ran out of excuses not to go. Armaine and I drove up, taking rural roads to see the countryside. That way we would enjoy something of the weekend.

We arrived at Ruth's cottage in the late afternoon and we had dinner with my mother and her aunt. After dinner I stood out on the porch and overlooked the lake. Ruth joined me.

"This is a beautiful view," I told my great aunt.

"Yes, it is, isn't it?" she smiled.

"The only shortcoming is that you don't see the sunset over the lake," I foolishly proposed.

"Sure we do," Ruth corrected. "It sets right there." She pointed across the lake at the shore to our right.

I looked over to where she was pointing. "But that's east," I noted. "Your cottage faces north so that's east. The sun rises in the east and it sets in the west, over there." I pointed to our left.

"Well," Ruth said in a haughty tone, "that may be how it is in Detroit. Up here, it's different."

The Gathering Storm

I later learned that my Aunt Ruth's lack of scientific knowledge was not limited to the earth's rotation. One time she and my mom were sitting on the cottage's porch. Clouds began rolling in from the west (to their left – Ruth's east) and my mother told Ruth that she was going to go in and get a sweater.

"Why, Iz?" Ruth asked.

"It's getting cloudy," Isabel explained.

"The sun's still out," Ruth corrected her.

My mother looked up at the sky. "But, I think that cloud's going to go in front of the sun soon."

Ruth observed the cloud in question. "No," she said. "I think that cloud is going to go *behind* the sun."

Now that was a very high cloud.

Where to Eat?

On another occasion my wife and I were visiting my mother's aunt at the cottage. It had been a particularly long weekend during which the four of us, my wife, my mother, Ruth and I, had passed time by playing board games. First came Scrabble.

When Ruth played Scrabble it was a scream. She cheated horribly. When she ran short of good letters she'd palm a Z or an X in her right hand and casually pass that hand and its mostly hidden tile over the "bone yard" of unpicked letters, dropping the offending letter as she did. Then, after a brief waited Ruth would suddenly notice she was short a letter and pick one from the other side of the letter pile from where she had dropped her unwanted one.

We never called her on this. It was too cruel to let her know that we knew.

We also played Monopoly, one of my favorite games. But when we played, Ruth had to be the Banker and Real Estate Agent so she could pay her rents from the bank and steal choice properties. We never called her on these cheats either. It was her cottage, after all.

The only problem with letting Ruth cheat her way to victories in these games was she'd rub in your loss.

"You just don't know how to play this game, do you," the cheater/winner would laugh.

If it looked like I was about to say something in response my mother would shoot me a look that said to keep the peace. I didn't have to live with Ruth. My mother did.

Sunday finally came and Ruth proposed we go out to eat breakfast in Traverse City. "Where do you want to go?" she asked me, a neophyte to the area.

"I don't know. I've never been in Traverse City before, Ruth," I replied.

"No. You're picking the place we're going to," she insisted.

"Give me a choice then."

"Okay. We could go to the Pancake Palace or to Huck's (not the real names)."

"Well, since we're going for breakfast – the Pancake Palace," I answered.

Ruth looked over at my mother. "Your son wants to go to the Pancake Palace, that dump. We haven't gone there in years. It's awful!"

Stupid me!

Presidents

I was once visiting my mother and, of course, Ruth was in the middle of our conversation. I was telling my mother about a book I was reading about the presidency of Chester Arthur, one of the more obscure of our past chief executives.

"I've never heard of him," my mother admitted.

I wasn't surprised. Along with Millard Fillmore and Franklin Pierce, Arthur is not a well-known president "Not well known but an interesting fellow anyway," I reported.

"Chester Arthur?" Ruth butted in. "I've never heard of him either. He must have been one of those presidents before George Washington."

"But..." I began. I looked at Ruth and kept my tongue.

Ruth's High Water Mark

One day my mother came home from grocery shopping and heard the shower running in her bathroom. She carried her purchases into the kitchen, putting them onto the counter there. Then the woman stepped down the hall to investigate why the door was open to her bathroom and the shower was running. She looked in to see the shower on full and the tub's drain closed so the tub was filling.

"Ruth?" she called out and her aunt appeared at her bedroom's door wrapped in a towel. "What are you doing?" mom asked.

"It's economy," the other woman said. "I heard on the TV that it's better for the economy and for the environment if you use the shower instead of the bath."

"But why is the tub filling?"

"I don't take showers. I prefer baths, so I'm filling the tub with the shower to save money and help the environment," Ruth explained.

Promo

When my mother was still working, Ruth would greet the woman with news from the various soap operas that she watched during the day. My mother would get the update on what Erica was up to in Pine Valley on *All My Children* and whether Luke and Laura were getting together on *General Hospital*. But one day my mother came in to other news.

"Iz, you've got to see this," Ruth said, noting a talk show on the television."

"What is it?" Isabel asked.

"It's all about promo," was the answer.

"Promo? You mean promotions"

"No, promo," Ruth said, a little exasperated at my mother's ignorance.

"Advertising?"

"No, promo. You know, dirty movies?"

That makes Larry Flint a "promographer", I guess.

The World's Standard

Once I was visiting my mother and helping her install a counter top in her kitchen. I measured the required space with a yardstick. "This section is twenty-four inches," I announced, laying the yardstick along an edge of the counter space.

"I don't think so," Ruth, who had been observing, declared.

"Twenty-four," I repeated, this time leaning down to get a closer look at my ruler.

"Can't be," Ruth insisted. "Here, I'll show you." I stayed in the kitchen as Ruth went to her room. My aunt came back with a box from which she extracted a silver necklace. "I bought this in the Bahamas and the man who sold it to me said it was twenty-four inches." She laid the necklace onto the counter and, sure enough, it was shorter than what my ruler measured as twenty-four inches.

"See?" Ruth said, triumphantly. "The space is more than twenty-four inches."

The thought that the man in the Bahamas may have shorted her when he sold her that necklace never occurred to Ruth. She was right. The ruler was wrong.

Heaven Can Wait

Ruth was watching television with my mother and saw news coverage of a proposed space program missile launch. The announcer reported that the space probe would be exploring the heavens by the end of the decade. She shook her head and frowned. "I'm against that sort of thing," she told my mom.

"What? The Space Program?"

"Yes," Ruth said. "Didn't you hear what he said? They'll be shooting missiles up to heaven and those astronauts will be looking at people there. After all they went through on earth to get to heaven those dead people deserve their privacy."

Really.

THE OPTION

"You're really miserable, aren't you, John?"

Peter looked across the high-top bar table at his co-worker. John was looking down into his scotch, swirling his drink clockwise to see the two ice cubes in his glass fight for positon. "Yes," he answered without looking up.

"The family?"

"Yeah. 'Family', if you can call it that. My wife hates me. My kids hate me."

"I've only met you wife that one time at the office Christmas party. She seemed alright to me."

John smirked. "Deceptive, isn't she?"

"You've been married – how long?"

"Thirteen years. Thirteen miserable years."

"Come on, man. Can't be that bad."

"It is. We got married young – real young."

"You met in high school, right?"

"Yeah."

"High school sweethearts?"

"Kinda."

"Huh?" Peter took a sip of his beer. "'Kinda?'"

"Yeah. Becky and I met in high school. We were in Senior Math together. Man, was she hot. Big boobs. Perfect ass. And those eyes."

"She has pretty eyes," Peter agreed.

"I couldn't take my eyes offa her. She almost made me flunk the class. I'd get all nervous and horny around her. She sat right in front of me and every time she'd get up to got to the board or something I had to put a book in my lap – if you get my drift."

"Been there," Peter smiled, remembering his high school years.

"It's funny how it happened, too," John went on with his high school recollections. "Becky pretty much ignored me. I always felt that I was out of her league but, one day when we were leaving the classroom we bumped into each other. I mean, literally bumped into each other. Those big boobs of her grazed my arm and instead of saying 'yuck' or something, she smiled. I smiled back and we talked on our way to our lockers. I asked her out to a dance and, well, we did it that night."

"Really?"

"Yeah and it was something, too. I was hooked." John looked over at his co-worker. "I knocked her up, Peter," he confided. "Her folks made us get married. It was a bad start and never got better. She was something, pal," John went on. "But, now…"

"Not so much?"

"Not at all. And it's not just that she put on weight – so did I – it's more about what she is."

"Huh?" Peter asked.

"A bitch," John answered. "She hates me but insists we stay together."

"For the kids?"

"I suppose so. Or for her. I think she's rather be miserable with me as long as she can make me miserable, too, than be on her own with those two kids of ours."

"They're at a bad age," Peter proposed. "Preteens?"

John nodded.

"And the sex?"

John laughed. "What sex? Maybe once a month, if that unless you count me in the bathroom with a magazine. And when we do it, it's all just mechanical. I'd say it was all worth it if I had great kids, but I don't."

"I had problems with my kids, too, at that age. And things get worse when they're into their teens unless you do something about it."

"Do something? Like what?"

"Change the way things are."

"Can't do that with Becky there."

"And if there was a way?"

"Yeah, kill her, right?"

"No, something better."

"Counseling? She won't go for that and I can't afford it, anyway."

"There's counseling and there's counseling."

"What's that mean?" John laughed. "No, I'm not joining your church."

"No, not the church. Something else."

"What?"

"An option."

"What option?"

"Something that can make things different – better."

"I wish." John lifted his drink to his lips and drained his glass of its scotch. He looked over at the server and lifted his empty glass.

"There may be something you can do, John. It's a bit drastic but guaranteed to work."

John smiled. "Come on, man. No BS."

"It's something I did and it changed my life."

"Okay, Mister Mysterious, what is it? Yoga? Vegan diet? Meditation? Hookers? Please say that it's hookers."

"There's a way you can change things, John," Peter said. "Make things different."

"Okay, come on, what is it?"

The server came over with another scotch and water with two ice cubes and put it on the high-top in front of John. "Anything for you, sir?" she asked Peter.

"No, I'm fine," that man answered and she left the table. John picked up his drink and took a sip.

"So, what is it?" he asked.

"It's changing things, from the beginning."

"Huh?" John asked with a wrinkled brow.

"It's changed the way things happened. You blame all your problems on getting Becky pregnant in high school."

John nodded, taking another drink of scotch.

"So, what if it never happened?"

"I wish it didn't, but it did."

"But, if it didn't…?"

John smiled. "I think about that a lot. If I hadn't knocked up Becky I coulda gone on to college instead of going right to work to support her and the kid. I coulda met someone who could really love me and I coulda really love. It'd be nice, but, guess what? You can't change the past."

"But, what if you could, John?"

"You nuts? Not possible."

"I've done it."

"Done what?"

"Exercised the option."

"What option?"

"The option to change the past. To make things better by changing something that went wrong."

"Yeah, sure. Tell you what, pal, I haven't had that much to drink yet to believe that crap."

"It's not crap, John. It's real."

"Changing the past? How?"

"By exercising the option. You interested?"

"If it wasn't BS, I would be." John smiled. "Good try, man."

"Tomorrow, after work. Can you go with me to see someone?"

"Someone who can change the past?"

"Exactly." Peter reached over and put a hand on top of one of his coworker's hands. "Believe me, John. It's true," he assured the man.

"Come on, Peter," John said as he pulled his hand out from under Peter's hand. "You're talking crazy stuff here."

"Just go with me. You'll see."

"After work tomorrow?"

Peter nodded.

"Okay," John agreed. "But this better not be Amway."

"Not Amway," Peter laughed.

The two men finished their drinks and left the bar. John drove home to his small house off the freeway. Becky was in bed. "Turn off the light," she shot out at her husband when he switched on a lamp near the bed. John turned off the lamp and changed into his pajamas in the bathroom. Becky's pajama-clad chunky body was stiff when John squeezed into their bed from his side.

"Good night," the man said.

His wife said nothing.

*

John left the warehouse where he worked with his co-worker, Peter. The two men drove in Peter's car to a downtown office building. Peter parked in the attached garage and led John to the elevator lobby. He pushed the up button and the two men entered an elevator.

"Well, it's differently not a church," John smiled.

"Not a church, John," Peter said. He had selected the fifth floor and when the elevator door opened he led John to suite 500. There was a sign on the door that simply said "OPTIONS"

"Day trading?" John guessed.

Peter laughed. "No, you'll see." He opened the door and the two men entered a normal-looking office reception area. There were the obligatory chairs along two walls and a reception desk. Various magazines were on top of small tables near the chairs. It could have been any office.

There was no one behind the reception desk when the two entered but, quickly, a young woman took a seat at the desk there. "May I help you?" she inquired.

"I called about my friend, John," Peter said.

"Yes, of course, the counsellor is expecting you."

"Counsellor, huh." John said. "I thought you said…"

"You'll see, John. Just talk to him. It's not what you expect."

"Fine," John relented and followed Peter through a door, into an office. There was a white-haired older man who was wearing rimless glasses at a desk. He rose as the two men approached.

"Peter, good to see you," the man said, extending a hand to Peter. "How are things going?"

"Wonderfully," Peter said.

John noticed that Peter had not used the term "doctor".

"Good to hear that, Peter," the older man smiled. He looked at John. "And you must be Peter's friend, John," he said, extending a hand to John.

"Yes, Peter and I work together," John said as he shook hands with the older man. He was a little uneasy about being called Peter's friend as the two only worker together and only began going out for drinks after work the last couple of weeks.

"Peter has told me about you, John," the older man said. "Please, both of you, have a seat." He gestured to two chairs before his desk and John and Peter took them.

"And just what had Peter told you about me?" John asked.

"That you may need to exercise the option."

John looked skeptical. "And, just what is this 'option?'"

The older man smiled. "I'm glad that Peter didn't tell you too much. It's better if I explain it to you." The older man paused. "My name is James Harris. I work for a foundation dedicated to making things better. The exact name of the foundation doesn't matter. What matters is what we do?"

"And that is?"

"To make things better."

"Yes, but how?"

"John, I'm going to tell you something that you will not believe at first, no one ever does. But hear me out, then I'll offer you proof."

"Go ahead," John said. He settled back into his chair a bit and listened.

"Our foundation has found a way to truly change things. We have the ability to go back into time and create an alternate reality, once for anyone who wants."

"'Alternate reality'? What the heck does that mean?"

"John, it's complicated but it's like this – time is like a flowing stream with many currents and eddies. What we do effects the flow, making things happen for us and for others. We have found a way to go to any spot in that flow and change an event so that it never happened. One person we helped had committed a terrible crime and we were able to undo it for him. His life changed to what it would have been if he hadn't committed the crime."

"You mean you can time travel?" John asked, suspiciously.

"No, not at all. We can't actually go back in time, we go back *into* time, to change one thing. We call it exercising the option. But it can be done only once in any one person's life. Would you be interested in exercising your option now?"

"If that was possible but I don't believe it."

"That's why I asked Peter to come with you, John," James Harris smiled. "Tell him, Peter."

"I did it two months ago."

"Did what?" John asked.

"Exercised my option," Peter smiled.

"Come on," John said with a disbelieving grin.

Peter looked at James Harris. The older man turned a computer monitor toward the two men. A recording began to play. It was Peter, telling his story:

"My name is Peter Johnson," the obvious image of Peter began. "I'm exercising my option of my own free will, knowing that it may grossly affect my life and the lives of others."

John looked over at Peter. This was the man on the tape, but not really. The man on the tape was a sullen and sad copy of his co-worker. The man on the tape was sickly-looking with a drawn look about him. John looked back at the computer monitor. "I have chosen to undo the wrong I did to a former employer that led to him firing me, sending me to jail and, in effect, ruining my life. I yielded to temptation and stole money. I have opted to undo that act and, in doing so, hope that it changes things in my life for the better."

"You're kidding me," John said.

"It's true, John," Peter said.

"Okay, how much did you steal?"

"I have no idea."

"I never happened," James Harris interjected. "Peter has no memory of the event because we were able to make it not happen. The day he stole the money was changed by our foundation's intervention into just another day at the office for him. There was no firing; no jail. It never happened."

"Not possible," John maintained.

"It's real, John," Peter said. "You can do it. You can change everything."

John was overwhelmed. As much as he wanted to believe this, it could not be. "But…"

"Yes?" Harris said.

"What about the change to others? If I never slept with Becky in high school and she never got pregnant, that'd change her life, too."

"Yes, and others."

"How many others?"

"Everyone," James Harris said.

"Everyone?"

"Yes. You see, all things are interconnected. All lives affect all other lives – some a little – some a lot."

"Becky?"

"Obviously, a lot," Harris said. "It's like ripples in a pond – the effect on nearby things is greater that the effect of distant things but all are affected. Once you exercise the option, everything will be as it would have been if the changed things changed – because it will be changed."

John looked at Peter. "It's true, John," Peter said. "All I remember is my life without any memories of jail or anything else. They had me make this recording so I could know what had changed but everything is different from it. Before I exercised my option, I had no hope. I couldn't overcome my past. I married the wrong woman, couldn't be a good father to my kids…"

"Kids," John interrupted. "If I could do what you say I could do, my kids…"

"Won't be," James Harris said. "You could go on to marry someone else but, if you had children, they'd be with that wife, not your present wife."

John thought about his two insolent, disrespectful and nasty children. He saw no problem there.

"So, everything would be changed?"

"Everything would be as it would have been if you hadn't slept with Becky then," Peter offered.

"But, you only can exercise the option once in your lifetime, John, so we recommend you be very careful in selecting to do so."

"I going for it," John grinned.

"Are you certain?" James Harris asked.

"Certain," John said. How could he lose?

"Then, we need to make a recording of your intensions, like we did with Peter."

"Okay," John said.

"But, first we much check…" James Harris logged onto his computer and searched files. "Oh, there's a problem," the man said.

"What?" John asked.

"John Olson, right? John Kenneth Olson?"

"Yes," John answered.

"I'm very sorry, John," Harris said, looking over at the man. "It seems you've already exercised your option. Five years ago, just after you got a big promotion at the law firm where you worked, you chose the option of having slept with a Becky Kennedy when you were in high school – something you said you always regretted not doing."

EMMA F. BEETLEBITER

As soon as I walked into the house I knew that something was wrong. My son was sitting on the sofa staring forward at nothing in particular and the television set was not on. The boy's face was pale and I thought I saw his lower lip tremble a bit.

"You okay?" I asked.

Jason slowly shook his head.

"What's wrong?"

"I got Beetlebiter," he replied.

"Did your mom take you to the doctor?" I asked. I assumed that Beetlebiter was yet another childhood disease.

"*Dad*," Jason said in that preteen voice of disgust that all parents hear when they ask a stupid question. He had tears in his eyes.

"What?" I asked, still not knowing how stupid I was sounding to my son.

"Beetlebiter," he repeated. "I got Beetlebiter as my teacher."

"Beetlebiter?" I smiled at the sound of that name.

"It's not funny!" Jason screamed from his place on our living room sofa. "Miss Beetlebiter is an ogre. Everyone knows that. She's the meanest teacher in our school. She's the pits. Horrible. It's the end of everything for me."

"There's really a person named Beetlebiter?" I asked, still smiling.

"**Dad**!" Jason shouted again. "This isn't funny."

"Beetlebiter isn't funny?" I protested, still being insensitive to my son's obvious pain. How, I thought, could anyone named Beetlebiter be anything but funny?

"You don't understand!" Jason roared. He pulled his knees up and got into the position in which he had lived during most of the nine months before he was born. He looked over at me and was crying.

"Jason," I began and the boy jumped up from the couch.

"You don't understand. You never understand!" he yelled and ran into his bedroom.

"I'm not supposed to understand. I'm a father," I called after my son.

It took me an hour to come to my senses. Finally, I remembered the advice I had read in all of those parenting books that I had purchased before Jason's birth and I went up to my boy's room to do some "active listening".

I dutifully knocked in Jason's door to "respect his space" and entered the second floor bedroom to "interface" with my son. By the time the active listening was over I had learned that Emma F. Beetlebiter was a homeroom teacher at my son's school and by the luck of a computer assisted draw Jason had been assigned to this lady's room. As Jason went on about the horrors of being in Miss Beetlebiter's class I remembered by own fifth grade experience in Miss Nastowski's classroom.

Eva Nastowski, naturally called "Nasty Nastowski" by my classmates, was the very image of what she was reputed to be. Miss Nastowski was short with dark brown hair that she always, and I mean always, wore in a tight bun pulled to the back of her head. Into that bun the woman stuck pencils so as to look more menacing in a porcupine way. She wore rimless glasses that were always, and once more I mean always, down on the lower part of her nose and she peered over them at her students in order to further terrorize the youngsters whom had been put under her control. I had always believed that there was nothing ever wrong with the woman's eyes and that those glasses of hers, like that awful bun, was only a prop used by her in her ongoing war against her students.

Miss Nastowski was also the last teacher in the Western world who required her students to learn to write with pens with replaceable points that needed to be dipped into inkwells. I remembered so vividly dipping my pen point into that ridiculous inkwell that was located in the upper right hand corner of my fifth grade desk and trying not to smear the black ink over my notebook page.

"Some banks still use this type of pen," Miss Nastowski explained as, without a hint of facial expression, she forced us to dip our pen points into our inkwells.

"Then go to another bank," the waggish boy who sat behind me whispered.

The funny thing is that I liked Miss Nastowski. I think that I was the only one. My fellow students could never understand why I refused to call our teacher Miss Nasty and I said stupid things like "but we sure learn stuff in her class."

I did learn in Miss Nastowski's class and the discipline the teacher enforced served me well in college when I could study as my roommate partied.

But, that was a long time ago. Miss Nastowski surely had gone on to her Heavenly Reward to teach the Angels how to write with inkwell-dipped pens. Now it was my son, Jason, who was entering the class of a teacher whose reputation alone could terrify a young boy. I knew there was no use in me saying anything comforting to Jason about how I had a teacher like Miss Beetlebiter and how I liked her. I knew from those parenting books how wrong that would be. I knew it but, being a father, I said it anyway.

"When I was your age," I said, beginning with exactly the wrong words, "I had a teacher just like Miss Beetlebiter." I went on to dig the hole even deeper. I told Jason how much I enjoyed the challenge of Miss Nastowski's class and how well I did in it. Jason listened like a dutiful son to this crap and rejected it all. He was smart enough to know when his life was over.

It was two months before I met Emma F. Beetlebiter. During those months I witnessed the total collapse of my son as a human being. The boy had gone from being the friendly, outgoing, bright-eyed youth he had been during summer vacation to being a shy, circumspect, hollow-eyed wreck. After our doctor ruled out the possibilities of any disease known to modern and/or ancient man, I began to believe my son when he claimed that it was Miss Beetlebiter who had sapped his strength and was leading him to an early death. My wife and I made an appointment to talk to my son's teacher.

I left work early on a Thursday to be at the school after classes were dismissed to meet my son's teacher. I picked up my wife on the way, parked in the school's parking lot, and the two of us walked into the school to go directly to Miss Beetlebiter's classroom. All along the way we passed schoolwork - drawings, maps and other artwork - that had been stuck on the walls. My wife and I were so determined to sort things out with Jason's teacher we did not even look for our boy's work on those walls.

As I walked the stairway to the school's second floor scenes from my childhood flashed into my mind. The smell of the school building, the sight of small lockers and the feel of the place all were exactly as they had been in my youth. This school was not my school but it could have been. The school's feeling was the same.

Walking along the halls with my wife I recalled the last time that she and I had come to school to meet one of Jason's teachers. "Old Lady Wilcox" turned out to be a petite blonde who looked to me to be just a few months out of teachers' college. I figured that Miss Beetlebiter would be the same.

When I turned into Room 217 I saw my old teacher, Miss Nastowski, sitting behind her desk. I do not mean that this teacher looked like Miss Nastowski. She WAS Miss Nastowski, right down to the pencil poked bun at the back of her head and those rimless pulled down glasses.

The woman rose upon seeing my wife and me and I recognized the plain dark blue dress she wore every day when I sat in her class some twenty-five years before.

"Are you Jason's parents?" the teacher asked and when I did not answer my wife stepped in.

"Yes we are," my wife said. She looked at me with a puzzled look. Miss Beetlebiter shook hands with both my wife and me and offered us seats at her desk. I still stared in silence at the woman.

"Is there something wrong, Mister Porter?" Miss Beetlebiter/Nastowski asked.

"I'm sorry," I said, finally breaking my untypical silence. "It's just that you look exactly like my own fifth grade teacher."

Miss Beetlebiter said something about all fifth grade teachers looking the same and she began talking to my wife and me about my son's progress in her class.

"Jason's a bright boy," she reported, "but seems distracted."

"If I can be frank," I began.

The teacher nodded without smiling.

"I think Jason's afraid of you," I offered.

"I know that," the teacher said, still without a smile. "They are all afraid of me, I suppose. It goes with the territory." Then the woman looked directly at me. "You were afraid of me at first, were you not, Paul?"

A cold chill ran through me. It was Miss Nastowski speaking to me.

"Yes, I was, Miss Nastowski," I replied

"He was a good boy," the teacher said, looking at my wife. "He was never trouble like the other boys in the class like that Gary Harris who sat behind him."

My wife looked puzzled. She looked at the teacher then at me.

"I told you about Miss Nastowski." I explained.

"Yes, but..." Ellen stopped short and looked at me.

"This is Miss Nastowski," I proposed.

"That's right, Mrs. Porter," the teacher said. "All fifth grade teachers are Miss Nastowski or Miss Beetlebiter or... Miss Greene."

"You... you are Miss Greene!" Ellen said, stunned as she recognized her own fifth grade teacher.

"'Mean Greene'," the teacher corrected.

"That's what we called her...er...you," my wife stammered.

"You see, Paul and Ellen," Emma F. Beetlebiter said, smiling only a bit at last and leaning forward in her chair. "Nothing ever changes. I'm always the fifth grade teacher."

We tried to explain all of this to our son but he just accused us of "screwing with his mind".

"It doesn't matter, Jason," I said. "Just be sure to print your name in careful block letters on the upper right hand corner of each page. That's the way Miss Beetlebiter likes it."

"And no talking in class", Ellen said. "And, for goodness sakes, don't pass notes."

My wife and I smiled at each other and my son returned to his homework.

THREE VIEWS

The Conservative Future

Jim left his desk at the American International Oil, Bread and Automobile Corporation and walked down the well-lit hall to the men's room. He entered a stall, the one he liked near the far wall, and began his business.

After he was done, Jim washed his hands, tossing the paper hand towel into the bin that was near the sinks and he returned to his office.

"Jim, come in here now," Jim's boss' voice said over the intercom and the man knew he was in trouble. He didn't know why he was in trouble, but from the tone of Ralph Richardson's voice, he knew he was in trouble. Jim's fears were confirmed when he saw a security guard, a large man with burly arms, stationed just outside of Richardson's office door.

"Mister Richardson is waiting," the guard said in a menacing voice and Jim entered the room.

Richardson's office was a large one with original artwork on the walls. There was a fish tank in one corner that contained tropicals. Jim waited for his boss to acknowledge his arrival.

"Over here, Jim," the man said and he waved Jim to his desk. Richardson, a tall blond-haired man with a mustache that always needed trimming, turned a monitor toward where Jim was standing at the desk.

"I've got something to show you, pal," Jim's boss said and the man pushed a key that started a playback on the monitor.

"That's you," Richardson said as Jim saw a tape of him entering the men' room.

"I see," Jim said.

"Now watch this." The tape continued with Jim on the toilet. Jim saw nothing wrong.

"There," Richardson said, stopping the tape as Jim was wiping his butt.

"Yes?" Jim asked.

"You're fondling yourself."

"I'm wiping my ass," Jim protested.

"I know sexual perversion when I see it," Richardson insisted. "You're fondling yourself in our men's room and we will not abide it."

"Honest, boss…"

Richardson raised a hand. "You're fired," he announced. "We have security cleaning out your desk now. You're history."

Jim knew that there was no use arguing. He left, escorted by the burly security guard and was given his things at his car in the parking lot.

The Liberal Future

Jim left his desk at the United States Department of Bread and Circuses and walked down the dimly lit hallway to the unisex toilet. The lights flickered as another brownout came to an end. The man entered a stall, the farthest one from the door, and sat reading a newspaper as he did his business.

After he was done Jim washed his hands in the cold-water sink and dried them under the warm air blower. He returned to his office to be summoned into his boss' office by an e-mail flashed on his computer screen. The number of exclamation points on that all capital e-mail let Jim knew he was in trouble. His fears were confirmed when Jim saw a security guard stationed in her wheelchair just outside Richardson's office door.

"Ms Richardson is waiting," the security guard told Jim and the man entered the supervisor's office.

Iris Richardson's office was a small one with no decorations except for Bob Dylan posters on one wall. It was Spartan in appearance and very efficiently designed. Jim waited for his supervisor to acknowledge his entry.

"Jim, come here," Richardson said with a wave of her hand. The woman was a short black woman with glasses. She looked over at Jim and turned a monitor toward him. "I've got something to show you, Jim," the woman said and she pushed a key that began a playback on the monitor.

"That's you," Richardson said as Jim saw a tape of him entering the toilet.

"I see," Jim said.

"Now watch this." The tape continued with Jim sitting on the toilet. Jim saw nothing wrong.

"See that?" Richardson asked, pointing to the monitor screen.

"What?"

"You're reading the newspaper, that's what."

"But I was going to the bathroom," Jim protested.

"Our consultants tell us that a person takes 15% more time going to the bathroom when the person is reading a paper. The time you wasted in there, although to you minimal, could have been used feeding a hungry child or helping a homeless person." Iris Richardson looked at Jim. "You're fired," she told him.

Jim knew that there was no use arguing. He left, escorted by the security guard in the wheelchair to the nearest bus stop.

The Libertarian Future

Jim left his desk in his office and went down the hall to the restroom. He took a crap and returned to work.

A DOG'S TALE

Puppy Thoughts

My name was not The Countess Co-Co San Leidesdorf in the beginning. When I was born, I had no name at all. I was just one of several puppies that had been all jammed together in my birth-mother's belly and expelled by the female dog, one by one; each one all wrapped up in a slimy coating that, for some reason, my birth-mother decided to eat – yuk! I barely remember my birth-mother. I remember that her belly was less hairy than the rest of her and that was good news to my brothers and sisters when we got hungry. It was easy for each of us, including my little brother, the Runt, to get to the milk my birth-mother provided us.

I never knew my birth-father and, I think that my birth-mother never knew him either. From what she said she really didn't get a good look at him the one time that they had met what with him staying behind her all of the time. My birth-mother raised me for a while and I remember sleeping tight against her along with my siblings. I remember her smell and the feel of her long hair on my body but not much else.

When I was finally eating semi-solid food, the people who cared for my birth-mother put all us puppies into a box and took us to a very noisy place that had cages and smelled like a lot of other dogs (and a few other animals I didn't see – but I knew they weren't dogs). One by one, people came and reached into the cage and took one of my brothers or one of my sisters until only I was left.

The people there called me "Cagney". Now what kind of a name is Cagney for a cute, longhaired redhead with black accents and floppy ears?

"Cagney?" a person would say, looking at a sign on the outside of the cage where I lived then. I assumed that that name was somehow put there. The person then would look in at me and say, "Are you Cagney" and I'd tell him I wasn't but it was as if each of them couldn't understand what I was saying.

"Cagney," he or she would laugh then go to another cage and pick out another dog to take away.

At the time I didn't know if that was good or bad. I had no idea where those other dogs were being taken. The unknown is always scary you know. At night the dogs in the other cages would speculate about that until someone would come in and yell something that sounded as if he or she was angry with us and we'd all be quiet for a while. I whimpered at lot. I was scared.

The night was the worst. There was always some light in the room of cages but not much. Shadows filled my cage and the other cages, I suppose, and I spend most of the night pressed into a corner of the cage, whimpering and shaking some.

I'd sniff and sniff to find out who else, or what else, was near where I was. The smells told me that other dogs where there but they also warned me that other animals were present, too. The awful stench of cats made me even more afraid. Even then I knew that cats were unpredictable. I'd see them go by my cage during the day being carried by people and each cat would look over at me with those weird eyes of theirs and make me afraid.

In the morning it was all right because that was when we were fed. A different person every day, I think (people looked pretty much all the same to me then), would come to the cage room and put a bowl of food in with me. I had it all to myself after my brothers and sisters were taken away but there was not as much in the bowl as there had been when they were there. I ate it all and I wanted more, but we were not fed again until much later in the day. In the meantime someone made sure we had water and my cage was cleaned.

You know, I pooped a lot and I kind of liked having my poop in my cage – it really made it *my* place – but the people wouldn't let me keep it there. They took it away. I have no idea what they did with it but I'd like it all back someday.

I was in that cage after my siblings were taken away for two days then *they* came.

I first saw my Mommy and my Daddy when they came to look in at me like so many others had. Daddy said something then Mommy said something and they went on to other cages. I tried to look out to see where they went but I couldn't see them after they walked away. Then they came back, opened the cage I was in, and picked me up. Daddy held me in his hands and lifted me up into the air. Mommy smiled and said something and Daddy put me back. That was the first time that someone had picked me out of the cage and the first time that someone who looked at me didn't call me Cagney.

But they left and I was alone in the cage again.

It was almost dinnertime. I could smell the food that was being put into other dogs' dishes and I wanted my helping. Then, suddenly, just like that, Daddy and Mommy were back and I was in Daddy's hands again. They talked to the woman who was supposed to give me my food and Daddy kept holding me.

It took two more nights of being alone in my cage before Daddy and Mommy came back for me. I was really afraid that they forgot about me or that they thought my name was really Cagney. In the meantime, the people there stuck a long sharp thing in my butt and poked me with terrible things that really hurt. I wanted Daddy and Mommy to come back and when they finally did I just kept saying "MY NAME'S NOT CAGNEY!" as loud as I could.

I guess they heard and understood me because when they took my out of my cage and put a strap around my neck and had me walk to them, they kept saying "Co-Co". I figured either that was my real name or it meant that I should pee, so just to be sure that I got it right, I peed on the floor.

That was how I became The Countess Co-Co San Leidesdorf, the dog of Daddy and Mommy. I was taken from that awful place where they found me and we went right to a big bright store that let mommies and daddies bring their dogs in and buy them things. I was in a basket with wheels on the bottom and pretty soon the basket was filled with all kinds of nice things like dog food, dog toys and some things that smelled good but I didn't recognize. I saw Daddy take a thin hard card from his pants and give it to someone up at the front of the store and the people there let us keep all that good stuff in the basket. I have to get one of those cards!

My home is big with a nice peeing place in the back where the grass is. I tried to pee other places like on the soft carpet in the house but that made Mommy very mad so I stopped doing it, except when I forgot. I settled in with Mommy and Daddy and GG (that's Daddy's mommy, I think) and we've been pretty happy ever since. I learned a lot of things at my home like not peeing on the carpet and how to bark at the people who come to the front door before anyone else even knows that there's someone there. I'm really good at that. I can hear someone nearing the house long before anyone else. I really think they're all hard of hearing.

Mommy and Daddy must really like me barking like that because when I do they both shout my name really loud. I like hearing them say "Co-Co" or "Co-Co San" and not Cagney. It makes me bark louder and wag my tail too.

I found out right away that neither Daddy nor Mommy speak dog. The say a lot of things I can't understand but I'm figuring out some of it. I know what the following sounds they make mean:

"Co-Co – Sit" – that means if I put my butt on the ground I get a treat.

"Co-Co – Stay" – that means that I must look at Mommy and Daddy then run to them so they can pull me back to where I started.

"Co-Co – Come here" – that means that I'm doing something that's a lot of fun and someone noticed.

"Co-Co – What's wrong with you?" – that means the same as above but that I'm really having a whole lot of fun.

I've tried to teach Mommy and Daddy some dog talk but they're not smart enough to learn it. I'll keep trying.

A Dog with a Family

I began growing fast. Mommy and Daddy would pick me up as much as they could until I was just too big for them to do that. After that they petted me and patted me on the head but couldn't pick me up. That was all right because I loved being petted and patted and I didn't want Mommy and Daddy to hurt themselves trying to lift a big dog like me.

Besides, I wasn't the only dog living at my house. I had an adoptive brother whose name was the Champion Siegfried von Baskerville but whom everyone just called Champ. At first my older brother, Champ, was much bigger than me, but I caught up with him quickly. At first I bit at his ankles and by the time I was his size I could bite his long bushy tail. Champ didn't seem to like me doing that, but I did it anyway because it was fun to do. I'd chase Champ too and try to get him to play, but he really wasn't interested in playing. All Champ seemed to care about was if he was getting enough food and I had to be careful not to eat out of his dish when he was watching. I had my own food dish his but the food in Champ's dish always seemed to taste better, so I'd wait until he was peeing and eat his food. Sure, he'd get mad and chase me but that was the fun part.

I love the peeing place in the back of our house where Mommy and Daddy entertained their friends. I have a big pond of water where Daddy swims and around which Mommy mostly sits. They call it a swimming pool. I went into that swimming pool once, by accident, and I didn't like it so I stay out now. I run around it barking and I poop behind it where there are some bushes but I leave the water to Daddy and others.

There are ponds with fish living in them near that big swimming pool for me to drink out of, although it makes

Mommy mad when I do. If she doesn't want me to drink the water, why does she keep filling those ponds? There are some things about Mommy and Daddy that just don't make sense.

At night, when it's dark outside, I sleep in the room with Daddy and Mommy. They sleep about eight hours there and that's all for the whole day! I sleep eight hours with them, then lots of more hours all the rest of the day. I sleep in the room in the front of our house and in a bigger room down some stairs. I sleep outside, near the swimming pool and under the bushes. I sleep just about everywhere. Daddy and Mommy don't. They sleep only those eight hours in the room we share. I'm concerned that they have some kind of medical problem. It doesn't seem natural to sleep that little.

The Dog in the Bottom of the Pool

After a while of running around and, that one time, falling into the big swimming pool and not noticing that it was there, I finally saw it. One day when it was quiet outside and my big brother Champ was sleeping near his food dish to keep me from eating out of it, I was next to the swimming pool. I like to lie there with one of my paws hanging over the edge of the pool but not in the water. I was there, feeling a slight breeze in my furry face and dozing a little when, for no real reason at all, I looked down into the pool. That was when I saw it. There was a dog in the pool! The dog looked just like me and it was looking up at me from under the water. I barked and so it that other dog but I could only hear my bark. Instantly, I stood and barked some more. That other dog just kept looking up at me and barking without making any sound.

I ran right over to where Daddy was sleeping on a long chair and I licked at one of his hands until he woke and pushed me back from him. I kept licking and I started barking too until Daddy realized that something was wrong. He got up from where he was and went with me to the pool. I looked over into the water and barked at that dog some more. Daddy watched and then he began to laugh. He said a few things I couldn't understand, patted my head and returned to his nap.

What does "reflection" mean?

The Squirrel

There is also an evil creature that lives in the back of the house where I pee. This beast is the vilest of creatures. It is called the Squirrel.

The Squirrel is a loathsome creature that inhabits the tops of the trees that surround Daddy's swimming pool and comes down to raid the food that my wonderful Daddy put out for birds. Daddy feeds the birds, big ones and little ones; red ones and brown ones (I can see shades of grays and identify them as various colors, you know); noisy ones and singing ones. He feeds the birds so that I can chase them. It's really fun to chase the birds and make them all fly away. I know Daddy loves seeing me do that because whenever I do, he shouts my name really loud. I also know that the birds like it too because they always come back for more.

But the Squirrel jumps a long way from a tree to where Daddy puts out food for the birds and it makes terrible faces at me. I chase it away but it doesn't fly like the birds. It just scampers right up the side of our house and then looks down at me and flicks its tail and makes a terrible mocking sound.

I hate the Squirrel.

The Squirrel makes me look bad, too. When I'm running along the fence that separates our house's peeing place from that man who makes a terrible noise when he makes his grass shorter, the Squirrel stays up in the trees far above me and drops things down on my head. It gets crab apples from another place and brings then over to our house so it can drop them down on my head. I bark up at that evil Squirrel and put my paws up on the tree's trunk but that only lets the Squirrel have a better aim when it drops crab apples on my head.

I hate the Squirrel.

I don't think that Daddy really understands that the Squirrel is as evil as it is. Daddy puts out food for it to eat! At first I thought that Daddy did that so he could catch the Squirrel and make it go somewhere else, but I don't know. Daddy never really tries to catch the nasty thing and just keeps putting out nuts, corn and other things that the Squirrel eats.

I don't understand that, at all.

The Squirrel has brought a friend, called Only-A-Raccoon, to my peeing place too. Only-A-Raccoon is bigger and fatter than the Squirrel and only comes to our house at night, after we've all gone to bed. There are those times when I'm asleep up on the bed with my Mommy and my Daddy and I hear Only-A-Raccoon out in the back of our house. I know it's there to eat the food that Champ and I have left in our dishes so we can have something to eat whenever we want it. That big fat Only-A-Raccoon waddles up to our dishes and eats our food and it's my job to tell Mommy and Daddy about it. I bark and run all around the bedroom where we all sleep and Mommy wakes and really lets me know that she's happy I woke her. She screams my name, Co-Co, not Cagney, and waves her hands at me to let me know how happy she is at the warning about the Only-A-Raccoon. Eventually, Mommy gets up, glaring at Daddy who's still asleep in our bed, and takes me to the back door to let me look out at Only-A-Raccoon who doesn't seem to mind us watching it eat.

Mommy tells me "it's only a raccoon," and that's how I know its name.

We do that game a lot.

There are lots of other games that we do at our house like when Mommy and Daddy put a collar around my neck and take me out for a walk so I can pull them as hard as I can. I know they really love me because the always take a bag they use to pick up any poop I make along the way so they can take it home for me. That's real nice of them. I have no idea what they do with all the poop they save – they're always using a shovel in my peeing place to pick it up, so they must have a lot by now. I hope I get it all back someday.

So, here I am, the Countess Co-Co San Leidesdorf, the dog and friend to Daddy and Mommy. I'll never be Cagney again and I love it all.

CODA

A WALK AFTER
MY WIFE DIED

How many times my wife and I had walked that trail together. Armaine so loved it. She'd pause to inspect a particularly interesting stone; or tree or to watch an egret fishing the river the trail paralleled for some of its length. I, on the other hand, usually had my eyes fixed upon the trail ahead and our goal of completing our walk before lunch.

Now I walked the trail alone. The previously interesting stones were still there as were the trees and water birds and I tried, and failed, to see them through her eyes.

I walked on, alone, but when the trail pulled up from the high river bank, to stretch out before me up into the hill, I saw him. A coyote!

I stopped. The coyote, off the trail to my right, stopped, too. Its eyes fixed on me then it lowered its head and I cautiously stepped on and so did the coyote. The trail pointed up a hill and I climbed in careful steady steps, looking ever to my right to see the animal join me. The coyote had its right paw raised and held raised; the feral canine glancing over at me from time to time as if to see if I were still there but not too close. So he and I continued on our walk; both injured by life but both still walking on. I reassured my new companion by not approaching him nor by starring as he hopped on his strong left leg while holding its obviously injured right paw in the air. I walked on, center path, and he walked on, paw raised and held-raised, to my right, ever vigilant and only slightly suspicious of my intentions.

My wife would have stopped to touch, or feed, or calm this injured animal. I was sure of that. But I did not. I recognized a fellow injured traveler in need of nothing but non-interacting companionship.

We walked on. The coyote moved slightly to his right to put a foot or so more between us but we continued on, my shaggy canine companion hopping steadily on his uninjured left foot.

The trail was well worn but also on occasion encumbered by a rut, a rock or washed out dry rill. Both of us navigated around or over these anomalies, both knowing they did not intend to block our progress but were only the naturally occurring things of natural life: a rut caused by a trickle of occasional rain; a rock left from a long ago slide of stones; a washed out dry rill, the evidence of a former heavy rainstorm.

We came to a sharp left turn in the trail. For a moment I thought the coyote was going to move off into the brush that filled the area to the right side of the trail but he did not. The wild canine paused; glanced over at me then continued on his side of our shared trail.

I dared not stop. I dared not slow. I had to maintain the pace that he and I had set. There was, for us, I felt, no goal, no destination, only the trail; our mutually shared journey. So I, and he, continued on in unabated pace – both suspicious of each other and both needing the company.

The coyote, still hopping on its left foot, still holding its obviously injured right foot in the air, and I, still mourning my wife's passing, reached the top of the hill. My companion looked over at me and, seem to wait until I was looking at him. Then eased its injured foot to the ground, at first putting no weight on it then pushing its pads more firmly to the hard-packed clay of the trail. I watched the coyote test his paw's strength and endurance then saw it turn and trot off the trail, hard to my right. The animal disappeared into the brush there. I looked for it to emerge. It did not. Its work was done.

ABOUT THE AUTHOR

Bert George Osterberg was born 1943 in Michigan. He was reared in Detroit and lived in Michigan most of his life. Mr. Osterberg has had a love of history since his school days and has authored several books on a variety of historic subjects. His works include **Our Silent Song: the True Story of an American Family; Forgotten Heroes: Detroit's Fight for Freedom; 1850 – 1910, One-hundred Years in America, A Black Family Story; 1850: A Year in the Life of America and Lion on the Loose: The Works of the Devil in the Twenty-first Century.** Among his lighter literary creations are **Silas Cully's Tavern Tales: Jokes, Stories and Recipes from a Nineteenth Century Barkeeper** and **Webb Untangled: The Life and Tines of Legendary Drummer Kenneth "Spider Webb" Rice**, a work co-written with Spider himself.

After working for almost thirty years for the Detroit Water Department where he became the Telecommunications Manager, Bert Osterberg retired and began writing more frequently. He soon had taken a job at The Henry Ford in Dearborn, Michigan portraying the historic character of the Greenfield Village's Eagle Tavern barkeeper, Silas H. Cully. In this role, Bert entertained and informed visitors to the eighty-acre outdoor museum while serving beverages authentic to the 1850s at the Eagle Tavern, an 1850's stagecoach stop. In addition, the author was certified as a Lay Minister and regularly provided preaching services to congregations in Southern Michigan. Bert also gave talks and first-person historical presentations to school and civic groups in the Detroit area.

Bert Osterberg married the former Armaine Yvonne Lacen in 1969 and is the proud father of three children, Bert Osterberg, Jr.; Lisa Thomas, and Margaret McFarlane. He also has seven grandchildren and three great-grandchildren.

Bert and Armaine relocated from Michigan to California in 2009 where Armaine began a heroic battle with cancer. She passed away in 2012 and Bert remains in California with his faithful dog and friend, Co-Co. Bert and his daughter, Meg, are now active members of the historic Johnson Chapel African Methodist Episcopal Church in Orange County, California where Bert was certified a Lay Minister. He continues his work in historical presentation in Southern California.

Printed in the United States
By Bookmasters